All Damian could do now was keep his promise to his father and bring justice to those who had profited from their downfall.

He hardened his heart against the fleeting memory: a fascinating dimple in one soft cheek when a small smile curved her lips.

He cared nothing for her innocence or her reduced circumstances. *He* had been innocent, before he had been forced to grow up among the stews of Marseilles. Innocence had offered *him* no protection. Scruples were nothing but a dead weight.

He entered what had once been his father's study—his own study now. It smelled of mold and dust. One day he would restore the house to its former glory. Perhaps. Or maybe, once his goal was accomplished, he would leave it to rot and move on. Only bitter memories and regrets remained for him here.

There was no need to think about the future. Right now he had to focus on the task at hand—bringing his enemies to their respective knees.

The thought usually warmed him. Tonight it left him feeling hollow.

Author Note

I hope you enjoy your visit to my vision of Regency England. As always, Damian and Pamela feel like family members, and it is with regret I must close this small chapter of their lives that intersected with mine for a few months. If you are interested in learning more about me and my books, please visit my website at annlethbridge.com. Do not hesitate to drop me a line. I always love to hear from readers.

A CINDERELLA TO REDEEM THE EARL

ANN LETHBRIDGE

ISBN-13: 978-1-335-59626-0

A Cinderella to Redeem the Earl

Harlequin Enterprises ULC
22 Adelaide St. West, 41st Floor
Toronto, Ontario M5H 4E3, Canada
www.Harlequin.com

Printed in U.S.A.

In her youth, award-winning author **Ann Lethbridge** reimagined the Regency romances she read—and now she loves writing her own. Now living in Canada, Ann visits Britain every year, where family members understand—or so they say—her need to poke around every antiquity within a hundred miles. Learn more about Ann or contact her at annlethbridge.com. She loves hearing from readers.

Books by Ann Lethbridge

Harlequin Historical

It Happened One Christmas
Secrets of the Marriage Bed
Rescued by the Earl's Vows
The Matchmaker and the Duke
The Viscount's Reckless Temptation
The Wife the Marquess Left Behind

The Widows of Westram

A Lord for the Wallflower Widow
An Earl for the Shy Widow
A Family for the Widowed Governess
A Shopkeeper for the Earl of Westram

Visit the Author Profile page
at Harlequin.com for more titles.

This book is dedicated to my greatest supporter—
my husband, Keith. Always and forever.

Chapter One

With a growing sense of dismay, Pamela gazed at Rake Hall, the address of her new employer, the Earl of Dart. Lit only by the moon. What must have once been a fine manor house built in the Palladian style was now a ramshackle hulk of boarded up windows, overgrown ivy and shrouded in darkness.

Clearly, the sly grin on the innkeeper's facc in the village of Rake had been a warning Pamela should have heeded. Not to mention the sniggers from a couple of the patrons in his taproom when they overheard her asking for its direction.

At the time, she had ignored the worry that had niggled in the corner of her mind. After all, the agency had been quite glowing in their recommendation. Not to mention the offer of a fabulous salary. This would definitely be a step up in her career as a cook.

On the other hand, if she hadn't been quite so desperate to find a new position after her third argument with the head chef at her last post, she might have wondered at the generosity of the offer.

It had come at a moment when she feared she might be dismissed without a reference, having tossed out one of the head chef's desserts because she had been quite sure he had used rancid butter, likely in order to pocket the funds provided to purchase fresh.

The chill of the evening caused her breath to mist before her face. Fortunately, the brisk two-mile walk had kept her warm, but there was no denying winter was just around the corner.

Having to walk should also have been a warning sign that all was not well. She ought to have been met by some sort of transportation from Rake Hall. But, no. The best she had got from the innkeeper was directions to the manor house and an oily smirk.

Now she was in two minds as to whether to cut her losses and run.

She glanced up at the sky sprinkled with stars. Even by the light of a full moon, she did not fancy the long walk back to the village. And what would she do when she got there? She had no funds to pay for board and lodging. Would she sleep under a hedge like the vagrants she had pitied over the years?

She shifted her valise to her other hand, flexing her arm for ease. Well, she had walked this far, she wasn't going to turn back now. Besides, she had used her advance of a week's salary to pay for her travel from Cornwall. At the very least, she needed to work that off.

Very well. In for a penny, in for a pound.

As advised by the agency, she made her way around to the back of the house and across the courtyard between the house and the stables. To her relief, things looked a little less run down on this side of the house and the glow of candles in a couple of windows seemed welcoming.

A lantern beside a low heavy oak door guided her steps. She put down her valise, clenched her fist and banged hard.

After a long pause, and right at the moment she plucked

up the courage to bang again, she heard the click of footsteps on flagstones inside.

The door swung back.

A startlingly handsome man of dishevelled appearance, his necktie loose and his coat an embroidered grey waistcoat with buttons undone, opened the door and held up a lamp.

His dark eyebrows drew together at the sight of her.

'Yes?'

Oh, Lord, what sort of house was this? Not a very well-run one if he was any example. She straightened her shoulders. 'I am Mrs Lamb, the new cook.'

His eyes widened as if he was surprised. He leaned one shoulder—one impressively broad shoulder—against the door, crossed his shirt-sleeved arms over his chest and his lips curled in wry amusement as he looked her up and down. His smile turned appreciative and devastatingly attractive. 'Are you now?'

Her heart did an odd little flip-flop accompanied with a strangely girlish sensation of excitement. She hadn't felt this way since the first time Alan had kissed her on one of their long walks. *Alan.* The pain of loss hit her anew, followed swiftly by a sense of shame at her untoward reaction to this fellow.

For a moment she had trouble speaking. 'The agency sent me,' she forced the words out. 'I have a contract.'

His eyebrows rose. He nodded his head slowly, his gaze pursuing her as if she was an insect under a microscope. 'You were expected two hours ago.'

Who was this person? The butler? She hoped not. If she wasn't mistaken, he had imbibed a little more than he should have and was far more arrogant than he ought to be. She lifted her chin. 'The mail was late. Still, I expected a conveyance to be awaiting me.'

'Did you now?'

Handsome or not, she wanted to take him by those elegant shoulders and give him a good shake. 'I most certainly did. That valise is heavy. May I speak to the housekeeper?'

'You may not.'

Shocked at his denial, she stepped back. There really was something wrong here. 'Why ever not?'

'Because we don't have one.' He stepped back and gestured for her to enter. 'Come.'

When she didn't move, he glowered and gestured impatiently. 'Inside.'

The man's peremptory tone was not a good sign at all.

Heaven help her, she really didn't have a choice.

Feet dragging, she walked past him into the house. The strong smell of brandy wafted on the air along with the heat from his body in the confined space of the narrow entrance. She sidled through, far too aware of his masculine presence for comfort.

Her breath caught in her throat. How could she find him attractive after his rudeness?

'This way,' he said, and squeezed past her again, his shirtsleeves brushing against her. Shivers darted down her back. Reproach rippled through her. How could she respond to this man in this manner? Perhaps Alan had been right.

She pushed the thought aside. She had far more important things to be concerned about. Such as exactly what sort of household she had arrived at.

Apparently, completely unaware of their physical contact, he plucked a lamp from a small hall table, and led the way down a set of stairs into another narrow corridor. He paused at a doorway and the lamp afforded her a glimpse of an enormous kitchen, all neat and shiny.

Pamela peeped in and glanced around in awe.

'This is the main kitchen,' he said. 'Yours is this way.'

Puzzled, she followed him as he held the lamp high to help them see their way. He turned into an even narrower corridor which ended in what was only a slightly larger kitchen than the one in the cottage she and Mother had rented for a short while after her beloved scholarly father died suddenly, leaving them destitute.

A week after his death, her hopes for marriage and a family with her fiancé Alan had been dashed—her parents had informed her of the terrible news of his death by a fluke accident. What an idiot she had been to let her passion overcome good sense and anticipate their wedding vows. Having grown up in a vicarage, she'd been taught better. But then, whoever would have predicted he would be killed by a runaway gun carriage?

Her world had tumbled about her ears. No longer marriageable because she had let herself be ruined, and not penny to her name, she had thought that not even her connections could overcome such disadvantages. She and her mother faced a life of poverty.

Until her mother married a widower she had described as a beau from her salad days within a few months. While the speed of her mother's marriage had been a surprise, the fact that she had chosen a wealthy husband had not. Mother had been very disappointed by her father's lack of ambition and his tendency to give their money to people less well off than himself. Pamela often wondered if their blazing row about money she'd overheard a few days before his death had been part of the cause of his fatal apoplexy.

Certainly, her mother's new husband was wealthy and a peer, and just as keen as her mother to see Pamela wed to one of his friends, a rather elderly bachelor, who was in need of an heir.

After enduring a Season in London as a debutante and with her suitor likely to make her an offer at any moment, she had done the only honourable thing she could think of: she'd fled London and hired herself out as a cook.

And why not? She loved to cook and was good at it, too.

While her mother had tried to discourage her visits to the kitchen, seeing it as beneath one of her station, her father had not minded and the cook at the vicarage had been only too pleased to pass on her skills to so willing a pupil. Together they had preserved fruits and vegetables, made pastries and pies and custards as well as roasted and fricasseed all sorts of meats. She had even begun experimenting with her own recipes. Not to mention that it saved the family money since they did not need to hire extra help.

Her interest had certainly proved fortuitous after she and her mother had been forced to leave the vicarage to make room for the new incumbent. Pamela had discovered she loved being in charge of her own kitchen. However, the moment her mother married again, all that was over. Pamela was back to being someone who was meant to care only for the latest fashion and how many invitations she received in a week.

A tug at her heart made her breath catch. A sense of betrayal. Nothing she said, no excuse or request for delay, dissuaded her mother from insisting Pamela marry the man she had chosen. When Pamela finally told her mother she could not bear the idea of being touched by such an old man, her mother said she was being ridiculously missish. That was when she knew her fate was sealed, unless she took matters into her own hands. Now she was in charge of her own future.

And yet sometimes, like now, she felt lost. She felt a yearning for her old life. For family and the comfort of home.

No. She would not think of that now. This kitchen was *her* domain. She glanced around. Unwashed pots filled the sink. The stove needed a good scrub. And on the scarred wooden table running down the centre, sat the remains of a roast that was little more than a charred lump.

'It used to be the summer kitchen,' he pronounced. He gestured at the table. 'The last cook was a bit of a disaster.' His chuckle sent a pleasurable tremor down her spine. Heavens above, this really would not do. She frowned, but whether at her reaction to him or at the mess, she wasn't exactly sure.

She pulled herself together. 'A mess indeed, Mr—I am sorry I did not catch your name.'

A mischievous grin lit his face. Her insides fluttered. 'I didn't give it. I am Dart.' His words stopped her cold.

Dart? Why on earth was the Earl of Dart answering his own door? What sort of establishment was this that he had no servants?

It certainly looked as if the last cook had left in a hurry. Perhaps she had jumped from the frying pan into the fire.

'My lord.' She sketched a curtsy. 'I am curious as to why you use this kitchen when the other is so much better?'

He shot her a hard look. 'I hope you do not plan to question my every decision.'

Taken aback at the swift change in his demeanour, she stared at him.

'I do a great deal of entertaining,' he said in more moderate tones as if he regretted his outburst. 'When my guests are here, a chef comes from London to prepare their food. Your job is to feed the servants who wait upon my guests, as well as send food out to their coachmen and grooms in the stable block.' He paused. 'And, upon occasion, feed me and Monsieur Phillippe, when I am here and not entertaining. Any more questions?'

'Yes.'

His frowned deepened.

'Where are my quarters? I have had a long journey and I need to rest.' She glanced with distaste at the kitchen. 'I will start work on this mess first thing in the morning.'

His unwilling chuckle lightened the atmosphere, though she had no clue why he thought what she had said was humorous. 'Your quarters are this way.'

He led her further along the narrow corridor through an antechamber and into the room beyond. The lamp revealed a chamber that boasted a narrow bed against one wall and a table with two chairs in the corner.

He lit several candles in strategically placed holders. 'This chamber backs on to the kitchen hearth. It is cosy in the winter and too hot in the summer, but there are lots of windows to open.'

There were indeed. A set of French doors led to somewhere outdoors. He pulled a set of heavy curtains over the glass. 'Better to keep these closed at this time of year.'

He glanced down at her valise. 'I will leave you to settle in.' He headed for the door.

'Wait.'

He turned back with a glare. He really did not like to be questioned. 'What is it now?'

'I have an offer of employment from the agency detailing salary and terms that requires your signature.'

'I will meet you in my office tomorrow, at ten, to finalise the details.' He sounded completely uninterested, but given that the offer was for what she considered an exorbitant salary, she was determined to have the contract signed and sealed.

'Very well. I will attend you at ten. Also, how many people require breakfast tomorrow morning, where and at what time?'

He huffed a sigh. 'Two. Me, Monsieur Phillippe, in addition to yourself. Something simple laid out in the servants' hall will do. By tomorrow afternoon there will be fifteen additional staff. They will require dinner at six, then will return to London before morning. They return again on Friday. They will require meals two evenings each week. I hope that is clear?'

Only two evenings each week? All that money for so little work? What was she to do the rest of the time?

Her earlier misgivings returned in a rush.

Damian frowned as he strode back to his study. *Mrs* Lamb, as she called herself, had not been quite as anticipated. When he had hatched his plans to take revenge on her and her family, he had not expected to discover her hiring herself out as a cook. He had also expected her to be delicate, less confident and easily influenced.

Until recently, his only experience with gently born ladies had been his mother, who had suffered greatly at their reduced circumstances. Her brave attempts to pitch in had been endearing, but more of a hindrance than a help. Her idea of adding to the family coffers had been to take in mending, but then had required his father to hire a woman to provide assistance. An expenditure they could little afford.

His father, who did his best to protect his wife, had not had the heart to tell her she was costing him money. Her sensibilities had been very delicate.

At first meeting, it seemed that Mrs Lamb was made of sterner stuff, both resilient and competent, which rather contradicted the tepid reference he'd received from the chef at her last place of employment. The reference had accorded with his expectation of a spoiled little miss, who, not getting her way over something ridiculous, had run off to be a cook, to blackmail her family into giving in.

But time would tell which of these was true.

He certainly had not expected to find her quite so lovely, or feel a tug of attraction. Until now, he had found most of the *ton*'s ladies not to his taste, being far too empty-headed and ingratiating.

Fortunate indeed. Had he found the spoiled miss repulsive, it might have made undertaking her ruin more difficult. Rubbish. Nothing would stand in his way. He controlled his future, whether it be divesting a young man of a fortune by the turn of a card, or tempting a woman to let down her guard. Every move he made was thought out and based on full knowledge of the risks.

The hard scrabble of the many years of gaining a fortune in the mean streets of Marseilles had taught him to identify what he wanted and focus his all on getting it.

He'd learned from the best, first as a lad, running errands for one of Marseilles's notorious criminals, and later setting up his own illegal gaming hell, which attracted a better class of gambler, where he made sure the gaming was honest and the premises discreet enough to attract the wealthiest of customers.

So it would be with his plans for Mrs Lamb. Pamela. Such a soft name for such a sharp-edged female. Well, pretty soon he'd blunt her blade and have her eating out of his hand, when and how he decided.

It was inevitable.

A twinge of guilt took him by surprise.

Guilt? Or pity?

Impossible. There was no way he would entertain second thoughts. Her father had ruined his family so she could live off the fat of the land while they languished in misery in France. She, and the family of the other man who had profited from the fraud perpetrated on his father, were going to suffer the same fate.

He deliberately recalled his father's agony as his mother wasted away from some horrible disease in what was little more than a slum. It was the night she died that Damian had learned who had brought about his family's downfall and made him promise to avenge his mother's death.

After her death his father lost all hope. Night after night he drank himself into oblivion until he finally succumbed.

If only Damian had been able to do more, provide more, he might have been able to save them both. The guilt of it racked him. He could have done more if he had not let his scruples get in the way. He'd been offered a chance to participate in a lucrative robbery, but the sight of the pistols and knives to be used if anyone got in the way had deterred him. At fifteen he still had notions of honour and right and wrong.

Until the night his mother had died and he learned the truth about the way his father had been lured into debt by a man he trusted and then who denied any knowledge of the plot and refused to help.

If Damian had taken the opportunity, his parents might be alive today to enjoy their old age in security and comfort. All he could do now was keep his promise to his father and bring to justice those who had profited from their downfall.

He hardened his heart against the fleeting memory: a fascinating dimple in one soft cheek when a small smile curved her lips.

He cared nothing for her innocence or her reduced circumstances. *He* had been innocent, before he had been forced grow up among the stews of Marseilles. Innocence had offered *him* no protection. Scruples were nothing but a dead weight.

He entered what had once been his father's study—his own study now. It smelled of mould and dust. One day he would restore the house to its former glory. Perhaps. Or maybe, once his goal was accomplished, he would leave it to rot and move on. Only bitter memories and regrets remained for him here.

There was no need to think about the future. Right now, he had to focus on the task at hand. Bringing his enemies to their respective knees.

The thought usually warmed him. Tonight, it left him feeling hollow. Perhaps because there was much left to be done and he wanted it over.

Pip, his friend who had helped him survive the streets of Marseilles, was one of those rare fair-haired men from the north of France. Glass in hand, he pushed his lanky six-foot frame from the overstuffed chair beside the hearth and went to the desk. 'Brandy, *mon ami*?' he asked.

Damian sighed. 'Brandy would not come amiss.'

Pip poured him a generous serving from the decanter. They chinked glasses and Damian gestured for Pip to sit. They had been together for so long they needed no ceremony. Pip was his partner in some would call it crime—Damian called it justice.

'Everything is ready for tomorrow evening?' Damian asked.

'Of course.' Pip's French accent was hardly discernible. Barely twenty-five and smart as a whip. That was what living on the streets since birth did for a chap.

Damian had been lucky to meet the younger man or

the streets might have eaten him alive, he had been such a Johnny Raw. He still didn't know what had moved Pip to befriend him rather than take advantage of his naivety. Together they had run rings around the local gendarmes.

But that was in the past. Now, after years of living in the backstreets of Marseilles, he was home. And he was well on the way to accomplishing all he had dreamed of these past fifteen years: revenge.

A return, with interest, for what had been done to him and his family by two self-serving noblemen. It wouldn't happen overnight, of course. But his plans were well underway. Already, news of the exciting new club called The Rake Hell, a short drive from Mayfair, had spread far and wide among the younger members of the *ton*.

Pretty soon, his fish would be in his net.

'The cook has arrived,' he said.

Pip cocked an eyebrow. 'Is she as you expected?'

'More or less.' More and less. More beautiful. Less pliable, but not invulnerable.

'We will have no more complaints from Chandon about feeding riff-raff who don't appreciate his talents,' Damien said. 'If she is half the cook she claims to be.'

Pip chuckled. 'The staff will be pleased if it is so. The meal Betsy cooked last week wasn't fit to feed to a pig. How many will attend this week?'

'At least thirty, by my reckoning. About a third of them female companions.' Up from the twenty last week. 'Now I wait for the other one to fall into our net and the real game can begin. In the meantime, we are making a fortune. The future bodes well.'

'You are a lucky devil, Damian.'

'So they say.' His luck at the tables was legendary. He was counting on it to hold.

After the successes of the past few weeks, every gentleman in London would do anything to receive one of his prized invitations to an evening at the exclusive Rake Hell Club. It catered to only the richest and most well-connected members of the *ton*—and their vices. Their need for excitement and titillation. Like children.

To Damian, the tables were the most important part of his venture, but the draw for his patrons was the club's exclusivity and its upstairs rooms. A sprat to catch a mackerel.

'Is the cook aware of the sort of house she's come to?' Pip asked.

'She has no reason to know anything apart from that she cooks only for the staff.'

'But servants talk, *mon ami*. Everyone working here is known to us. Is loyal to us. This cook is a whole different story. Will you be able to keep her from going to the authorities?'

He shrugged. 'She needs money or she would not have taken the lure. Besides, there is nothing illegal about what we are doing.' Although they walked a very fine line and it would not take much to tip them over on to the wrong side of the law.

Pip sipped his brandy. 'Let us hope you are correct. I look forward to meeting this cook of yours.'

A spark of something hot rose in Damien's chest. Anger? Since when did he care about Pip's legendary romantic adventures? Nonsense. He merely didn't want Pip causing his plan to go awry. 'This is one female I insist you stay away from.'

A charming smile broke out on his friend's face. 'She is so lovely, then?'

'Ugly or fair, it is all the same to me. I don't want you getting in the way of our plans.' He caught the twinkle in his friend's eye and relaxed. 'Stop roasting me, I will deal with her.'

Pip tossed back his drink. 'It shall be as you request. I bid you goodnight. Tomorrow will be a busy day.'

Tomorrow would be a good day. Everything was coming together exactly the way he had planned.

Pamela dried her hands on a cloth and inspected the fruits of the labour she had started at six that morning. The little kitchen—her domain—sparkled. The wooden table top shone, as did the floor, the copper pots hanging from the wall rack gleamed and the stove had been scrubbed inside and out.

Four hours of hard work and well worth it.

To her delight, the pantry was exceedingly well stocked with everything she would need for at least two weeks. Now she began to explore the rest of her surroundings. Since the house was built into a small rise, while she had come downstairs from the front door to reach the kitchens, at the back of the house, it was above ground. The kitchen windows looked out over a herb and vegetable garden, long neglected.

Following the corridor, she had walked down the previous evening, she passed the servants' hall where she had laid out breakfast for three as ordered and opened the back door to the outside. This was how one accessed the garden and a collection of buildings for storage, smoking meats and laundry. Which had her wondering who was responsible for washing the linens.

Another question to ask her employer when she saw him in...not very many minutes' time.

Time to get ready for her appointment. At the thought, her heart gave an odd little skip. Not afraid, but a kind of eager anticipation. It really would not do. She must not let herself find him attractive. He was her employer. She peeked into the servants' hall and was disappointed to see no signs that Dart or Monsieur Phillippe had availed themselves of the breakfast she had laid out.

She had wanted his reaction to the food. She wanted to make a good impression. But alas, apparently the exceedingly handsome, somewhat brooding Earl of Dart clearly was not an early riser.

The more she thought about him, the more she wondered at the strangeness of his abode. Opening his own door. Hiring his own servants. And the odd arrangement regarding meals for the servants and guests.

She had heard that some members of the nobility were eccentric and she had an uncomfortable feeling about this one. Well, as long as he left her in peace to do her work, she didn't see why she would have a problem with his foibles.

Returned to her kitchen, she took a deep steadying breath, hung up her apron and glanced at her reflection in the bottom of a pot.

She smoothed a stray lock of hair back into her bun. Neat as a pin, like her kitchen. Satisfied, she climbed the stairs and pushed open the baize door into the main entrance hall.

Where was Dart's study?

She walked along the corridor to the right and peeked into the first room she came to. She could not believe her eyes. The floorboards were rotted and haphazardly patched, a broken chair lay on its side and odd bits of wood covered many of the window panes. If she wasn't mistaken, those were mice droppings all over the floor.

She tried the next room and found it worse.

Perhaps the other wing… She retraced her steps back to the entrance hall.

'Are you looking for something?'

Her heart gave a startled thump.

She spun around to see a young fair-haired man strolling down the grand staircase. An Adonis of a young man, no less.

She took a quick breath. 'Yes. I am seeking my employer. Lord Dart.'

The young man tilted his head and let his gaze roam from her head to her heels.

'Yes, of course,' he murmured. 'The cook.'

Her face heated. 'You have me at a disadvantage, Mr…'

He beamed winsomely. 'I am Phillippe. My friends call me, Pip. But then I only have one friend.'

She did not trust that charming smile for one moment. This was the Monsieur Phillippe Dart had spoken of the previous evening. 'Do you know where His Lordship is?'

'Bien sur,' Monsieur Phillippe said.

'Would you care to share the information?' she said coldly.

'So haughty a cook. Interesting.' He gestured to the other corridor. 'You will find him in his study.' He frowned. 'Do you offer breakfast, or should I help myself as usual?'

Something about this young man annoyed her. 'You will find bread and cheese and fruit laid out in the servants' hall. I was not asked to provide a hot meal until this evening.'

He nodded and walked off whistling. Very annoying indeed. And if he was responsible for the mess she had just cleaned up—he'd clearly stated he had been helping himself to her kitchen—she wanted to get back to her domain as soon as possible to keep an eye on him.

She hurried down the corridor. The set of large, ornately carved double doors she came to first did not look as though they would lead to a study, but she opened them anyway.

She gasped at the sight of gilt and glass and tastefully arranged tables arrayed around the rooms. It was one of the most sumptuous rooms she had ever seen in her life.

Nothing like the shambles in the other wing.

It looked as though it was set for a ball or a rout. Or a card party, perhaps, but on a very grand scale.

She backed out and continued along the corridor. Further along, a door lay ajar. Perhaps this was where she would find the elusive Lord Dart.

She pushed the door open and there he was, seated at a desk, wearing a pair of spectacles on the end of his aristocratic nose. He wore a tweed coat and belcher handkerchief at his throat. The uniform of a gentleman farmer. And he wore it with impeccable style.

By comparison, she felt suddenly dowdy.

As was right. After all, he was an earl and she merely a cook.

The room, however, was nothing like the luxurious ballroom. The furniture had seen better days and the air had a stale smell.

He looked up upon her entry, removed his spectacles and pushed to his feet.

That she had not expected. Courtesy to the lower orders was rarely observed in her experience.

She dipped a curtsy. 'You said we should discuss the terms of my employment this morning.'

'I did. You found everything to your satisfaction with your new quarters?'

Startled, she stared at him. Most of the employers she had come across since leaving home hadn't cared a farthing whether she found her quarters, let alone if she found them satisfactory. 'They are perfectly adequate.'

They had, in fact, been deliciously cosy and the bed had been so comfortable she had drifted to sleep in an instant.

He indicated a chair in front of the desk. 'Please, be seated.'

She hesitated. Then took the chair offered.

'You have the contract for me to sign?' he asked.

She laid the sheaf of papers on the desk. 'The agency contract.'

He perused the paper. 'All seems in order.'

He didn't even blink at the ten pounds per week the agency had proposed and she had wondered if he might argue about it, as had happened before when an employer discovered her youth.

An uneasy feeling rippled down her spine. Everything about this man—this house—seemed out of kilter with her experience. Perhaps accepting this position, no matter how lucrative, was a mistake.

But then everything she attempted seemed to be a mistake. Such as giving herself to Alan and trusting her mother to have her happiness at heart.

Unfortunately, each new undertaking she had embarked on had proved to have drawbacks.

It seemed this one might be no different.

The question was—would the drawbacks be untenable?

Chapter Two

Damian eyed the young woman sitting calmly before him. For someone who had chosen hard work after being raised in the lap of luxury, she seemed remarkably sanguine.

The self-assurance of the overprivileged miss. It seemed she hadn't learned her place. Or was she merely playing at being a member of the lower orders? Was her family supporting her, while they let her play with her patty pans?

He wouldn't be surprised.

He scrawled his signature at the bottom of the contract and handed it back.

'I had expected to find I would have a scullery maid to help,' she said.

Aha, here it was, just as he had expected, the lady needing someone else to do the real work. 'I doubt there is enough to keep two people busy.'

Her lovely mouth tightened. 'It took me four hours to clean the kitchen this morning, My Lord. A cook does not normally undertake that sort of labour. Why don't I seek help from a woman in the village for the days each week your household is in residence? It will not cost that much.'

He felt a sense of disappointment. As if he had wanted her to be different. Which was nonsense, of course.

'If the work is too much for you, perhaps I need to look for someone else.'

Her soft grey eyes focused on his face.

Dammit it. She was going to call his bluff.

She straightened her shoulders slightly, a stiffening of her resolve no doubt. But what was it she had decided?

'Very well,' she said briskly.

He let go the breath he hadn't realised he was holding and nodded.

'I will see how it goes,' she continued. 'I reserve the right to revisit the issue if necessary.'

If necessary. He could not help but admire her gall. But having passed one hurdle, he wasn't going to erect another. 'As you wish.'

She rose to her feet.

He stood up and opened the door. She paused on the threshold and glanced up at him. 'And I am not required to feed your guests?'

Oh, yes, she really did not want to work too hard. She was exactly what he had expected.

He narrowed his eyes. 'No. My London staff will take care of their needs, you have no need to worry that you will be overburdened.'

'I see. Thank you.' She turned and walked away. Her stride was purposeful, but exceedingly feminine. Quite enticing, in fact. Womanly and elegant at the same time. He muttered a curse under his breath.

He had the odd feeling she would prove to be more of a challenge than he had expected. Now if he could only figure out why that would be, he could solve the problem.

He glanced down at the papers on his desk. Some bills from tradesmen, an estimate for a new roof on the east wing from a local carpenter, and a bill for feed, which reminded him—he had planned to visit his horses this morning.

He put on his coat and headed across the courtyard.

In the stables, he found Pip in his shirt sleeves, already at work. No point in hiring a stable master and grooms when the animals were only here a couple of days a week, so he and Pip took on those duties.

The same logic did not apply to his cook, of course. Her wages were a small price to pay for the punishment he planned to exact.

He glanced at the bay standing patiently under Pip's ministrations. 'Is Caesar all right?'

Pip straightened. 'He seems fine. I was worried he had the colic last night, but everything is right this morning.'

'Glad to hear it.' Damian picked up a pitchfork and began mucking out the stall.

'I met your cook,' Pip said.

An odd sensation tightened his gut. Damian straightened his forkful of manure and regarded his friend. 'Did you?'

'On her way to see you. *Une belle petite fille, mon ami.* Be careful she does not turn the tables on you.'

He grunted and heaved the load of stinking straw into the barrow. 'Unlikely. She's not my sort of female at all.' He preferred the earthy experienced type who expected nothing but a generous gift at the end of an association.

Pip chuckled. 'You are right, of course. She struck me as very prim and proper. Perhaps she is more my sort.'

Damian snorted. 'Prim and proper would have *you* running for the hills. Prim and proper is looking for marriage.' He was banking on it. He leaned on his fork and glowered at his friend's grinning face. 'I meant what I said. Stay well away from her. This is mine to finish.'

Pip grimaced. 'You don't have to warn me off. I am not in the market for a wife, I assure you.' Pip put away his brushes and tossed a blanket over Caesar. 'You, however, are a different story. A nobleman needs an heir, does he not?'

Damian grabbed the barrow's handles and lifted it. This conversation was pointless. 'The title is nothing but a means to an end. And when that end is accomplished, I'll have no use for it.' He stomped out into the yard and tipped his load on the manure pile.

Behind him he heard Pip's laughter.

Damn him.

He could laugh. But Damian had decided long ago he cared nothing about the title or the duty it entailed. He had set himself one purpose in life and that was to make those who had caused him and his family to suffer humiliation and degradation suffer it tenfold in return.

Nothing would ever get in the way of that, even if it took him the rest of his life.

He certainly didn't want to marry. Women came with a whole set of expectations of their own. And if you failed to meet them, they did not take it well. His own mother had died of a broken heart, her sensibilities weakened and living in squalor too much to cope with after his father's failures.

Their family had lost everything because Father had believed the smiles and promises of a couple of noblemen he admired and who hadn't hesitated to use his admiration to their advantage.

Now the tables were turned. He, Damian, was the one the *ton* admired and fawned over. And he would have no hesitation in turning the tables on them and their offspring when the time was right.

He gazed across the courtyard at the house he had lived in until he was ten. The last twenty years had not treated it kindly. The bailiffs had taken anything of value that was not nailed down, but since it was entailed, it could not be sold to clear their debts. His family had been forced to leave England or face debtors' prison. Over the years several renters had come and gone and ultimately it had been abandoned to its fate. The cost to put it right would be enormous.

The estate belonging to the title he had recently inherited he would sell at the first opportunity, if anyone would buy it. He didn't give a damn. He would have loved to have sold it all—this estate, this house—and be rid of the financial and emotional burden, but its entailment meant he had to make do.

Once his plan had borne fruit, it could fall down for all he cared. He and Pip had set their sights on a new life in the New World.

The staff who had arrived earlier in the afternoon was a strange lot indeed. Pamela had expected housemaids and footmen and, indeed, when they had arrived, they had apparently gone about those sorts of tasks in the upstairs rooms, but the chattering jolly bunch who had come down from their quarters for dinner were like no servants she had ever seen.

The men wore the powdered wigs of footmen to be sure, and a livery of sorts, but rather than being of all the same discreet colour designed to fade into the background, their coats were bright blues, reds and greens and embellished with quantities of gold braid.

The women wore evening gowns and elaborate coiffures and glittering jewellery at throat and wrist. Stones made of paste, no doubt, but they sparkled in the candlelight of the plain servants' dining hall. And they all carried masks.

At the direction of the head footman, who had introduced himself as Albert, his underlings carried the tureens of stew from the kitchen to the table. She joined them, seating herself at one end of the table with Albert at the other.

The moment Albert finished saying grace everyone helped themselves to stew and fresh baked bread.

She turned to the young woman beside her, who was tucking in with apparent relish. 'I expect you will be busy when the guests arrive?' Dressed as she and the other women were, Pamela could not imagine their tasks were limited to bed making or fire lighting.

The girl eyed her up and down somewhat suspiciously, Pamela thought. 'Ain't that the truth?' She broke apart a slice of bread and dipped it in the gravy. 'Good grub for a change.'

A woman further down the table shot her a glare. 'Anything is better than what you got at the workhouse, Meg,' she called out.

A tall handsome young man in a red coat seated on the other side of Pamela chuckled. 'Don't take any notice of Betsy, down there. She's cross because you are a better cook. I'm Johnny, by the way. How do you do?' He raised his voice. 'Isn't that right?'

There were mutters of agreement around the table.

A sudden silence descended and people rose to their feet. Surprised, Pamela glanced up to see His Lordship in the doorway.

Clearly dressed for the evening in a black form-fitting coat that showed off his broad shoulders and lithe body, a dazzling white cravat with an emerald glinting in its folds and an emerald-green silk waistcoat, he looked gorgeous.

Her stomach gave an appreciative little flip. She was horrified to notice similar reactions on the faces of the other women.

'Please,' he said with a charming smile, 'sit down. Do not let me interrupt your meal.'

Everyone resumed their seats.

Pamela schooled her expression into one of cool enquiry. 'May I be of assistance, Your Lordship?'

Albert frowned, as if he thought she should not have spoken.

'I came to assure myself all is satisfactory,' Dart said. His gaze took in the table and the food before falling on Albert.

'Mrs Lamb has done us proud, My Lord,' Albert said.

Others at the table nodded their agreement.

Pamela could not quite believe her eyes and ears. What nobleman ever came to the servants' hall to ensure his staff was well fed?

His Lordship sent a glance of approval in her direction. 'It certainly smells wonderful.'

It seemed she had passed muster. Was that what this was all about, him checking up on her performance of her duties?

'Would you care to try it?'

He hesitated. 'Perhaps another time.'

The clock on the wall struck six. 'Come on, you lot,' Albert, said. 'Finish up. There's a lot to do before the chickens arrive.'

'Chickens?' Pamela said. Her voice was lost in the scraping of chairs on flagstones and the general hubbub.

Or perhaps not. 'Birds ripe for the plucking,' Johnny said in a low mutter, leaning close as he got up.

His words had a distinctly ominous undertone. She glanced over at His Lordship who stood back to allow everyone out of the door.

A strange sensation curled in the pit of her stomach. There was something not quite right here. Something she did not understand. Something she had the feeling she should have been told before she accepted the position.

There was no chance to ask any questions. In moments, the dining hall was empty, His Lordship having followed them out.

Pamela huffed out a breath, stacked the plates and carried them to the kitchen sink.

She might be inclined to find out just what was going on here. And if it was something unpleasant, as she was starting to suspect? She would have to decide if she would go or stay.

Leaving would require she pay a heavy penalty for breaking her contract. And the employment agency might refuse to send her any more offers of work.

That would not be a good outcome.

If she could not find other work, she would have to return home—to her mother and the prospect of accepting her elderly suitor.

She finished clearing the table and headed back to her sink.

A portly man in a chef's hat was standing at the stove with a ladle in his hand.

'Good evening,' she said.

The man turned. His face reminded her of a jolly elf, rosy red cheeks, brown eyes and hair which was clearly receding. His mouth turned down at the sight of her. 'Who are you?' His tone was definitely belligerent.

She eyed him calmly. 'Mrs Lamb, the new cook. And you?'

'Chandon. His Lordship's chef.' He took a sip of her stew. 'Adequate. Fit for those who serve.'

'They seemed to like it,' she said, trying not to let him bait her into saying something she would regret.

'They know nothing.' He stalked out.

He was wrong. Her stew was more than adequate. It

was delicious. Her father, who liked his food, had said so. Chandon was another of those men who feared female competition.

Well, this was her kitchen. Her domain. Next time he set foot in it, she would demand his departure.

She filled her sink full of dishes with hot water and soap and began the mindless task of washing up.

The sound of horses' hooves and carriage wheels crunching on gravel came from outside.

His Lordship's guests, no doubt. Along with their coachmen and grooms, who also required an evening meal.

They would definitely appreciate her stew, Chandon be hanged.

Damian surveyed his domain.

Now the obligatory meal was over, the tip of the hat to a legitimate house party, here, in the gaming room, he felt comfortable and in control.

The rattle of die and the clink of glasses amid the chatter and laughter played like a perfectly conducted symphony. Every table overflowed with players watched over by his female croupiers, smiling and nimble, while the footmen moved through the throng with trays of the very best champagne.

The more the pigeons drank, the more they played. The more they played, the more money he made.

A movement at the door caught his eye. A brief flash of drab skirt whisked out of sight.

What the devil?

There was only one woman in this house dressed in dreary grey. He passed through his guests, smiling and bowing, showing no sign of the anger building inside.

Pip, currently entertaining a couple of ladies at a game

of vingt-et-un, glanced up as he passed. An eyebrow rose in question. *Something wrong?* the look asked.

Nothing he couldn't deal with, he replied with a tilt of his head. They had been communicating with these silent signals since they were lads when the gendarmes would have carted them off to jail had they discerned the tricks they were up to.

Outside in the corridor, there was no sign of his quarry. He walked quietly along the hall to the nearest room, the library. He pushed at the door and it swung open.

On the other side of the room, his cook, in her prim grey gown and severe cap, was staring up at a portrait of one of his female ancestors in powdered wig and Elizabethan ruff, trying, no doubt, to give the impression she was completely absorbed. The tension in her shoulders indicated she was fully aware of his presence.

He stalked across the room and stood inches behind her. The severe bun beneath her cap meant her nape was bared to his gaze, soft and white and vulnerable. How would her skin feel against his lips? Would she shiver if he kissed her? Or would she turn and slap his face?

'Mrs Lamb,' he murmured.

She swung around as if startled, then backed up when she realised his nearness.

'My Lord?' Her voice was breathy, a little shaky as if her heart was beating too fast for comfort.

'Was there something you required?' he asked.

'I…er… I was wondering if the staff would require supper at the end of their day?'

Quick-witted, then. It was a perfectly reasonable explanation, even if it wasn't the truth. But then he hadn't expected the truth from her father's daughter. Deceit ran in her blood.

'There will be plenty left over for them once my guests depart, should they feel the need.'

'Oh, I see. Thank you.'

She made to move around him. He cut her off. She frowned.

'What was your real purpose for being in this wing of the house?' he asked.

She lifted her chin in a little show of defiance, but pink stained her cheeks. Guilt at being caught in a lie? 'I was curious.'

'You know what curiosity did?'

She looked him right in the eyes. 'I am not a cat, My Lord.'

And not a meek little mouse either. But then she hadn't been raised to be meek, unless she was dealing with someone she considered her better, or a good marriage prospect. 'I see. Is your curiosity now satisfied?'

She hesitated.

What would she say next?

'Why would members of the *ton* drive all the way out here to gamble when there are plenty of hells and whatnot close to hand in London?'

Interesting that she instantly saw right to the hub of the matter. 'Why indeed?'

She shot him a piercing stare. 'That is hardly an answer.'

'I don't answer to you, Mrs Lamb,' he said in bored tones. 'I fail to see how it is any of your business, to be honest.'

She flinched slightly, but, to his surprise, held her ground. 'It is my business if you are engaged in some sort of nefarious activity.'

Devil take it, did she think to cause trouble? He closed the gap between them once more. She held her ground, but her hands tightened convulsively at her waist.

'As far as I know, house parties are not outlawed in England,' he said evenly.

'I—no. It is rather reprehensible for a nobleman to be setting up a gaming establishment, however. Relieving people of their money.'

And it wasn't reprehensible to defraud a gentleman of his fortune as her father had done? 'This is not a gaming establishment. Everyone here is a guest, invited to spend an evening among their peers, enjoying each other's company and playing cards or die to while away the time.'

Her expression said she did not believe a word of it. 'At every one of the tables a member of your staff holds the bank. How is that different from a gaming establishment? Everyone knows that the bank almost always wins.'

'Unlike most gaming establishments, this house plays fair. While the odds are naturally stacked in favour of those who hold the bank, those who gamble here have a fair chance of winning large sums of money.'

Her lips thinned. 'Only to lose it all again the next time.'

How dare she look down on him? 'Do you think they would not be gaming elsewhere under much less favourable circumstances, if they were not gambling here?'

Her shoulders slumped. 'I suppose not.'

Surprised that she acquiesced so readily to his logic, he stepped back and gestured for her to leave. 'Now you have satisfied your curiosity, I would prefer it that you return to your domain and leave my domain to me. Is that clear?'

'Very clear, My Lord.' She looked as though she wanted to say more, inhaled a deep breath and marched out.

He watched her go. Felt the tug of his heart again. Pity? Regret that she would eventually receive her comeuppance at his hands?

How was it possible?

Had her father felt any regret about what had happened to him and his mother? It was only right that the daughter suffer a similar fate.

He strode back to the chatter and laughter in the ballroom. Everything was moving along very nicely. Nothing and no one would stop him from dealing justice to those who deserved it.

Chapter Three

Pamela stretched and snuggled back beneath her covers. She hadn't been this cosy since she had been forced to leave her bedroom at the vicarage behind.

In those days her dreams had been full of Alan, her future husband. Both sets of parents had approved their marriage and she had romanticised her future as a soldier's wife. His death, an accident while on manoeuvres, had been a terrible shock, not the least because they had anticipated their wedding vows. An awful truth she would have to admit to any man who might propose marriage in the future. She shook her head at her foolish thoughts. As if that was ever going to happen. Marriage was out of the question.

She was now an independent woman, earning her own living. It wasn't quite as easy as one might expect, but it provided a good deal of satisfaction.

Somewhere in the distance a cockerel crowed. She had work to do. A kitchen to ready for the next onslaught of His Lordship's 'servants', people who earned their keep by turning cards and rolling dice in the employ of a man she didn't trust an inch. She grimaced. She did not believe a word of his explanation the previous evening and not just because he had made her stomach flutter in a most inappropriate way.

That he had done on purpose. Standing so close. Looking down at her as if she was a mouse to be gobbled up by a cat.

She could not help recalling how handsome he had looked in his evening clothes, the way he'd surveyed *his domain* as he called it. He'd looked elegant and devastatingly charming when he'd smiled at one of his guests. Her stomach fluttered anew.

Dash it. She would do very well to avoid him if that was the sort of reaction he caused.

She forced herself to throw the covers back, but instead of the usual chilly air of a servant's attic, the room was warm and welcoming.

She lit a candle and prepared for her day.

As she washed and dressed, she found herself humming. She paused. What was that song?

A waltz. How odd. She must have heard it the previous evening.

She brushed her hair and pinned it neatly under her cap, then went to prepare the breakfast table in the dining hall. Most of the houses she had worked in fed the servants early in the morning, before they began their duties, but here there were no servants except her. All she had to do was prepare a breakfast for the Earl and his friend Monsieur Phillippe.

At the kitchen door, she halted on the threshold. Her heart gave an odd little thump.

Oh! What on earth was *he* doing here? The Earl himself.

'Good morning, Mrs Lamb.'

She glared at him. 'I hardly expected to see you so early this morning, My Lord.'

He blinked and shook his head as if to clear it. No doubt he had imbibed too much the previous evening. 'Really—why not?'

'If I am not mistaken, your guests did not depart until the small hours, which means I expected you to be still abed. Now if you will excuse me, I have breakfast to prepare.'

'That is why I am here—I am starving.'

'Breakfast will be available in the servants' hall shortly, as per your instructions.'

He gave her that charmingly boyish smile, the one that caused her mind to go blank and her heart to flutter. 'I am hungry enough to eat a horse right now.'

He sounded like a wheedling lad instead of the arrogant nobleman she knew him to be. But she could hardly deny a meal to her employer.

'Very well. Would scrambled eggs suit you?'

'A bit of bacon with it wouldn't go amiss.'

She couldn't hold back a chuckle. 'Very well, bacon and coffee. Shall I bring it to the servants' hall or…?' There had to be a dining room, she just hadn't seen it.

'I don't want to put you to any trouble,' he said, almost meekly. 'I can eat here.' He sat down at the end of the kitchen table.

Meek? Hardly. This man would never be anything but demanding and commanding. And his presence in her kitchen unnerved her. 'I have a great deal to do this morning.' Oh, dear, that sounded a bit rude.

He seemed to take it in stride. 'Then you should not waste your time bringing me a tray.'

He was clearly determined to have his way. And she did have a great deal to do. Instead of arguing, she needed to give him his breakfast and send him on his way.

She gathered her supplies from the pantry and set out what she needed. She would have to wait to break her fast until he was gone.

As she worked, he sat silently watching. She tried hard

to ignore his presence, but failed. Her hand shook as she poured coffee into a mug for him and one for her.

She passed him the cream and sugar, which he refused. She added generous dollops of each to her own cup.

The fire was now hot enough for cooking and so, after a few sips of coffee, she fried the bacon, scrambled two eggs and cooked two slices of toast.

'That bacon smells delicious,' he said as she served him.

'It is excellent,' she replied. 'Not too lean, but meaty.'

She handed him a knife and fork and a napkin and began scrubbing down the stove.

'Where is your home?' he asked.

'My home?' The question took her aback. She turned to face him.

He picked up his coffee cup with one eyebrow raised. He wanted an answer.

'I grew up in a small village in Kent, Bexley.'

He nodded slowly. 'I see.'

'And you?' she asked feeling emboldened by his interest.

'Here, at this house. And in Marseilles.'

'France. I have never travelled outside England. How interesting it must have been.' She turned back to her work.

'Interesting is one word for it.'

'What word would you use?'

'Educational.'

There was a tinge of wryness in his tone, but she could not read much in his expression when she glanced back at his face. 'Travel broadens the mind, they say.'

He chuckled and there was a warmth in that soft sound this time. Her stomach gave a little hop.

Most unnerving.

'They do say so indeed,' he said and bit into his toast

with strong white teeth. Why did he have to look so gorgeous simply chewing on a bite of toast?

She forced herself to turn back to her work. Keeping her hands busy meant she would not be tempted to stand gazing at him like a besotted fool.

By the time she had cleaned the top of the stove, His Lordship was rising to his feet. To her surprise, he took his plate and cup to the sink, passing close behind her. She froze, but he did not touch her or even seem to notice.

'Thank you for accommodating me,' he said.

'You were quick,' she said, then wished she had bitten her tongue. It was not her place to comment on his speed and she could not help but feel pleased that he had enjoyed his meal. She put a pan of water on the hob to heat for washing up.

'I learned early to eat fast or risk going hungry,' he said, seemingly unperturbed.

'At school, I suppose,' she said. She'd heard that some of the schools the boys attended were quite beastly.

His chuckle had a bitter edge. 'I suppose you could call it a school.'

Puzzled she turned to face him, but he was already halfway out of the door and did not turn back to explain. What on earth could he mean by that cryptic comment?

Replete from the delicious breakfast, Damian made his way to his study. He needed to tally up last night's income. Setting up Rake Hall had cost him a pretty penny, but it was starting to pay for itself.

He sat down at his desk and pulled out the tin box containing money and vowels.

He paused for a moment, thinking about breakfast. He could not recall when he had enjoyed a meal more.

The eggs were light and fluffy and seasoned just right, the bacon curled at its crispy edges and she had presented him with some perfectly browned toast, butter and preserves to finish it off.

But more than that, he had enjoyed watching her work. The swift sure way she beat the eggs, the turning of the bacon and the toast at just the right moment.

She knew her business.

Which, when you thought about it, was exceedingly odd for the daughter of a vicar and the cousin of at least one earl and a couple of barons. Daughters of the nobility did not know how to cook as a rule.

His investigations had revealed that the vicar had not left his family well off when he died, which was strange in and of itself, but somehow, he had not expected her to support herself by her own industry. Her mother certainly had not, marrying at the first opportunity. It was odd that the daughter had not chosen the same path to comfort.

Fortunate, given his plan. And that was *not* a pang of regret.

He had buckled down to work and by midday had finished.

Time to check in with Pip. He stretched his arms over his head. Paperwork: it was the bane of his life. A necessary evil. He shrugged into his coat and strolled out to the stables.

He met Pip in the courtyard on his way into the house.

'Good morning.'

Pip grinned and shook his hand. '*Bonjour, mon ami.* Are we rich?'

'Not yet.' He grimaced. 'We still have some way to go before we have recovered our investment. But we will. A few more evenings like last night and you will never need to work again.'

'Good. You have no need to check on the stables, if that is where you were going. All is under control.'

'Then you have no need to check in on the kitchen.' Now why the hell had he added that?

Pip's eyes gleamed with amusement. '*Bien sur*. I will be heading back to Town once my bag is packed. Will you come with me?'

'No. I will return in a couple of days. There are a few things here that require my attention. I noticed another leak in the roof. It would not do to have the ceiling fall down on our patrons.'

The smile on his friend's face became more mischievous. 'Or on the new cook.'

Damian let the comment pass. He was used to Pip's teasing. Or at least he should be, but he still felt a surge of irritation at his friend's obvious interest in Mrs Lamb. 'Well, if there is nothing for me to do in the stables, I'll take my walk around the property and see what other repairs are needed.'

Pip nodded. 'Very well. I look forward to seeing you in London in a few days.'

Damian meandered across the lawn with no clear destination in mind and found himself approaching the orangery—a glass structure set facing south against the wall along one side of the formal gardens.

He frowned. Someone had left the door open.

He hadn't been in the building since he had returned from France. Nor could he recall whether, the last time he had passed by the building, the door had been open or closed.

Perhaps the door had been left ajar years ago when his family fled for the Continent.

The dark sky made it gloomy inside. That and the smell of rotting vegetation. Bare branches added to the sense of death.

To his astonishment, Mrs Lamb was poking around in one of the large containers at the far end. It contained a small tree sporting the only green leaves in the building. She was the last person he wanted to meet.

Or was she? He sauntered between the rows of clay pots, the carpet of dead leaves crunching underfoot, wondering how long it would be before she noticed his approach.

She glanced up as he drew near. 'Oh. It is you.' Displeasure filled her expression.

What had he done? 'Why are you in here?' He sounded a little more brusque than he intended.

'It is an orangery. I was looking for oranges.' She must have seen his disbelief because she continued, 'I thought to make some marmalade.' She shook her head. 'Unfortunately, most of the trees are dead. They have been left without water.'

Another act to lay at the feet of his enemies. Dead fruit trees. Not the worst of their crimes, to be sure.

She tipped her basket towards him and in the bottom sat three small oranges. 'I did find this one tree with fruit. There is water dripping down from somewhere. It kept the tree alive. Let me show you.'

She spoke as if she had found a treasure.

Bemused, and very slightly enchanted by her enthusiasm—only very slightly—he followed the direction of her pointing finger.

'I think the water must come in somewhere up there.'

The glass panes above their heads were filthy, but he

could indeed see streaks in the dirt cause by trickling water. Higher up the glass was cracked.

He grimaced. 'Something must have broken the pane. Perhaps a tree branch in a storm.'

She gave a little shiver. 'Indeed. Well, I suppose it is an ill wind. The other trees are truly dead, but this one can be saved, if you've a mind.'

About to say it wasn't worth the trouble, the hope in her voice gave him pause. 'Perhaps.'

She tipped her head. 'Don't you care that this poor tree has struggled onwards in the face of terrible neglect?'

'There are other things more important than an orange tree demanding my attention at the moment.'

Disappointment filled her expression. 'Your house parties.'

'Indeed.'

She made a face of distaste. 'As you wish.'

How was it possible she could make him feel guilty about a tree? And what right had she to judge him about his way of making a living? Damn her. If not for the actions of her father, it would never have been necessary.

'I shouldn't think those oranges are worth the time. Better to put them in the slop bucket.'

'Well, I don't know about you, but I like marmalade with my toast and, since it is my time, I—'

'Time I pay for is *my* time,' he said mildly, but still she shot him a glare.

'You do not pay for all of my time. There are hours that belong to me, My Lord.'

Should he point out that the sugar she would add to the fruits, the wood she would use for the stove and the pots and pans and jars were all his? He opened his mouth.

Off in the distance, thunder rumbled.

Mrs Lamb froze. 'A storm?'

Genuine fear. The desire to put a protective arm around her shoulders took him by surprise. He restrained the urge. 'Yes,' he said, coolly, unfeelingly.

She glanced upward with a shiver. 'Excuse me. I will return to the house.' She moved past him.

The clean smell of soap blended with, of all things, the scent of orange filled his nostrils. A surprisingly enticing combination. The desire to inhale more of it had him following her, the rustle of dead leaves marking their passing. Outside, she pulled her shawl over her head, picked up her skirts and ran for the house.

Only by strength of will did he refrain from following to ensure she arrived safely.

Devil take it.

Never mind the orange trees. Lives had been ruined and that required payment.

To Pamela's relief the storm that had threatened earlier in the day had passed by with only a few distant rumbles. She'd spent until mid-afternoon organising the kitchen cupboards and preparing dinner for her employer—since he had not left with Monsieur Phillippe—a roast of beef and a selection of vegetables along with a game pie and some soup. To be served in the servants' hall.

It really was not right that a titled gentleman should eat in such lowly quarters, even if he was the only person dining.

She removed her apron and, taking the ring of keys she had discovered in a drawer, set off to explore the house, to see if she could discover a more suitable dining room.

Clearly the ballroom and the dining room used for his guests were too large. His study was unsuitable since it lacked a proper table, so she wandered along corridors, peeping into each room she passed. The library she had visited yesterday was devoid of any furniture and the empty shelves were covered in dust.

Without much hope, she threw open the last door along the wing and peered into a dark room with chinks of light showing here and there through the shutters along one wall. She picked her way across and with a little effort opened one of the heavy wooden shutters to reveal a magnificent view of the park.

The room was not large, but it was exactly what she had been seeking. Pleasant surroundings and no dust. A drawing room. No doubt the table in the centre was intended to be used for playing games of chance rather than for eating, but with a table cloth, it would perfectly adequate for one or two diners.

She threw back the rest of the shutters. Given the state of most of the house she was surprised to find this room in such good order. The only drawback was its distance from the kitchen.

A problem she could solve, surely?

If she got everything ready beforehand and put all the hot items on one large tray, perhaps it would work.

And when Monsieur Phillippe was also in residence, he could do the fetching and carrying.

It was exceedingly strange that neither one of them had a valet and His Lordship did not keep at least one footman to take care of the house. Instead, they ferried servants back and forth from London at what must be a considerable expense. If the gambling was not illegal, as His Lordship claimed, then there must be something else nefarious going on.

She recalled the way Meg and the others had laughed

about the upstairs rooms being ready. Perhaps it was there she would find her answers.

She picked up the keys from the table where she had put them while she opened the shutters and made her way to the narrow staircase at the end of the hall.

She hesitated. It really was none of her business.

She glanced down the staircase. Was it possible there was a shorter route to the kitchen beneath the courtyard? If so, it would make using the room a great deal more convenient. Would it not make more sense if she explored in that direction instead?

His Lordship might say everything was above board, but, from what she had learned over the past several years, many men said anything to get their own way.

Like her stepfather trying to push her into a marriage with his friend, a man old enough to be her father. She quelled a shudder.

Before she could change her mind, she ran upwards. A quick glance was all she would need to satisfy her curiosity and hopefully put her mind to rest.

The first door she came to did not open when she turned the handle. Locked.

She tried first one key, then another. None of them fit. Bother.

'Can I be of assistance?' a deep voice enquired.

His Lordship. Her heart sank. She turned to face him. To her surprise and relief, his expression was one of interest, not anger.

'I…er… I was seeking a place where you might dine, other than the servants' hall.'

A dark brow winged upwards. 'Among the bedrooms?'

Dash it. 'No. I found the perfect room downstairs and

then came up here, curious about something one of the maids said.'

He drew closer. 'What sort of something?'

She tried to ignore his proximity, the way he loomed over her, the way he made her feel overwhelmed and breathless.

It was hard to ignore when her heart galloped so hard.

She took a deep steadying breath. 'It wasn't so much what she said, as the way she giggled when she was asked if the bedrooms were ready. It struck me as odd since you said your guests were not staying the night.'

A rather mischievous smile curved his lips. 'I can see how that would pique your interest, Mrs Lamb. Why she would giggle, I cannot guess, but these rooms are used by my guests when they require a little privacy. They are generally called retiring rooms, *n'est ce-pas*?'

Oh. Retiring rooms, where a lady must go to use the necessary. And possibly a gentleman, too. It was so obvious, why hadn't she thought of it? Was she so determined to see problems at every turn in regard to this man? 'I see. Thank you. Well, if you will excuse me—'

He reached out a hand. 'Where did you get the keys?'

Swallowing, she glanced down at the ring of keys clutched in her hand. 'I found them in a drawer in the kitchen.'

'May I see?' His tone brooked no argument and, indeed, why would she argue? This was his house after all.

She held them out.

His wary expression cleared. 'Those are for the cellars. Now, you said you had discovered a suitable dining room. Would you care to show it to me?'

As if she had any option.

He shepherded her towards the staircase. Not that she

had any objections to showing him. She was pleased with her find.

'This way,' she said.

He followed her downstairs and along the ground floor corridor. She opened the door to the small chamber. 'What do you think?'

His silence caused her to look up. The genial expression had been replaced with...sadness?

How ironic that this woman had declared this room as perfect. This had been his mother's favourite place to spend her days with her needlework or taking tea with her friends. It was the room whose loss his mother had bemoaned constantly in their draughty two-room apartment in Marseilles.

When he first returned to the house, Damian had suffered an urge to restore this chamber to its former glory. His memories of the house and park were vague, but this room remained etched in his mind by way of her description. He'd done his best to recreate it and had been pleased with the result.

Even so, whenever he entered this room, he felt the pain of loss. That his mother had not lived long enough to return here, to redo it herself, saddened him.

He should have left it well alone. It had been pointless and he couldn't step foot in it without remembering her, and now this woman wanted him to eat in here. Damien tamped down his emotions. Or at least he attempted to sound calm.

'It is not a dining room.'

'No, but...' she opened one of the shutters '...the view of the park is quite lovely and the table, while small, would work for two people. I would cover it with a heavy cloth so the wood is not damaged—'

'I will dine in the servants' hall as previously arranged.'

She spun around, obviously surprised and obviously planning to attempt to make her case.

His frown must have stopped her words, because she closed her mouth and folded her hands at her waist. 'Very well.'

What the devil did she have to be disappointed about? 'What does it matter where I eat as long as I do eat? You cannot tell me this is more convenient, for I am not a fool.'

'No. No, indeed,' she said hastily, edging towards the door. 'If you wish to eat in the servants' hall, it is of no matter to me.'

Damn it all. This was not what he intended to happen. He was supposed to be charming her, not acting like a bear with a sore head.

He strode to the window and looked out. In his mind's eye he saw himself as a small boy running across the expanse of lawn trailing a kite, or sitting astride his first pony being led by a groom. But he no longer knew if these idyllic mental pictures were memories or merely stories told by his mother.

His clearest boyhood memories were of the stink of Marseilles's streets lined with tenements and running with filth. Of stealing pocket handkerchiefs to buy food. More recently they were of making money gambling in taverns until he had enough saved to buy an establishment of his own.

He heard a sound behind him. She was leaving.

'Wait.'

He turned back to face her. She straightened her shoulders as if bracing against more of his ill humour. 'I will eat in here.'

Surprise crossed her face. 'If you are sure?'

'Why not? As you say, the surroundings are far more

pleasant than downstairs. I will even show you a shortcut to the kitchens, if you wish.'

'That would be most helpful, thank you.'

'I am pleased to be of use.' He could not keep the wry note out of his voice.

She stifled a chuckle. He grinned at her. 'Come on. It's this way.'

He guided her down the stairs. After lighting one of the lamps set on a chest at the bottom, he led her along the gloomy tunnel he had discovered when exploring the wine cellars.

She shivered.

'Not afraid, are you?' he said recalling her previous reaction to thunder.

'Not at all. Just a little chilly.'

Yes, it was a great deal cooler down here and damp, too. He resisted a sudden urge to give her his coat and picked up his pace instead. 'It won't take long.'

'This goes under the courtyard?' Her voice echoed off the brick-lined walls.

'It does.' As they neared the end, he pointed to the doors on either side. 'These are the wine cellars. They used to be full of wine sent down by my father and his father before him. All gone now, apart from what I have purchased myself. Everything from before was sold off to cover my father's debts.'

'Oh, dear,' she said. 'Was he also a gambler?'

He gritted his teeth at the implied criticism. His father had never gambled a penny in his life until her father had tempted him down the road to hell. 'He certainly had a run of bad luck. But he wasn't what you would call a dyed-in-the-wool gambler, no.'

'I am sorry. It is none of my business.'

It *was* her business. But she did not need to know that yet. He pushed open the door at the end. 'And here we are back at the kitchens.'

She looked up at him with a smile. 'That is indeed a much faster way. I can deliver your food much more easily. Thank you.'

He smiled back. 'My pleasure. Now if you will excuse me, I have some business that requires my attention elsewhere.'

'Of course.' She dipped a little curtsy.

A mad idea bounced into his head. He hesitated. When had he become so tentative? He always followed his instincts. They never let him down. 'Since there is no one in residence at the moment, apart from you and me, you may as well join me for dinner.'

Her mouth dropped open. 'I could not. It would not be right.'

The more he thought about it, the more he liked the idea. 'Where is the sense in us each dining in a solitary state, using up candles in two rooms instead of one, when it would be far more economical to dine together?'

'It isn't appropriate.'

He sensed her weakening. 'Who is to know? I won't tell if you won't. Either dine with me in the drawing room or provide my dinner in the servants' hall and dine with me there. I am not asking.'

She huffed out a sigh. 'Very well. I will dine with you in the drawing room, if you insist.'

'I do.'

Before she could change her mind, he walked away. For

several moments, he felt her watching him, as if trying to understand the reason behind his invitation.

The wariness in her face after he had made his suggestion warned him he would have to tread very carefully if he was not going to scare her off.

Having dinner with her employer was the stupidest thing she had ever done.

She should have left the issue of where he dined well alone and she would not be in this mess. But, no. She had to interfere.

She had already got a fire going in the drawing room, lit the candles and set the table. Now all that was required was the food.

She eyed the trays she had prepared to deliver to the dining room. Three trays, each platter with its own cover. By the time she had delivered all three, no doubt the dishes on the first one would be barely lukewarm.

Oh, yes, a very stupid idea.

And then there was what she was wearing. She had been torn between her usual serviceable grey gown and the gown she wore to church. A rare occurrence since she had been in service. The pale blue muslin had won out, but now she was regretting her choice. Too late to change. She slipped a shawl around her shoulders to keep out the chill in the tunnel and picked up the heaviest of the three trays.

'Here, let me help you.'

She almost dropped the tray in shock.

He grabbed it.

'I can manage,' she said, hanging on to it a second longer than she should have.

'I am sure you can.' He smiled at her. 'But it occurred

to me that you might need to make more than one trip, unless you had some assistance.'

He looked lovely in his evening clothes. Suddenly she was very glad she had chosen her best dress. She could not help smiling back.

'Thank you.'

He picked up the second tray, easily holding each tray in one hand, whereas she had struggled with the weight using both of hers. 'Can you manage the last one?' he asked.

'Of course.'

'Good, then we can make it in one trip, if you would be so good as to get the door.'

And so, with her opening doors for him, they made their way to the little drawing room.

'If you would put your trays on the sideboard, there by the window,' she said as they entered the room, 'I think we can serve ourselves.'

He glanced around. 'This all looks very cosy.' He set the trays where she directed. 'What delights do you have in store for me?'

She swallowed. Tonight he was clearly trying to be pleasant. Trying? He was devastatingly charming.

In the hopes of impressing him with her skill, she had thought most carefully about the menu. After all, feeding him was a great deal different than feeding his servants.

'Would you care to pour yourself a libation,' she said, 'while I make things ready?'

She had set decanters of brandy, sherry and madeira on a small circular table beside one of the armchairs beside the hearth, where a fire burned merrily.

He walked over to inspect the offering. 'Sherry for you?' he asked.

Startled, she almost dropped the platter of vegetables.

'Oh, no. Nothing for me, thank you. I will have water with dinner.'

Carefully, she organised the dishes on the sideboard and turned with a smile. He was watching her, while sipping on what must be sherry judging from the glass he was holding.

'I hope the sherry is to your liking,' she said. 'I found it in the cellar you pointed out earlier.'

'It is a very good sherry,' he said, smiling at her. 'I selected it myself.'

She felt her cheeks heat. She resisted the temptation to press her palms against them, to cool them.

'Yes, of course. I beg your pardon.'

'No need to apologise,' he said cheerfully.

She finished laying out the dishes. 'We can eat whenever you are ready.' She gestured to the plates.

He set his glass down beside the decanters and strolled over to inspect her offerings. 'I say, this looks marvellous.'

He seemed to be in the mood to be pleased. She began to relax.

'If you would carve the beef and the chicken, and then help yourself to the other dishes, I think that would work very well. There is white wine in the cooler, or red wine, if you prefer.'

'Wonderful,' he said. He carved thin slices of the meat and put them on a plate, which, to her shock, he handed to her.

'Oh, but—'

He chuckled. 'Fill your plate with vegetables, Mrs Lamb, it would be a shame for everything to get cold while you dither.'

She repressed a smile and did as instructed. It was no good standing here arguing about protocol.

She took her plate to her place at the table and, to her

surprise, he was there, pulling back her chair, helping her to sit. She could not remember the last time she had been treated like a lady.

Her heart picked up speed. She sat and smiled up at him. 'Thank you.'

She waited for him to fill his plate and sit down.

He poured water for them both and then chose the white wine from the cooler and, without asking, poured them each a glass. 'You have gone to a great deal of trouble, Mrs Lamb. Thank you.' He raised his glass in a toast. 'To the chef.'

Once more her cheeks felt hot. She picked up her glass of wine and tilted her head in acknowledgement of his toast. They both sipped.

The wine was delicious. Crisp and cold and slightly fruity.

'Bon appetit,' he said and began to eat.

Her heart felt so full, she wasn't sure she could eat a bite. But she had to, or he would wonder if there was a problem.

She cut into the chicken and was pleased to find it juicy and tender. The scalloped potatoes were cooked just right and the vegetables were perfect. She gestured to the small gravy boat. 'Would you pass the gravy?'

'I most certainly will. Can you pass the mustard, please?'

For a moment or two there was silence as they both took the edge off their hunger.

Abruptly, he put down his knife and fork. 'Good Lord.'

She froze. Was something wrong?

'This is far beyond anything I expected.'

'I beg your pardon.'

'This food. It is delicious.'

He sounded so disbelieving, a surge of anger rose up

from somewhere deep inside. 'Why would you be surprised?'

'Because you are—' He stopped and shook his head.

'Because I am what? A woman? You did not think a woman would be able to cook as well as your fancy French chef?'

A guilty expression flashed across his face. He gave her a shamefaced smile. 'I apologise. I must say, this meal is as good as, if not better than, anything Chandon has prepared over the past year. In my experience, all the best chefs are men. And usually French.'

She had the feeling he wasn't speaking the entire truth. His reaction had been too extreme to match his reason.

But she was pleased by his compliment. She could hardly argue with his praise, even if something about it did not feel…honest. On the other hand, she was quite prepared to take issue with his premise. 'I learned how to cook from a woman, actually. We females are not as incompetent as some men seem to believe.' She hadn't meant to sound quite so stiff or so censorious. 'I am pleased you are enjoying the fruits of my labour.' That was hardly better.

He picked up his knife and fork. 'I am indeed.'

Damian covertly eyed his dinner companion. He had stupidly ruffled her feathers, when he had intended to enchant her.

What was it about this woman that caused him to lose his grip on his famous ability to charm birds out of trees? There wasn't a woman in London who wasn't susceptible, so the story went.

Pip would laugh his head off, if he knew how he had fumbled this one so badly.

'You are right, my dear Mrs Lamb. Women are often underestimated.'

'By men.'

He looked up and saw she was staring at him narrowed eyed, daring him to contradict her. Challenging.

He liked a challenge.

He finished his mouthful. 'Are you saying that women do not encourage us males to think of them as weaker, less able, more in need of protection? Indeed, do not ladies like to think of themselves as the weaker sex, both physically and mentally?'

Her spine straightened. 'Are you blaming women for their subjugation?'

'It was a question.'

'It was men who made the laws that define a wife as an extension of her husband, rather than a person in her own right. It was men who decided that an older daughter would be pushed aside by a younger brother.'

These were truths for which he had no answer. He had not thought about them terribly much, either. 'Do you have a brother?' He knew very well she did not, but she would not know that.

'No. I am an only child.'

'So you were not pushed aside?'

'No. But I knew girls who were. What I could not understand was their meek acceptance of the situation. Or their willingness to marry whomever their father picked out, even if they loved another.'

He really had not expected her to be quite so militant. 'This is a friend you are speaking of.'

'Yes. A friend who gave up any chance for happiness, though she would never admit it.'

'Because she did not stand up for herself, in your opinion.'

She gave him a suspicious glance, as if to see if his intention was to mock her opinions. Seemingly satisfied, she nodded. 'She could have said no. Under the law, one cannot be forced into marriage.'

'I think you are the sort of woman whom no one could force into anything. I admire your courage.'

A pained expression crossed her face. 'Sadly, I do not believe I am at all courageous.' She began eating again, as if to forestall herself from saying any more. He decided that it was best to change the subject.

'And where did you learn to cook so masterfully?'

'At home.'

'Without wishing to pry, I would say that you were brought up to be a lady, rather than a cook.'

She frowned, looking worried. 'Why would you think so?'

'You are well educated, well spoken and well versed in the finest of table manners, for a start. And I noticed that among the items in your room is an embroidery hoop already decorated with the finest of stitches. Your family was never among the poor.'

She pressed her lips together, clearly deciding how much to admit. 'You are observant, sir. It is true. My father was a gentleman. I learned to cook because I discovered a love for creating good food at a young age and I was indulged enough to be able to follow my passion. Now it is no longer a hobby, but the way I earn my bread, I am fortunate that passion and necessity collided.'

He raised his glass and smiled at her. 'No, my dear Mrs Lamb, I believe it is I who am fortunate.'

Her eyes widened. A smile curved her lips. In that moment pleasure and beauty shone in her face. 'Thank you, My Lord.' She picked up her glass and drank.

He leaned back in his chair, replete with fine food and fine wine and finally able to relax. He had made her smile.

She cleared the dishes from the table and set them on the buffet.

'Let me help you with that,' he said. 'Would you like me to help you carry them to the kitchen?

'No need. I will collect everything in the morning.' She offered him a shy glance. 'I have one last treat in store, if you would care for dessert.'

Dessert? It was she who looked like a sweet treat in her gown the colour of forget-me-nots. Good enough to eat. 'You are spoiling me.'

She rose and went to the buffet table. She bent to open its doors, presenting him with a view of her derrière, a beautifully rounded firm little bottom that he could imagine naked— He cut the thought off. What the devil was wrong with him?

She opened a door to reveal another, smaller cooler.

'May I assist you with that?' He was pleased that he sounded calm. Unaffected.

She glanced over her shoulder with a provocative smile. His heart skipped a beat.

'I can manage, My Lord.' She removed two small dishes, bumped the door closed with a seductive swing of her hip, leaving him dry mouthed, and brought the dishes to the table.

He forced himself to look at what she had placed before him and not the curves of her body that had just sent his body into a frenzy of lust the like of which he had not suffered since he was a youth.

'Ice cream!' he said, unable to resist grinning like a schoolboy.

'Lemon ice, actually,' she said as she sat down, 'with a touch of orange.'

'Made from the oranges in the greenhouse?'

She beamed. 'Yes. How did you guess?'

He thought about it for a moment. He recalled their conversation, about her desire to save that tree. 'You want to prove to me that the tree is worth saving.'

'Oh, dear, am I so easily read? Please, try it. Tell me what you think?'

'About the tree?' he teased gently.

Her light laugh made his body hum. 'No. About the dessert.'

While she watched him closely, he dipped his spoon into the oval yellow ice with a swirl of orange running through it. The taste was heavenly. Tart with a touch of sweetness and he could definitely distinguish both flavours. 'It is delicious. Ambrosia.'

She nodded, clearly satisfied with his reaction. And he felt supremely glad that she was happy.

He smiled wryly at himself. This was what he had wanted, wasn't it? To gain her trust. To seduce her the way her father had tempted his down a ruinous path.

He finished the dessert. 'Thank you. That was indeed a treat.'

She took those dishes from the table and stacked them neatly.

She glanced over at the table with the decanters and glasses. 'I expect you would like to partake of your port now.'

Was she trying to escape him? He wasn't ready to let her go just yet.

'Won't you join me?'

She looked shocked.

Damn. 'If you do not wish to partake of port, then I would be happy to join you in a cup of tea.'

Confusion filled her expression. 'I did not think of bringing a tea tray, My Lord. I presumed that once dinner was over…'

'I have an idea. Why don't we carry the dishes back to the kitchen and have tea there?'

She looked doubtful. 'Are you sure?'

'It is the perfect solution. That way I can help you with the dishes and we can have a perfect ending to a delicious meal.' He got up and started putting the leftovers on a tray. Somewhat unwillingly she filled the other tray.

'Ready?' he asked.

Chapter Four

With the dishes all stacked neatly in the scullery out of sight, Pamela concentrated on making tea for His Lordship, who had disposed himself on the settle beside the large hearth where she baked her bread.

She poured the boiling water into the teapot and waited the requisite number of minutes.

His Lordship, gazing into the fire, clearly deep in his own thoughts, looked a little sad. Or was that just her imagination?

Why on earth had he wanted to take tea in the kitchen?

It felt strange. Almost scandalous.

Of course it was scandalous. Single women didn't entertain single men like this. *Be honest.* Dinner had been scandalous.

But then she wasn't a 'single' woman, was she? While she might never have been married, she used a married woman's title and she wasn't exactly an innocent. If she had been, she might have seriously considered her mother's suggestion that she marry.

But she'd foolishly let her heart rule her head, let passion overcome good sense and given herself to the man she had expected to marry, Consequently, there was no point thinking about making any kind of marriage, let alone a good one. And besides she was perfectly happy as a cook.

On the other hand, she was nobody's fool and she was beginning to wonder if His Lordship had some sort of ulterior motive for insisting she eat dinner with him, then inviting himself to tea in her kitchen. Unless he was as lonely as he looked at this moment.

How could a man in his position be lonely?

She poured the tea and took it over. He glanced up with a faint smile. 'Thank you.'

He patted the seat beside him. 'Please, make yourself comfortable.'

Sit beside him? 'I—'

'I do not bite, Mrs Lamb.'

She winced. Now he sounded offended. 'Very well.' She fetched her cup and sat down making very sure to leave a few inches of space between them. The settle was certainly a good deal more comfortable than the bench at the table.

He stretched out his legs. 'This reminds me of my youth. We always sat around the hearth and had tea on cold days.'

'Did you toast bread over the fire?' she asked. 'I love hot bread toasted on one side with the butter melting into it on the other.'

He grinned boyishly. 'Me, too. Nothing tastes like bread you have toasted yourself.'

'I was never allowed to hold the toasting fork. Father said it was too dangerous.'

'Oh, I was official toaster in our home. Mother said I made a better job of it than Father. I had more patience. He always held the bread too close to the flames, trying to hurry it along.'

She grimaced. 'Burned edges.'

'Exactly.'

They both laughed and sipped their tea in a comfortable silence.

'Thank you again for a wonderful meal,' he said. 'And for granting me your company. I don't know when I have enjoyed an evening more.'

She looked at him askance. 'More than your parties with all your guests? I find that hard to believe.'

A thoughtful expression crossed his face. 'You are right.'

A little pang of disappointment took her aback.

'I do enjoy my guests,' he said. 'I suppose what I am trying to say is that I enjoyed this evening in an equal but different way.'

Indeed, it must be very different. His party had been a hubbub of laughter and excitement. Even she could see that from her brief glance through the door. But it was kind of him to say he had enjoyed this evening. 'I have had a very pleasant time also, though I really do not think it is something we should repeat, since it is not really appropriate.' There, she had said it. Much as she hadn't wanted to, it was the right thing to do. She didn't want him getting any false notions, thinking she was fast, or available, or something. Just thinking about it made her feel hot.

'There won't be much opportunity,' he said with a chill in his voice. 'I will be heading off to London in the morning.'

Had she made him angry? If so, it was for the best.

'To make arrangements for your next party, I suppose,' she said. 'To pluck more chickens.'

He glared at her. 'Indeed.' He got to his feet. 'I will bid you goodnight, Mrs Lamb.' He bowed, put his cup on the table and left.

She sighed. Why could she not keep her thoughts to herself? They had enjoyed a perfectly respectable dinner and then she had ruined it. No doubt he was regretting giving her a job and would be looking for a replacement.

No. It had been the right thing to say. To remind herself of his true colours. To stop herself from falling for his charm.

Because falling for his charm would be a very easy, and a very stupid, thing to do.

She took the tea cups through to the pantry. Should she do the dishes before bed or leave them until morning?

If His Lordship was off to London after breakfast, she would be here all alone. And she would need to be up early in the morning to ensure he had breakfast before he departed. Besides, it would give her something to do tomorrow.

The dishes could wait.

She picked turning down the lamps, picked up her candlestick and headed for bed.

His Lordship had indeed headed out for London early in the morning. Pamela surveyed the breakfast she had prepared. No plates or utensils had been used. He had seemingly taken a couple of bread rolls and departed.

She went to the buffet and helped herself to scrambled eggs and bacon. She might as well enjoy the fruits of her labour, even if he had not.

She should not have bothered with the eggs. He had told her he wanted very little prepared in the mornings.

A rap on the kitchen door startled her.

Who could that be?

She went to the door to find one of the shopkeepers from the village. 'Good morning, missus,' he said doffing his cap. 'Dobbs at your service. Dobbs Greengrocers.'

She eyed the box clutched in his arms. 'I didn't order anything.'

'Came by way of His Lordship,' the man said.

'You better come in.'

He put the box on the table. 'Will there be anything else you will be needing?' he asked, glancing around.

She thanked heavens she had got the kitchen cleaned up from last night's dinner. Village gossip was notoriously cruel. Any sign that the new cook wasn't up to scratch would be reported immediately.

'Not at the moment, thank you.'

'You only has to send word, missus, and I'll do my best to accommodate. His Lordship said as how you wanted to make preserves. Took a few days to get them oranges, but I found them, so I did.'

'Oranges!' Her heart gave a little jump.

She could scarcely believe he had been so thoughtful.

It was three weeks since Pamela had arrived at Rake Hall, or Rakehell's Hall as she learn that the locals called it. The arrival and departure of the London servants, the master of the house, and his guests twice a week had become routine.

She had become acquainted with the members of the London household and they now treated her as one of their own.

She had not dined with His Lordship again, though she had served him and Monsieur Phillippe dinner in the drawing room twice since that first evening.

She glanced at the kitchen clock as it struck four. At any moment, she would hear carriages on the drive and the house would be full again. Today she had made a suet pudding with beef and kidneys and all kinds of vegetables as well as fresh bread and a treacle tart for dessert.

Albert loved her sweet desserts, as did most of the others, and Dart spared no expense to keep his household happy. Lord Dart was unusually solicitous about the welfare of his servants, she had noticed. And they were all devoted to him. Never a complaint or a cross word had she heard from any of them. Was that his way of ensuring they kept his secrets?

The sound of horses and wheels on gravel wafted through the window. She checked her cap and apron. All neat and tidy. Not that His Lordship ever noticed her appearance, since he entered the house by the front door. She made her way outside into the stable courtyard to greet the arrivals.

'My dear Mrs Lamb,' Albert said. He was always the first to step down. 'You are looking well.' He, on the other hand, was looking anxious.

'Is something wrong?'

'Betsy took off this morning. She said her ma was sick and she had to go tend to her. Then Giles twisted his ankle and had to be left behind. So I'm short-handed. We can manage without one, but two will be difficult. I'll have to leave one of the tables empty. It would have to be Betsy. She's always very popular with the punters.'

The other servants were climbing out of the carriages and heading into the house.

'Now what?' Albert said, glancing behind him. 'Lord have mercy. Meg, what the devil is wrong with you?'

Meg was bent double, her hand pressed to her stomach with one of the other girls hanging over her.

'It's her monthlies,' the other girl said. 'Always takes her bad.'

'Shut your mouth, Sukey,' Meg said. 'I'll be fine. I just got rattled about in that there box on wheels.'

Albert looked grim. 'Hurry along then. Lots to do before dinner. Sukey, you will have to take on Betsy's work.'

The girl, Sukey, looked back over her shoulder from where she was bent over Meg. 'And this 'un's, too, I should 'spect.' She didn't sound happy. 'I'll do me best, Albert, but you should've brought another girl.'

''Ow could I get another girl, when I didn't know I was going to be missing one? I ain't a bloody mind-reader.'

'Can't I help?' Pamela said, feeling sorry for him and for Sukey. Over the past few weeks she had learned that His Lordship was a stickler for everything being just so for his guests and the staff never wanted to let him down. They really cared about his good opinion.

Albert blinked. 'You've got your own work to take care of, Mrs Lamb.'

'My work is all done. Everything is prepared. I can do nothing more until after you have eaten and, even then, the cleaning up can easily be left until tomorrow.'

Sukey left Meg, who, arms wrapped around her waist, plodded her way up the steps into the house, and came back to Albert. 'I can manage the extra rooms, Albert, truly I can, but why not let her help at the tables tonight. The punters will like a new face to flirt wiv, you know they will. You know how His Lordship hates an empty table.'

This last apparently clinched the matter for Albert. 'All right, but you will have to help Mrs Lamb dress. Hopefully you can find a good costume.'

The parties at Rake Hall were always masquerades.

'Ooh, perfect,' Sukey said. 'You and me will have a quick bite, Mrs Lamb, then I'll take you up to the dressing room.' Sukey put her arm through Pamela's and they walked inside. 'I am sure we have something to fit.'

'Teach her how to deal the cards, too, Sukey.' Albert called after them.

Pamela felt a smidgeon of doubt, a slight sinking feeling in her stomach. She had never attended a masquerade. Father hadn't thought them at all proper for a young lady.

But then, she wasn't a young lady any more. Nor was she 'attending'. She would be safely behind a card table.

Damian glanced around the ballroom. Everything was as it should be. Guests floating around in masks and outlandish costumes, this week's theme was set in Versailles under Louis XIV, the Sun King. The tables buzzed with the rattle of dice boxes, the chink of tokens and coins, and the cries of winners and losers. Masquerades were always popular among the *ton*. For some reason they liked dressing up. As usual, he wore a mask as a nod to the event, but kept to his usual black evening coat. It made it easier for his guests to find him, should they have need.

One of the tables seemed particularly crowded. A cheer went up and he strolled over to see what was holding his guests' interest.

The woman dealing cards wore an elaborate grey powdered wig, a gold mask that covered her face from her forehead to her lower cheeks and a gown of gold tissue that skimmed the rise of her breasts. She shimmered under the light of the chandelier above her head.

Her hands handled the cards with a graceful elegance and skill he had never seen among any of his ladies. Her smile, a mysterious curve of full lips, emphasised by the small black spot at their corner, seemed to hold the gentlemen at the table completely enthralled as she encouraged them to risk their chips.

Vingt-et-un was always one of the most profitable games and, judging by the chips at her elbow and the growing pile of vowels, tonight would be even better than usual.

As she glanced up and the lovely grey eyes regarded him briefly, the breath left his chest in a rush. What the devil was Mrs Lamb doing dealing cards?

He felt a strong urge to haul her out of the room by her arm and demand an explanation. He clenched his hands at his sides. To do anything so rash would invite unwanted comment.

Her eyes widened as if she sensed his anger, then she smiled at him and her eyes twinkled with mischief. Devil take the woman, she was enjoying herself.

And why would he feel anger when she had played right into his hands? What did it matter that every red-blooded male in the room was ogling her with lascivious interest, when he had now started her down the path to ignominy?

It could not have worked better than if he had planned it.

He smiled back, bowed slightly and moved on. Phillippe, dressed as the Sun King himself, sidled up to him. 'Your cook is making *l'impression grande*,' he said softly.

'You knew she was here and didn't think to say anything?' He tamped down his temper once again. What the hell was the matter with him?

Phillippe shrugged. 'The staff is in your care. I assumed it was by your orders.'

Of course he should have known. Albert was the one who should have informed him. Well, he knew now and there was no more to be said about it. It would be many more hours before tonight was over, and a plan began to form for how he might use the time to his advantage.

As the evening wore on, Damian noticed that although the crowd around Mrs Lamb's table ebbed and flowed somewhat, it was always the busiest. It was the younger crowd who seemed to be drawn into her orbit. For the most part these young men were harmless, though not above sowing their wild oats in any available pasture.

He drew closer. He was surprised at how comfortable

Mrs Lamb looked in her new role as she deftly dealt a hand to those sitting at the table. A king of hearts landed face up in front of her.

The men around her groaned at the sight of the royal card.

'Your bets, please, gentlemen,' she said calmly.

'How about a kiss for luck?' the lad on her right said.

Damian frowned, ready to step in if this sort of loose talk made her uncomfortable.

Mrs Lamb laughed lightly. 'How about you make your wager, or give up your place to a gentleman who will, Lord James? You know full well I do not play favourites.' Her tone was friendly, but firm.

Lord James grinned good-naturedly. 'It was worth a try.' He pushed forward a pile of chips representing a guinea.

Clearly Mrs Lamb was not in need of assistance.

She glanced around the table, ensuring all bets were placed, then dealt the next card with a graceful turn of her wrist. She paused for a moment with a little dramatic flair that made Damian want to chuckle, then put her own card down with a tiny snap in the silence of bated breath. 'Bank pays twenty-one.'

Which meant the bank paid no one. She gathered up the chips.

'You have the most devilish luck, Mrs Lamb,' one of the fellows said.

Mrs Lamb's steady grey gaze rested on his face. 'Would you like me to call for a fresh deck?' she asked sweetly.

'Hey!' Lord James said. 'No need for that, Smythe. Mrs Lamb runs a straight-up game. Besides, that was a fresh pack.'

Smythe looked embarrassed. 'Didn't mean anything. Just saying Mrs Lamb's luck is in and mine is out.'

'Idiot,' someone in the crowd said and there was general laughter, including from Smythe.

All was well here. Better than well. It seemed Mrs Lamb had a real talent for keeping the young puppies in order. He moved on to check on the other tables.

After a while, he signalled to Albert that it was time to start the dancing. The croupiers needed a break. He needed to collect up some of the winnings and the ladies who were guests would not be happy if gambling was the only thing on offer.

He'd learned early that if he wanted to keep the men spending their money, he had to keep their lady friends suitably entertained.

Albert moved from table to table, helping each croupier wrap up her game and clear the winnings from each station. It was always a risky time, though unlike the hells where he had learned his craft, there were no ruffians ready to spot the slightest weakness and steal the proceeds.

Each of his guests was selected by him personally. They would deem it dishonourable to steal anything, or at least dishonourable to be caught stealing anything. He smiled grimly.

When Albert reached Mrs Lamb's table, some of the men complained good-naturedly about ruining their luck. Albert jollied them along and they drifted away. Mrs Lamb stood up and stretched her back, chatting with Sukey who had clearly taken her under her wing.

The footmen began moving the tables to the edges of the room, clearing a space in the centre as the two women left arm in arm for the room set aside for the staff to rest.

Leaving Pip in charge, Damian accompanied Albert back to the safe in his study. He put all the notes and coins in the safe, apart from a number of coins to act as a float when the gambling started again later, and locked the door.

'Mrs Lamb seemed to be doing very well,' he remarked mildly. 'I was surprised to see her working tonight.'

It must not have been said as mildly as he intended because Albert started and turned red. 'We were short two girls, My Lord. I hope that was all right.'

It was better than all right. Wasn't it?

'Of course. She seems very popular with the gentlemen. How is it that we were missing two girls?'

'As you know, Your Lordship, since you yourself gave her permission, Betsy went to visit her old mum. Then Meg went and took a bad turn on the way down here. I had to do something.'

He could have removed one of the tables. But that would have been less than satisfactory to his guests. Not to mention considerably reduce his profits since only a finite number of gamblers could sit at each table at one time.

'Besides,' Albert continued, 'she must have seen it was a problem because she offered.'

Now that was interesting.

He nodded. 'She seemed to take to it very well.'

'Like a duck to water,' Albert said. 'She said she had played cards with her pa. Seems to know all the rules. I watched her for a while just to be sure.'

'Very good. But please inform me of any changes to the staff in future, would you, Albert?'

'Of course, My Lord.'

The sounds of the orchestra in full swing wafted along the corridor as they made their way back. As usual, he stopped to speak to the staff where they were resting. The room had once been known as the music room, but he had filled it with comfortable sofas and chairs and there was lemonade to drink if they wished.

'Good job, everyone,' he said, giving them a broad grin. 'The night is going very well indeed. I look for the second half to be as good as the first.'

There were nods and smiles all around. They received a bonus based on the night's takings, so they were always cheered to hear things were going well.

He wandered the room, speaking to this one and that as he went until he arrived beside Mrs Lamb, seated with Sukey on a sofa. Sukey got up to let him sit down.

Mrs Lamb had removed her mask, but she still looked remarkably stunning in her old-fashioned costume. 'Thank you for coming to our aid,' he said.

'Oh, it was no trouble. I am enjoying myself.'

'Are you now?'

'I am. I must say I was glad of the mask. Although, I think…'

She hesitated.

He gave her an encouraging smile. 'You think?'

'Well…it is possible that I recognised a couple of people among the guests. I would not want them to recognise me.'

'People you have met at the houses of your other employers?' he asked, knowing full well that was not what she meant.

Her full lips tightened slightly. 'Not exactly. People I knew before I became a cook.'

For someone living a lie, she wasn't very good at concealing things.

'Do you think they will recognise you?'

She sighed and shook her head. 'If they haven't recognised me by now, I doubt they will. It was a long time since I met them.'

He rose and clapped his hands. 'Ladies.'

All heads turned in his direction.

'There are quite a number of unaccompanied gentlemen here this evening if you have a mind to dance.'

There were smiles of enthusiasm. Dancing with the guests would mean generous tips for the girls themselves. 'Please remember, dancing only. No one is to go upstairs, that area is strictly for our guests.'

If his lady croupiers started going upstairs with gentlemen guests to earn money, then his perfectly respectable card parties would become something else. A bawdy house. Something that would leave him open to criminal prosecution.

He glanced down at Mrs Lamb. 'You need not dance if you do not wish to.'

'Oh, come on, Pammy,' Sukey said. 'Half the men in that room was eying you up...they will be tripping over themselves to get a dance.'

Pammy looked a shade doubtful, then smiled. 'Why not? In for a penny, in for a pound.'

Much as he imagined his father had said when her father had seduced him into gambling away his fortune.

'That's the way,' Sukey said. And off the ladies went.

Damian followed them with every intention of keeping an eye on Mrs Lamb. He did not want her scared off by some lustful lout or, worse yet, inadvertently revealing her true identity. At least not yet.

He wanted everything to go along at his pace.

Chapter Five

When Pamela returned to the ballroom, she discovered that indeed several gentlemen were desirous of leading her on to the dance floor. Monsieur Phillippe seemed to have taken charge of keeping them in line, since he introduced her to her first partner, whom he named as Valencourt. A very young fair-haired and rather tongue-tied gentleman, whose steps had obviously been honed by a dancing master who had failed to impart any style or grace.

She recalled that he had spent a considerable amount of money at her table earlier in the evening, but had thankfully stopped when his chips ran out.

'Mr Valencourt. How kind of you to ask me to dance,' she said with a smile intended to put him at ease.

He blushed. 'Mrs Lamb. The honour is mine. Most grateful. I m-mean…' He stuttered into silence.

'The weather is very mild for this time of year,' he said, after a few minutes. He sounded as if he was following some sort of script called 'The Rules for Conversation while Dancing'.

She kept her tone light and friendly. 'Perhaps the winter will be mild also?'

He grinned and seemed to relax a little. 'You are not like the other girls,' he said, leaning close and dropping his voice. 'They always make me feel as if I have two left feet.'

'Surely not? You are an excellent dancer.'

His blush deepened. 'Thank you. It… Umm… I mean… one dances better when one has…' he swallowed '…a partner who…'

He swallowed again.

Oh, dear. Poor young man. She felt sorry for him. 'A partner with whom one feels comfortable.'

'A partner who dances beautifully,' he said in a rush.

'Why, thank you, Mr Valencourt. You are very kind.' She twirled under his arm and they promenaded down the length of the ballroom side by side.

'Not kind,' he said, sounding rather strangled.

Glancing up at his face, she saw he was once again struggling for words.

Fortunately, the music was drawing to a close and Monsieur Phillippe was trying to catch their attention.

Valencourt dutifully walked her back to him. 'Can I ask you to dance again?'

She smiled. 'Not tonight. It would not be seemly.' Actually she had no idea of the rules, but she didn't want to give the poor young man any false ideas.

The next gentleman waiting to dance with her was Lord James, the young man who had jumped to her defence when it had looked as if one of her players might accuse her of cheating after losing badly. She had been horrified by the accusation. If there had been any cheating going on, she would have refused to take part. But she had also been a little scared by the young man's outburst, though she had tried not to show it.

She smiled at Lord James as he led her out on to the floor. The music began and they danced in silence for a while, each getting used to the other as they moved through the opening steps. So far every dance had been a waltz and the patrons seemed to be enjoying themselves.

'I must thank you for your kind assistance earlier, with Mr Smythe.'

'Smythe was making a cake of himself,' he said. 'And not for the first time. Everyone knows Dart's parties are the one place one can be assured the die are not weighted and the cards are not marked. He's a gentleman, for heaven's sake.'

'Nevertheless, I appreciate your intervention.'

'I haven't seen you here before. You are not like the other girls.'

He was the second man to make this observation. 'In what way?'

He looked thoughtful as he twirled her around. 'You are more refined, and…nicer, somehow.'

'Nicer.' She chuckled. 'A milk-and-water miss, am I?'

He grinned. 'No. I didn't mean it that way. Perhaps I should have said kinder.'

'Have the other ladies been unkind to you?'

'They are not unkind. They are just not kind. For them it's all about the chips on the table. You seem to take an interest in a chap. And Betsy would have slapped Smythe down instantly, whereas you tried not to hurt his feelings.'

'Which did not work very well, until you spoke up.'

'But you see, if Betsy had been there, we might have egged him on a bit, enjoyed the argument, but tonight everyone at the table was on your side. So he left.'

'Well, I am glad for his sake he left, because he had lost a lot of money, I think.'

'And that's what makes you different. You care.'

'Now you are making me sound like some sort of saint. And I can assure you I am not.'

His laugh was infectious. 'That is the last thing I would say you are.'

Good heavens, what did he mean? Better not to ask.

On the way back to Monsieur Phillippe, Pamela was surprised to see him approached by a couple who looked—well, they looked mischievous and perhaps a little excited. Monsieur Phillip smiled at the pair and pulled something from his inside breast pocket, which he handed to the man, with what she could only describe as a knowing grin.

The pair left the ballroom at speed.

'Where are they going?' she asked Monsieur Phillippe once Lord James had delivered her safely.

'Who?'

He knew very well whom she meant. 'The couple that were with you right before I returned.'

He waved a vague arm. 'I am sure I have no idea what you mean.'

He's lying.

But there was no time to question him further, her next dance partner was already eagerly reaching for her hand. Besides, what business of hers was it when they had looked so pleased?

'Who is the new girl?'

Damian didn't have to follow the direction of Lord Hill's gaze to know he was referring to Mrs Lamb. The dancing had finished a half-hour before and the croupiers were back at their tables.

Hill, a retired army colonel, was gazing at her as if he was a wolf who had just spotted an unattended sheep.

Damian gritted his teeth and replied pleasantly, 'Mrs Lamb? She is no one in particular.' At least no one he was prepared to admit to just yet. Fortunately Lamb was a common enough last name and no one was likely to associate a croupier at his parties with the well-connected Lambs of Bexley. 'She is one of my staff who agreed to help out this evening in the absence of one of our regular croupiers.'

'If I were you, I would make *her* one of your regular croupiers. These parties of yours were getting a little mundane, old fellow. Quite dull. She has livened things up considerably.'

Mundane? Dull? What the devil was he talking about? Damian glanced around. Was the crowd thinner tonight than usual? Was the *ton* in need of more excitement?

Damn them for a bunch of spoiled wastrels.

'She's quite the beauty,' Hill went on. 'By the time I got to Monsieur Phillippe, all her dances were spoken for. All the young fellows are enchanted.'

He had noticed that much for himself. 'Why is that, I wonder?'

'I was asking myself that. She is not as intimidating as the other gals. She don't scare them. But she don't put up with any of their nonsense either. And there is an aura of mystery about her. A sense of secrets.'

Damian forced himself not to smile at the description. Mrs Lamb did indeed have secrets. And she had done well this evening. Much better than he had expected.

Perhaps he should strike while the iron was hot. Something to consider.

'I thank you for your advice. Do you have other thoughts on how we might enliven the evening for our guests?'

He had, though. Making the club exclusive would be temptation enough, along with the provision of private rooms where guests could pursue their peccadilloes, no questions asked.

'Higher stakes.'

Some men liked to live on the edge of disaster. But higher stakes meant higher risks for the house. That he would have to discuss with Pip.

Hill wandered off to join one of the other tables and Damian, as was his wont, wandered the room, checking on each of the tables in turn, except that he seemed to return to Mrs Lamb's table more often than any of the others.

What was it that drew so many of the young men into her orbit? The *ton* did indeed like novelty. It was part of the reason his club had taken off so quickly. There was nothing else like it.

But if they became bored, then that would not suit his purposes at all.

'Do you know you have the most beautiful eyes?' Mr Galt said, gazing adoringly at Mrs Lamb. 'Won't you remove your mask and let me see your face? I am sure you must be the loveliest woman here.'

Damian had to restrain himself from planting the fellow a facer. As it was he took a step closer, ready to usher the young man out.

The rules were clear. No one was to touch the lady croupiers.

Mrs Lamb smiled at him calmly. 'I take no responsibility for the eyes the Lord gave me, Mr Galt. Or the curve of my lips, Lord Raif,' she added, smiling at another of the young men. 'And, no, I will not remove my mask simply to edify your curiosity.'

There was some good-natured laughter and a fair bit of jostling of the young men who had been so bold. The sort of laughter that suggested the others also were dying to see behind her mask, but were a smidgeon glad Galt had not been successful because they wanted to be the ones who convinced her to reveal herself.

'Do you plan to make a wager, Mr Galt, or will you give your place to someone who will?'

Tonight would not be the night when she unmasked.

'Wagers, please, ladies and gentlemen,' Mrs Lamb said firmly.

Chips and sovereigns were pushed forward on the green baize. 'Blast,' said Lord James. 'I am out of cash.'

He was one of the fellows she had danced with earlier.

Lord James pulled out a notebook, clearly intending to write a vowel.

'Are you sure, you want to do that?' she said, putting her hand on the scrap of paper. 'You have lost rather a lot already.'

Damian frowned. The pile of winnings at her elbow was large, but included not one vowel? Unusual. How many more young men had she discouraged in this way?

He stepped forward. 'Your vowel is good with us, Lord James,' he said smoothly.

Mrs Lamb shot him a startled glance. 'Oh, but—'

'My dear Mrs Lamb, you have been on your feet for hours, not to mention the way these young fellows were stepping on your toes not so very long ago.' He gave her a glare when she didn't move. 'Off you go. Take a well-earned break. I will look after things here.'

A couple of the fellows gave a groan and for a moment he thought Lord James would argue, but Damien smiled at him and glanced around at the other players. 'Place your bets, please, ladies and gentlemen.'

After a brief hesitation, Mrs Lamb left the table and glided away.

A few moments later Pip arrived at his side. 'All well?' he asked *sotto voce*.

'Take over for me,' Damian said and went off in search of the blasted woman.

He found her in the retiring room pouring herself a cup of tea. They were alone.

The taste of the anger at the back of his throat was as familiar as his face in the mirror. Anger at those who had made his family flee their home. Anger at his father for playing the gentleman when he could not put food on the table. Anger at what circumstances had forced him to become.

Damn it. He had nothing to be ashamed of.

'Why the devil were you stopping him from writing his vowel? What next? Will you be letting them win?'

She glared up at him. Her eyes narrowed and her mouth thinned to a straight line.

'I beg your pardon,' she said stiffly.

'Are you deliberately trying to ruin me?'

'Are you trying to ruin that young man? He had run out of money.'

'Lord James is a wealthy young man. What he loses here tonight he will make back tomorrow on the 'Change. He would not be here if he could not afford the stakes.'

'Oh. I see. I had no idea, but—'

'Exactly. You had no idea. But you decided anyway.' He took a deep breath. 'The evening is about done. I have no further need for you. You may return to your chambers.'

'As you wish.' She put down the teacup.

She looked hurt and he felt as if he had kicked a puppy or drowned a kitten. Dammit it, she was the one at fault.

He followed her out and down the hall, making sure she made it safely to her part of the house. He didn't want some wag from his party attempting to see behind the mask, or worse. By this hour they were all half-seas over.

He and Pip always made sure the girls were not importuned by their guests, male or female. It was simply good sense and had nothing to do with feeling protective towards this woman.

Pamela was still seething about her abrupt dismissal the day before when she entered her kitchen. She halted at the sight of the man seated at her kitchen table among the dirty dishes which she had not had time to deal with the previous evening, because she had done him a favour.

How dare he? He needn't think she was going to cook him a special breakfast today.

'Good morning, My Lord,' she said stiffly. 'Breakfast will be available in the servants' hall at seven.'

'I am leaving for London in a few minutes so no need to prepare anything.'

He gave her a shamefaced glance. A rather boyishly endearing look, if she was to be honest. Her stomach gave a strange little pulse. Clearly, she needed to give that part of her a good talking to. He was definitely in her bad books.

'I came to apologise for my outburst last night.'

Well, blast the man. Here she was happily being annoyed with him and now he had completed melted her defences.

'Apology accepted.' She worked her way around him to the stove and picked up the coal scuttle.

'Allow me.'

He had moved so swiftly, so silently, she hadn't heard him come up behind her. She jumped. And he took the scuttle from her now rather nerveless hands.

'Not too much,' she said. 'Or it will smoke. Er… I mean, thank you.'

'Tell me when to stop.'

He shook the coal in a few pieces at a time. 'Yes, that is enough.'

He put the scuttle down and brushed the coal dust off his hands. 'That thing is heavy.'

'Yes.'

He looked around. 'And where do you fill it?'

'In the coal cellar. Beside your wine cellars,' she added when he looked vaguely about him.

'Oh, I see. Do I need to order more?'

'You are being very conciliatory this morning.'

He grimaced and it really was a naughty lad's expression. 'I…er…well, I was talking to Pip and he mentioned that of all the tables last night, yours was the most profitable. So I thought I would ask if you would continue on as a croupier on party nights.'

She looked at the mess. Normally she would have had this all cleaned up before she went to bed. Not that she really had anything else much to do today since there would be no one else at the house but her.

She shook her head. 'I don't think so. I am a cook. That is why you hired me. And besides,' she went on, thinking about what her taking on these additional duties would mean, 'I don't want to put Betsy or Meg out of work.'

'You don't need to worry about that.'

'Oh, but I do. You might not care about what happens to those ladies, but I do. They rely on the money you pay them.'

'I mean, you won't be putting them out of work. They will continue as before. I have had another idea. I ran it by Pip and he thinks it is a grand idea.'

'What sort of idea?' He was looking too pleased with himself.

'I would like you to become my hostess. To be in charge

of the girls while Pip and I look after the guests and security.'

'I don't think I understand.'

'You would attend the parties, dinner and, afterwards, when we play cards, move from table to table, ensuring the guests are happy, talking with them, making sure they have drinks. Generally acting as the hostess of the evening. You could also relieve each girl in turn so we never have an empty table and that way all the tables will benefit from your presence. You will, of course, be well recompensed, based on earnings for the night.'

The girls were paid according to the earnings at their table. 'Based on earnings at all the tables?'

'Yes.'

'Why?'

'I think—well, we think the house will do better, to be honest.'

Last night had been fun. At least, it had until the end. And there had been no one there who had shown any sign of recognition. The two men whose names she had recognised had visited her father only, not the family. Besides, the mask had protected her identity. But the next party might be different. What if someone she did know was one of the attendees. A relative, or a friend of Alan's. It was too much of a risk.

She shook her head. 'It is a kind offer, but I prefer to remain as your cook.'

He looked at the dishes stacked on the table. 'I suppose you did not have time to clear up last night.'

'Neither time nor inclination.'

'Yes, of course. You must have been tired. It was a long night for everyone. I will get you some help from the village, so you won't have to face a pile of dirty dishes in the morning, if that would help change your mind. Oh, I almost forgot.' He pulled a sheaf of banknotes from his pocket and handed them to her. 'This is your share of the takings from last night.'

She stared at what looked like a king's ransom. 'You cannot mean it.'

'I do.'

'So much money lost at the tables?' It seemed immoral.

'That and payment for your dances.'

'Oh. I did not realise they were paying…'

He shrugged. 'Why would the girls want to dance with the patrons for free when they could be putting their feet up in the withdrawing room?'

'Why, indeed. And what else do they do for money?'

'Now, now, Mrs Lamb, you have a very earthy turn of mind. My staff does not do anything of that sort under my roof. It is against the rules.'

'I saw couples leaving the dancing—'

'Couples who came together. Not my ladies. Now what do you say?'

He seemed very anxious for her to say yes. And if she made that amount of money each evening, she could retire to a little cottage in the country in no time at all.

It was so very tempting.

But she couldn't risk being recognised.

She shook her head. 'I am sorry. It is out of the question.'

'I see.' His voice was full of disappointment.

She felt guilty. As if she had let him down. 'You see, it is possible that I might know someone among your guests. My mother isn't pleased about my becoming a cook, but since I am always tucked away in a kitchen, no one is likely to know. On the other hand, if I was recognised acting as a hostess at what is really a gambling hell—whatever you say about it being respectable—I think it would be ruinous. Reputations other than mine would be destroyed.'

'And last night you were not concerned about this, because you knew you would leave before the unmasking?'

She nodded.

'Then continue to leave.'

'Won't people wonder why I disappear?'

'Let them wonder. The *ton* loves a bit of intrigue.'

'I really don't think—'

'Give it a try for a couple of weeks. If you don't like it, you can go back to your kitchen and I won't hold it against you.'

She looked at the wad of banknotes in her hand and back at his face—he was grinning like a schoolboy.

Her dream of her own little cottage seemed as though it could become a reality. 'Very well. I will try it for two weeks.'

'That's the ticket.' He whirled her around in a circle and took off out of the door, leaving her gasping for breath.

Oh, my word! What had she done?

Let him charm her. That was what she had done.

Chapter Six

Damian had been very careful to keep his distance from Mrs Lamb for the past two weeks. They had exchanged the odd remark relating to her new position, but for the most part he had left her in Pip's charge.

He had been shocked at how pleased he had felt when she had agreed to his proposal. It wasn't like him to feel so...giddy? He was used to being in charge of his emotions.

As a consequence, he had given himself some space. Got himself under control. After all, he wasn't the sort of man who needed anyone else to make him happy. And now it was time to put the second part of his plan in motion.

Having dressed for the outdoors, he wandered down to the servants' hall for breakfast.

Mrs Lamb was already sitting at the table, reading a newspaper.

She rose upon his entry. 'My Lord. I am sorry I did not realise you had stayed over last night or I would have prepared more of a breakfast.'

He had purposely not relayed his intention to stay the night—the first time he had done so for two weeks.

He had wanted to take her by surprise.

'No matter.'

'Were you planning on staying for dinner?'

'I was, if that won't put you out too much.' He could see her mind racing to take stock of what food she had on hand.

He browsed the offerings on the buffet. A couple of slices of cold ham, toast, marmalade, some sweet breads, and fruit.

'Did you make this marmalade?' he asked.

'I did. From the oranges you provided and the last of the little oranges from your tree.'

A sly reminder that the tree needed some care, no doubt. Well, she need not bother. He was leaving England once he had accomplished his purpose. He had decided.

He poured himself coffee and put the ham on his plate with a slice of toast and a scoop of marmalade.

He took the seat opposite her and, having eaten the ham, slathered the preserve on to his toast. He was aware of her watching him.

He took a bite of toast. 'Oh.' He had not been expecting it to taste so extraordinary.

'Is something wrong?'

'What on earth did you put in it? It isn't marmalade, its ambrosia.' It was. It had all the flavour of oranges, but more.

She chuckled, clearly pleased with his reaction. 'It is a secret.'

He wanted to smile back. Damn the woman. It seemed he had no armour against her charm. 'You had better be careful. I may end up sending you a cartload of oranges instead of a box.'

'Unfortunately, I have run out of the secret ingredient.'

'Which is?'

She smiled enigmatically.

He laughed. 'I will find out, you know.' He tasted the marmalade again. 'I think it is some sort of liquor.'

She raised an eyebrow. She definitely did not intend to reveal a thing. And he was enjoying teasing her, he realised.

She got up and poured herself another coffee and sat down again. 'How long will you be staying, My Lord? Only I may need to send to the village for supplies.'

'A day or so. I thought I might see if I could bag a duck for dinner before I started on some paperwork.'

'A duck would be a welcome addition to what I have on hand.' She looked as if she would say more.

'What?' he asked.

'I was thinking I could use a walk. I would like to see if there are any mushrooms in your woods and there is a chestnut tree I have been meaning to have a look at over near the river. Unless you prefer your own company.'

'Not at all. You would be more than welcome.' It couldn't be better. He had been thinking of broaching the matter on his mind over dinner, but he had a sense she might be more amenable to his proposal while wandering outside in the woods. As long as he didn't overplay his hand.

'Do you think it will rain?' she asked. 'It looked pretty overcast when I looked out earlier.'

'It might. I can lend you an oilskin, if you wish and some boots, too. I think there are some smaller ones, left from—' Damn it, he did not want to think about his mother.

'No need. I have my own. I am quite used to tramping around in the wet.'

Of course she was. He kept forgetting she was supposed to be a servant, because she did not talk or act like a servant.

'If you can give me some time to clear up here and get ready,' she continued, 'I will accompany you.'

'No need to hurry. I have to clean my gun and that will take a bit of time. I'll meet you outside in, say, an hour?'

'Perfect.'

And suddenly the day, although gloomy, seemed much brighter.

He must be losing his mind. He left before he did something stupid.

When she entered the courtyard, Pamela discovered Dart waiting, leant against the stable wall, his gun beside him looking like a typical English nobleman off on a hunt. Sensibly clothed in raincoat and hat, his hunting accoutrements slung on straps crossways over his chest, he looked ready for anything. Not unlike herself. In addition, he wore a pair of gaiters to protect his trousers above his walking boots.

Seeing him so dressed reminded her of when she used to go with her father on the occasional shoot. Not that Dart was anything like her father. Not in the least. Even in his heavy rain gear, he looked fit and healthy and terribly attractive.

Gah. Not something she should be thinking about her employer.

He greeted her with a wave, shouldered his gun and side by side they set off across the park.

It had rained the day before so the long grass was wet. 'This would be a beautiful lawn, if it was mowed,' she said.

'There is no one here to see it.'

True. His guests never arrived before dark and were gone long before the sun rose. At least, at this time of year. 'Still, it seems a shame. It looks more like a hayfield than a lawn.'

'Yes.'

She sensed he was not pleased with her line of conversation.

There was no pleasing the man. If she owned a house like this, she would want it to look its very best. Not only did he not seem to care, he seemed almost opposed to any sort of restoration that did not directly relate to his parties. To the making of money, in other words.

Rooks cawed somewhere ahead. 'Noisy creatures. They must have a rookery nearby.'

'Yes.'

Why had she bothered to walk with him? She would have been better company alone. She might not have bothered trekking as far as the woods either. No doubt she would have found a few field mushrooms hiding in all this long grass.

They reached the edge of the beech woods to the west of the park. Wet leaves slid underfoot, making the path treacherous.

Here and there brambles stretched long barbed tendrils to grab on to her skirts and his coat. Clearly this path was rarely used, though at one point it must have been a well-trodden route to the river.

They walked in single file and now and then he would turn to hold back a bramble or an encroaching thorn bush.

The air smelled of earth and damp. A typical autumn scent, dark yet not unpleasant. She kept her gaze peeled for any signs of fungi. They loved this sort of environment.

She spotted a blood-red ox tongue fungus clinging low on the trunk of one of the few oak trees in this woods. It was not a flavour she preferred and passed it by, remembering its location in case she did not find something more appetising.

Dart halted without warning. Looking for mushrooms off to the side, Pamela bumped into him. 'Oof,' she said. 'What is wrong?'

'Shh.' He cupped his ear, gazing off to their right.

She listened. Nothing. And then she heard it. A sort of squeaking. Some sort of rodent? She grimaced. She wasn't all that keen on mice or rats. As a cook she had to deal with them, but that didn't mean she would seek them out.

'Wait here.' He pushed off through the undergrowth.

She followed.

He gave her a dark look over his shoulder as if to say on your head be it and continued on, but she noticed he was careful not to let twigs or brambles snap back at her.

A clearing opened before them and at its edge on the other side she could see the source of what she now recognised as whimpering.

A dog. Large and black and rangy.

Its ears flattened at their approach and its lips curled back from sharp-looking teeth.

'Careful,' Dart said as she moved around him. He unshouldered his gun. 'Stay back. I may have to shoot it.'

'What? No.' As she drew closer she could see the source of the problem. Twine around the animal's paw. 'It is caught in a snare. Oh, you poor thing.'

'Don't get too close. It is liable to bite and you are now in my line of sight.'

She turned to see him loading his gun.

'You are not going to shoot it,' she said, horrified.

'I will shoot it if it attacks. Have you ever seen a case of hydrophobia? No? I have. Believe me, you won't want to take the risk.'

She knelt beside the dog warily. It whimpered and flattened itself to the ground. 'It is not attacking.'

He hunkered down beside her and reached out. The dog snarled.

'It's all right,' he said gently. 'I'm not going to hurt you.' The dog whined, then dropped his head. Its tail gave a hesitant wag.

He pulled out a knife from his belt and reached for the twine.

Pamela could see the dog was anxious by the way it tensed. She stroked its head. 'It's all right. He won't hurt you.'

The dog looked up at her and in that instant Dart reached for the snare. The dog, quick as a wink, jerked its head around and snapped.

'Damnation.' Dart sucked on one finger.

'Did it bite you?' she asked.

'No. I cut myself. Just a nick.' He dived into his pocket and pulled out a pair of gloves. 'I should have put these on in the first place.

The dog, some sort of retriever breed, though a bit of a mix of more than one something else, she thought, licked at its paw.

'Now,' Dart said firmly, 'hold still.'

The dog whined, but surprisingly held still while Dart cut the snare.

The dog rose and shook itself.

Pamela peered at its paw. 'I don't think it's been caught long. It doesn't seem to be bleeding.'

She petted the dog's head and stood up. Dart had removed his glove and was looking at his wound.

'Let me see,' she said.

'It is nothing.'

She glared at him.

He rolled his eyes and held out his hand. 'See. Nothing.'

The cut wasn't deep, but it was still welling with blood.

'Let me bind it up until we can put some salve on it at the house.' She picked up the knife he had dropped beside his gloves and, turning away from him, cut off a strip of her petticoat.

Looking rather surprised, he held out his hand for her

to bind the strip of material around his finger. 'That will keep it clean,' she said.

The dog was sitting watching them, its bright red tongue lolling and its tail wagging.

'I wonder where he came from?'

Dart regarded the animal for a moment. 'He looks a bit on the thin side. He might be a stray.'

He did look a bit scruffy.

'Off you go,' Dart said to the dog. 'Go home. And try to stay out of poachers' snares in future.'

The dog cocked its head, but didn't move.

Dart looked about him. 'It will go when its ready, I suppose. The river is this way. Not far now, as we have taken a bit of a shortcut.'

The dog followed them, occasionally leaving their trail to explore on one side or the other, but always returning after a few moments.

'It looks like you have gained a new friend,' she said with a chuckle.

Dart glared back at her. 'Someone in the village will know who owns him.'

He sounded annoyed.

An Englishman who didn't like dogs. Her father had always said you could judge a man by his dogs, how they responded to him would tell a lot about a man's character. Did his lack of liking for dogs mean something?

The trees thinned out and changed from beech to the occasional willow and the grass grew longer and the ground became wet and squelchy. And then, before them, there was the river. Not terribly large as rivers went, about ten feet across, and quite sluggish with a low muddy bank and reeds growing along its edge.

Dart checked his gun, then walked quietly towards the

bank. 'I will see if there are ducks on the water. Please remain here,' he said softly.

She nodded.

The dog disappeared off into the long grass. A moment later a duck broke cover with a whirr of wings and a quack.

'Sacre bleu,' Dart said softly, lining up. He fired. The duck came down in a flutter of feathers and landed in the river.

'Devil take it,' Dart said.

Without warning, the dog leapt from the bank into the water a little further down.

Pamela almost laughed at Dart's helpless fury at the sight of the dog about to have duck for dinner.

Dart stomped back to her. 'It is not funny. I didn't come hunting to feed a dog.'

They watched as the dog snagged his prize and swam strongly for the bank.

Once out of the water it dropped the duck and shook itself from stem to stern. Then, to Pamela's astonishment, it retrieved its prize, brought it to Damian and dropped it at his feet with a big doggy grin.

Dog and man regarded each other for a moment. 'Well, that is a surprise.' He patted the dog, picked up the duck and tied it to the lanyard at his belt.

'Good boy,' Pamela said.

The dog gave a half-hearted tail-wag, but its gaze was firmly fixed on Damian.

Damian shouldered his gun.

The dog looked puzzled.

'We only need one,' Damian said to it. 'You will get your share. Now we have to find a chestnut tree, I believe.

Damian was enjoying himself, he realised to his great surprise as they wound their way back through the woods.

He had forgotten that he had hunted in these woods with his father. The longer he had lived in France, bearing the responsibility for feeding his family, by fair means or foul, his life before Marseilles had begun to seem like a dream or one of those interminable stories his father used to tell about the good old days.

Providing for your household by hunting was somehow a great deal more satisfying than he expected. Far more satisfying than some of his nefarious activities.

He pushed the thought aside. That part of his life was behind him. Stealing scraps of food and robbing the poor box was something he would never have to do again.

He was sorry that his mother and father had not lived long enough to see how successful he had become, how he was restoring the family fortunes. And, in the process, exacting a fitting revenge.

The dog had wandered off for a few minutes, but returned as if to check on their welfare. Heaven help him, the last thing he needed was to be adopted by a dog.

'What will you do if you can't find its owner?' she asked.

Like some sort of mind reader.

'Find someone who will take him, I suppose.'

'He seems like such a good dog. Why would anyone abandon him?'

In other words, why would he not want to keep him? If she thought she could pull on his heart strings, she was in for a disappointment. He did not have a heart.

'Do you recall exactly where this chestnut tree is located?' he asked.

'Somewhere up ahead, I think.'

How did she even know one tree from another? He preferred the bustle of city streets. Trees he could do without. 'What sort of trees are these?'

'Beech.'

'How do you know?'

The look she gave him was one of astonishment, mingled with pity. 'By the shape of the leaves, the ridges on the trunk. All sorts of things.' She chuckled. 'And by all these little nuts underfoot.'

Oh. That's what those were. 'Are they edible?'

'Somewhat. Not really a delicacy.'

'The only thing I can recognise with any certainty is an oak tree.'

'That is something, I suppose, since you are an English nobleman and there are oak leaves decorating your coat of arms.'

He laughed at her wry tone.

He looked around, to see if he could spot anything that might be a chestnut tree.

'There it is,' she said.

He glanced back and she was pointing off to his right.

And then he saw it. A tree of larger girth than the others around it and with golden leaves still clinging to its branches along with clusters of green fruit.

When they reached the tree, she looked about her on the ground. 'I think it is a bit too early. There really aren't many here.' She gingerly picked up a twig with a couple of bright green whiskery-looking balls attached to it.

He reached for it.

'Stop' she said.

The dog barked at her sharp tone.

'Enough,' Damian said to him.

She laughed. 'He is protecting you. Don't touch them. They really are horribly prickly.'

'Oh, now I remember.' He remembered something else.

He took the twig and dropped it on the ground. He gently

captured one of the casings between his boots and split the soft shell open. Out spilled three bright glossy reddish-brown nuts. He picked them up and popped them in her basket.

'I do remember this tree. Not its location, exactly. But I remember doing this when out on a walk with my mother.'

It was a strangely painful memory he wished he had not recalled.

'It is a good thing you have sturdy leather gloves,' she said. 'Mine are far too thin for the task. Perhaps, if you wouldn't mind, you could gather up whatever we can find and I will shell them when we get back.'

He raked through the leaves and found quite a few more spiky shells. Almost enough to half fill her basket, but the majority of the harvest remained up on the tree. 'Shall I climb up?' he asked.

She glanced upwards. 'Actually, I think it is time we returned to the house, because I think it is starting to rain again. Much harder than before.'

The sky had indeed got much darker.

And, if he wasn't mistaken, the wind had picked up, too. He took the basket.

'And we still haven't found any mushrooms that you promised me for dinner,' he teased.

She pulled her hood up over her hat. 'Then we had better hurry.'

And hurry they did. They were almost to the edge of the forest when she dove off to one side. 'Yes,' she called out. 'Exactly what I was hoping for. Chanterelles.'

She foraged around, popping small, yellow, frilly fungi in the basket he held out to her as she went.

'There. That will be enough,' she said.

The rain was coming down harder, but she was grinning from ear to ear as she looked up at him. She looked positively lovely. Sweet. Happy. Full of joy at such a simple accomplishment.

And he couldn't stop himself. He bent his head and kissed her cheek. She tasted of fresh cold air and sweet, sweet smiles.

She gasped.

He stepped back, mentally shaking his head at his madness. What the devil had come over him?

She touched a gloved finger to her face as if she could still feel his touch. 'Oh.'

And he wanted to kiss her again.

Properly. On her mouth. With his hands on her, instead of clutching a basket full of prickles.

A gust of wind brought raindrops splattering down on them.

She laughed. He grinned back at her. Indescribably relieved that she didn't look the least bit offended. To his shock, she rose up on her toes and, holding on to his lapels, she kissed him back. A soft sweet brush of her warm plush lips on his mouth.

Instant arousal.

If there had been the slightest chance of a warm dry spot anywhere close, he would have pulled her close and devoured that delicious mouth. A pang seized his heart. Sweetly painful.

Another cold splat hit his cheek and brought him to his senses.

'Hurry up,' he said, his voice strangely rough. 'Before we get soaked and you catch an ague.' He took her hand and urged her forward, to the house. As they ran, the dog circled them, barking excitedly.

'Foolish animal,' she said, breathless and laughing.

He, Damian, was the foolish one. He wanted more of this.

But that wasn't the plan.

They entered through the side door and discarded their outer layers and boots in the mud room while the dog remained outside, whining and yapping his disapproval at their disappearance.

Damian carried the basket through to the kitchen and set it on the table.

He opened his mouth to say something, but the vision of her glowing from exertion, windblown, and damp tendrils of hair clinging to her cheeks, robbed him of speech.

They stared at each other silently. The air tingled with unspoken longing. Not something he had ever experienced.

The dog scratched at the outside door. Dammit it.

'I better...' 'You better...' they said at the same moment and laughed.

'I will see to the dog,' he said. 'I am looking forward to our dinner.'

'Six o'clock,' she said, smiling.

His heart felt the warmth of that smile all the way to the stables. He didn't even care that the dog almost tripped him up twice.

It seemed he had reached a new understanding with Mrs Lamb and now he must use it to his advantage.

A pang of regret slid down his spine.

No. He regretted nothing. From here on, everything would go according to plan—as long as he remained in control.

Chapter Seven

Safe in her own room, Pamela unpinned her hair and set to work drying it with a towel. Inside, she was shaking. Mortified.

Alan had been right when he said there was something wrong with her. He'd been shocked at what he called her lasciviousness. He said her carnal appetites went far beyond what he would have expected from a lady. And this, after they had engaged in what she had thought was the most wonderous feelings she had ever experienced.

She recalled how in the throes of passions she had taken control of their lovemaking, rolling on top of him and…

She cut the thoughts off.

Terrified that he would not want to marry her, if he found her too unbridled, after that she had tried to restrain her unnatural passion, to be less responsive and more ladylike.

And now she had done it again. She had kissed Damian. The sensation of the brush of his warm firm lips against her skin remained like an indelible imprint.

On her lips. Humming in her body… Reminding her…

How could she feel so much when all he had done was kiss her cheek?

She went hot, then cold at the recollection of his look of shock and the way the atmosphere between them had turned awkward.

There really was something wrong with her. Some sort of aberration in her nature. Other women—other ladies, she corrected—did not rouse the way she did when kissing. Alan had assured her of this.

She had tried her best to control these sensations, to conquer her unnatural yearnings, but as demonstrated in those few moments with Damian, she had failed miserably.

Her hands trembled as she touched her lips. She had not imagined that he had returned her kiss with enthusiasm. Gently, yes. Hesitantly, yes. But there was no mistaking their mutual spark of attraction.

Clearly, she had let a handsome face get the better of good sense. Yet his male beauty wasn't the source of his allure. Not for her. It was something else. Something she had the feeling he tried to hide from the world. Kindness? Was that what she saw in him?

Certainly, he was kind in his deeds. Look at the consideration he showed for the people who worked for him. And how caring he had been with the dog, despite his denials.

She liked him. A great deal more than she should. And he seemed to like her. But if she gave in to the passions roiling inside her, he would no doubt feel the same sort of distaste Alan had felt and it would ruin everything.

She would lose his friendship. She could not bear the idea of him turning away in disgust.

And since she could not trust herself around him, from now on she really would maintain a proper distance. Keep everything strictly business and avoid any further slips.

A knock on the door brought her to her feet. 'Who is it?'

Oh, how stupid. They were the only two people in the house.

'Dart.'

'One moment.' She scooped the scattered clothing and

bundled them behind the sofa, then opened the door to see him with, one arm resting high on the doorframe, looking down at her, his dark hair tousled, his gaze intense. The man was too gorgeous for words. Breathtaking.

She clung to what little remained of her sanity. 'Yes, My Lord?' Her voice shook a little. She sounded breathless. 'Please, come in.' She stepped back to allow him to pass. 'How is the dog? Well settled?'

He paced to the window and then turned with a gesture of defeat. 'The stubborn animal refuses to remain in the stables. It is now happily ensconced beside the fire in my study.'

'Oh.' She tried not to chuckle at his chagrin.

'I will enquire for its owner in the village tomorrow, but that was not what I wanted to discuss. I came to apologise.'

She stared at him, her heart sinking oddly. 'For what?'

'For allowing myself such ungentlemanly conduct—'

'No, indeed! I turned a brotherly peck on the cheek into…' heat rushed into her face '…into something more.'

'Brotherly?' He stared at her. 'I can assure you, it wasn't in the least bit brotherly.'

She swallowed. 'I thought you might think I was far too forward for kissing you back as I did.'

A wicked smile lit his face and sent shivers down her spine. 'I liked it. I wanted you to do it again.'

Her toes curled into the carpet. Oh, goodness, she hadn't put on her slippers.

He stalked towards her and brushed her hair back from her face, peering at her expression, and what he saw seemed to take the worry from his gaze.

'I think you and I have been dancing around each other for quite some time.'

He drew close, took her hand and rubbed his thumb over her knuckles.

'I think we have. I should probably hand in my notice.'

'Why?'

'I am your employee. A servant. It is not fitting.' Not the full truth. But it would do to keep him at bay. She hoped.

'Sit,' he said and drew her down on the sofa.

She perched on the edge. If her heart had been racing before, now it seemed ready to gallop out of her chest. He did not let go of her hand. And she did not pull it away.

She could not, did not want to give up the feel of his skin on hers. Her body hummed with pleasure at his touch.

'Let me say, firstly, you have become much more than a servant,' he said. 'You have become indispensable to the success of my endeavour here. The staff is happier than they have ever been. The guests are happy. The tables are more profitable than ever. You may think I have not noticed the way you have made things run more smoothly, but I have.'

Oh. This was about the club. Not about... She shook off her feeling of disappointment. He appreciated her work. She should be pleased.

She had actually thought he might not like the changes she had wrought, making sure some of the young men did not dip too deeply, teasing them into good spirits when they lost and celebrating the occasions when they won. The very rare occasions.

'Thank you. Your words mean a great deal.'

'I wondered if you would like to become a partner, with me and Pip.'

'A partner?' She stared at him blankly. Never in her wildest dreams would she have expected such an offer. As usual, her thoughts had been focused on far more carnal matters. Shame filled her.

He must have taken her silence for doubt because he

quickly added, 'Don't answer now. Think about it. We will discuss more at dinner.'

A vision of her little cottage in the country flashed into her head. It was larger than before. A great deal larger. Was it possible that such a dream could become a reality?

He got up with a smile. 'I should leave you to dress.'

She winced. Right. She was still in her dressing gown.

He lifted a lock of hair from where it draped over her shoulder and rubbed it between his finger and thumb. 'If I may say so, your hair is quite beautiful.'

Speechless, she watched him leave.

Never in her life had she felt quite so confused. One moment he was talking business, the next he was offering compliments intended to make her blush.

She wasn't sure if she was on her head or her heels. And, truth to tell, she was feeling like a woman for the first time in a long time.

Was it possible she was losing her heart, when she had sworn she would never do so again? Or was she just missing the pleasures of the flesh?

Knowing herself, the latter was more likely.

Damien put down his knife and fork and lifted his glass. 'My compliments to the chef. That was absolutely delicious.'

Happiness made her heart feel lighter. 'Thank you. I am glad you enjoyed it. I expect you are used to a great many more dishes when Monsieur Chandon prepares your meals, but there is no one here to eat leftovers.'

He glanced down at a pair of entreating eyes. 'Except this dratted dog.'

She smiled. 'Well, yes. But I don't think he has a very discerning palate. He would be just as happy with raw meat.'

Damien grinned. 'Without a doubt. And I am just as

happy with a few plates of delicious food, than a whole table full of stuff I do not recognise covered in slimy sauces that taste nasty.'

'Oh, no. I am sure Monsieur Chandon does not make anything so unappealing.'

He grunted. 'I like food I can recognise by names I know.'

'Hmm. Then I hope you don't dislike the dessert I have made.'

'Apple pie?' he said hopefully.

'Eclair, with a chestnut purée filling.'

She got up and went to the sideboard and brought back two chocolate-topped oblongs.

'I love eclairs,' he said. He had spent many afternoons gazing longingly at a tray of them in the window of a nearby patisserie in Marseilles. Watching them disappear and never able to afford a taste—unless he managed to steal one.

He grimaced. 'I like them with custard inside, though. I don't know about chestnuts.'

'You won't know, until you try them.' She placed the plate in front of him.

He cut into the pastry with the edge of his fork. 'Mrs Lamb, or may I call you Pamela?'

'You may. But only when we are in private, My Lord,' she said primly. He liked prim. It was very sensual. At least with regard to her.

'Then you must call me Damian.' He ate a mouthful of the dessert. It was light, it was chocolate and the creamy filling was like nothing he had ever tasted. It was delicate and rich and nutty. 'Oh, good Lord.'

Her eyes widened. 'Is something wrong?'

'I have never tasted anything like it. It is absolutely amazing.' He finished the rest of it. 'Is there another.'

She laughed and got up. 'I thought you said you couldn't eat another bite.'

'That was before I tried this.'

She put another one on his plate and sat down. 'I have a feeling you were going to ask me something before we got on to the subject of dessert.'

He finished the most amazing pastry down to the last crumb. He forced himself not to ask for another.

'I am sure you guessed I was going to ask if you had considered my offer.'

'With regard to the partnership?'

He leaned his elbows on the table and leant forward. 'Yes.'

'I gave it some thought while I was cooking. I am not opposed to the idea and I certainly appreciate the honour you are doing me by asking…' She took a deep breath. How did she explain her misgivings?

'But?'

'I still do not understand why you would wish to reduce your own profits for no benefit that I can see. I am already undertaking the work you need of me. Usually a partnership requires some sort of equal financial investment. I have very little to offer in that regard.'

Of course. He certainly could not make it sound like some sort of charity. 'Naturally, you will no longer receive wages, but rather a draw from the profits the same way Pip and I do.'

'Should there not be some sort of legal undertaking? A guarantee that I would not make any less than I do under our current agreement?'

'Naturally. If you agree to this plan, I will contact my solicitor and have him draw up the agreement.'

She frowned. Was she going to turn him down? He really hoped not. 'Do you have other concerns?'

'There are things going on in this house, other than gambling. I see couples leaving the ballroom and returning throughout the course of the evening. I know they go upstairs and I have strong suspicion they pay for the privilege. There must be something amiss or it would not be done so secretively.'

'Ah, that.'

'Yes, that! Not to mention the giggles of the maids when they speak of cleaning and tidying the rooms up.'

He frowned. 'The girls are not supposed to discuss what goes on in those rooms. Indeed, it is why we all wear masks at my parties. Discretion is the watchword and one of the reasons the *ton* attend.'

'They said not one word. Just giggled and shushed each other. And I did not ask them to explain. However, I do not see how I could become a partner in a business when I am not fully informed of what the business *is*. I will not mince words. I will have nothing to do with loose women.'

Without a doubt, she was nobody's fool. 'Of course. As a partner, you would not be kept in the dark about any aspect of the business.'

'I would need full disclosure before coming to any decision.'

She was definitely intrigued, but would she be shocked? It was a gamble. She might pack her bags and leave. He thought not. Well, it was time to roll the die.

'Why don't I show you? Then you can make a decision.'

She looked surprised, as if she had expected an argument.

He rose to his feet. 'Are you ready? I just need to collect the keys from my study.'

As they walked along the corridor together, he deliberately matched his steps to hers so that she neither felt hurried nor as if he was dawdling for her sake.

In his study, the dog lay on a carpet in front of the fire. The animal opened one eye, thumped its tail in a very desultory manner as a way of greeting them and went back to sleep.

'He really is making himself comfortable,' she said.

Dart groaned. 'He has no shame.'

She laughed.

Her laughter made something inside him feel lighter. He liked it when she laughed.

Damian picked up the ring of keys from the table and a candlestick.

The dog raised its head.

'Stay,' Damien said.

The dog lowered its head with a sigh.

Damian escorted her up the main staircase.

Pamela's heart was beating a little too fast as they climbed the stairs, not the servants' stairs she had crept up the first time she had visited this floor, but the main staircase. It wasn't the climb making her breathless. She was about to discover the secrets of this house and she was both excited and worried.

Damian hesitated upon entering the corridor then, rather than choosing the first door they came to, he put a key in the lock of the second one.

She peered into the darkness. Damian plucked a candle from the wall lamp and used it to light several torchières in the corners of what proved to be a room clearly meant for bathing. A large square tub sat on a dais in the middle of the room, with a canopy of heavy red fabric which puddled on the floor at each of its four corners. Towels and bottles of perfumes and oils covered a table against the wall. There were cushions on the floor and an assortment of silk dressing gowns hanging on a stand in the corner.

She looked around in astonishment. 'You said these were withdrawing rooms, but I did not expect them to contain baths.'

He smiled gently. 'I believe I said that this is where my guests came when they needed a little privacy.'

'Couples come here to bathe together?'

He shrugged. 'Among other things.'

'Oh.' It dawned on her what these other things might be. 'In the bath? How—?' She covered her mouth with her hand before she said anything she would regret.

He clearly was trying not to laugh. 'It is challenging, but most enjoyable.'

'This is the sort of thing they do in a bawdy house. You said—'

'No. The ladies and gentlemen arrive together. Some are wives. Some are lovers. I do not question them. Whatever arrangements they make, financial or otherwise, are nothing to do with me. They simply pay for the use of the key. That ensures only one couple is in here at a time.'

'Are all the rooms like this one?'

'They all have different…themes.'

'Themes?'

He huffed out a breath. 'The themes are based around fantasies. There are some common ones and some not so common. I simply provide the venue.'

Themes? She tried to imagine what those might be.

Damian must have taken her silence as disapproval because he gave her a hard look. 'This is a way for people to indulge in their fantasies, to play sensual games, without the fear of embarrassing others in their lives, such as servants and other family members.'

Sensual games? She had never heard of such a thing. 'But surely there are other…places they can go for this sort of thing?' She swallowed. Was she really having this sort of discussion with a man and her employer?

'It is certainly possible to satisfy certain desires at a house of ill repute. Have you ever been to one?'

Her jaw dropped. She bridled. 'Of course not.'

'I didn't think so. Well, let me tell you, they tend to be none too clean and the women are likely not as healthy as they should be. Whereas here, a couple attending my party can have a nice clean room and they know each other. Some of those who avail themselves of these rooms are husbands and wives.'

Her jaw dropped.

But she knew he was right. She had seen them. Did women enjoy these games? Had Alan been wrong about her after all? 'I see.'

What did she 'see'? She certainly looked decidedly flushed and, yes, just a tiny bit shocked. Whether it was at what he was telling her, or her own reaction to it, he wasn't quite sure. He had a feeling, though, that it was the latter.

Well, she would be shocked, if she felt some sort of response. She was an innocent. And he was intent on leading her down a dark path.

Guilt rolled over him.

He could end this now. Forget the need for justice and send her back to her kitchen, her reputation and innocence intact.

The image of his mother's face flashed before his eyes. Her sadness. Her bitterness. Her lingering death.

His resolve hardened. It wasn't right that those who had

destroyed their family should live their comfortable lives on the proceeds of what his family had lost.

He had vowed to his father that no matter what, he would see justice done and visit the sins of the fathers upon the children, as was right.

Had not their parents' wicked deeds been visited upon him as a child? Had any one of them ever given a thought to the pain they had caused him?

Now was not the time to weaken. Not when everything was falling into place. This woman meant nothing to him, apart from being a means to an end.

'Would you like to see more?' The expression on her face showed intrigue, even if she remained a little nervous.

He sorted through his keys. He opened the door to the room he always thought of as the most ridiculous, though it had proved very popular. A bed, shaped like a baby's cradle but big enough for an adult, took up centre stage. There were lacy curtains at the window, rattles and a baby bottle and large-sized nappies folded neatly on a chest. Everything one might find in a nursery except on a larger scale.

'Here they play mother and baby, or nursey and baby or some such.'

'Oh.' She stifled a laugh. Clearly, she also thought it ludicrous.

He continued down the corridor. He stood in front of the door at the far end. It held the most grown-up sort of games. Something he didn't mind playing once in a while, as long as he was the one in control. It was also very popular.

He paused, key in hand.

This one might be a bit too much.

'This one is a little more risqué. Perhaps we should save it for another day.'

Wide-eyed, she stared at him.

Clearly she was tempted, but also concerned. He certainly did not want to scare her off. He waited for her decision.

'It is getting rather late,' she said breathlessly. 'Perhaps another time would be best.'

'I don't want you to think I am hiding things from you.'

'No. No. Not at all. This has been most illuminative.'

In a way, he was disappointed that she had retreated, but it really was probably just as well. 'Then it is enough for tonight?'

'Yes. I think I would like to retire now. You have given me a great deal to think about.'

'Please do not take too long to consider my offer. I should like to have this settled before I return to London tomorrow. I will need to see my solicitor and arrange to have the necessary paperwork drawn up.'

'You are leaving tomorrow?'

She sounded regretful. As if she would miss him. Good. 'For a day or so. As is usual.'

'Of course.'

He held out his arm. 'Let me escort you to your chamber.'

After a little hesitation, she took his arm and they walked back down the way they had come up.

He wished he could tell what she was thinking. Perhaps he should have waited to show her these rooms. Yet his instincts said she would have baulked at his offer if he had tried to put her off.

They arrived at her door.

She smiled up at him. 'Will you take the dog to London with you? He will miss you when you're gone.'

He gazed at her hopeful expression. 'I was thinking I would drop into the village shop and see if anyone knows who owns him.'

She nodded. 'Of course.'

'Did you want me to leave him with you? For company?'

'No. I don't think he would stay. I was just wondering what you were planning. What if no one claims him?'

'Then he will travel to London with me, I suppose.'

'I am sure he will enjoy that.' She chuckled. A low husky sound that strummed chords in his body and made his blood run hot.

'And what about you? Will you miss me?'

Her gaze dropped to the floor.

He tipped her chin up gently with one finger. 'Will you?' he murmured, his voice huskier than he expected as a sense of longing twisted deep in his chest.

She lifted her gaze to meet his. 'I prefer it when you are here.'

'Because you are lonely?' He ought to have thought about that.

'Not at all. I do not mind my own company. But I find myself wondering about what you are doing when you are in London.'

As he found himself wondering about her from time to time. Too many times.

'Did I tell you how much I enjoyed our walk today? I don't think I have enjoyed a day so much in a long time.'

Even the flickering light of the candle in the sconce by the door could not hide the way she coloured up at his words.

'I enjoyed it also,' she said softly.

Was she remembering their kiss? It seemed to hover between them. A memory filled with joy.

Her lips parted slightly on a sigh. He could not resist. He bent his head and brushed those delicate lips with his own. When she angled her head for better access, he tasted her lovely mouth with the tip of his tongue.

She made a small sound in the back of her throat and to his utter delight she wound her arms around his body, pressing close and kissed him back.

His body responded instantly. Hardening with desire. A desire long pent up and simmering beneath the surface almost from the day they met.

Not something he wanted to admit.

He moved his mouth over hers, gently encouraging, and her lips parted, welcoming him to taste and explore the delicious depths.

Even through their layers of clothing he could feel her hands moving over his back, while her soft breasts pressed against his chest. He flicked her tongue with his and heard her slight groan of approval.

Her stance widened and he pressed his knee into the space, aware of her body arching into him.

Moments passed in deep sighs and heat.

He found the doorknob behind her and turned, kicking open the door with his foot, backing her into the room.

He raised his head, looking for… Reason came flooding back. He drew back a little, staring down into her face. Dazed eyes full of sensual promise gazed back at him.

'Oh, my,' she said.

Overcome by a strong desire to kiss her again, he closed his eyes briefly. He needed to take this slowly. She was, above everything else, a lady. An unmarried one at that. If he rushed his fences now, she would run like a startled hare.

He drew in one or two deep breaths, smiling down at her. 'The perfect end to a perfect evening. Now I will bid you goodnight.'

'I… Yes. Goodnight,' she said, in barely more than a whisper.

Chapter Eight

When Pamela brought the teapot into the servants' hall the following morning, she stopped short on the threshold when she realised Dart had arrived and was already tucking into the scrambled eggs she'd prepared earlier, along with a slice of toast and some rashers of bacon. A book lay open beside his plate.

The sight of him was almost enough to make her regret her decision of the previous evening. The morning light from the high windows cast his face into chiselled relief, like that of a sculpture. His lithe elegant figure encased in forest green was a delight to the eye.

Her pulse quickened. While last night she had been determined to resist his allure, this morning, apparently, she was having trouble dredging up one reason why she should. She was no innocent miss with prospects of making a good marriage. Who would know what she did tucked away in the countryside?

Not that she should read much into that kiss. While delicious and enticing, it had been all too brief. He had withdrawn so swiftly she had the feeling he regretted it. Or perhaps—a flush of shame rose up from her chest—he thought, like Alan, that based on her responses she was unnaturally lascivious.

The memory of Alan's faint air of distaste stung her

anew. Never again would she show that side of herself and leave herself open to mockery.

She pasted a cool smile on her face and strode in.

He glanced up from his reading. 'Good morning, Pamela.'

She jumped at the sound of her given name on his lips. It sounded so warm and friendly. She should never have agreed he might use her given name when they were alone. 'Good morning, Damian.'

Strangely, she liked the way his name rolled off her tongue.

She poured tea for them both, filled her plate and sat down. It was then that she noticed the dog on his other side. It wasn't begging exactly, but it did have a hopeful look in its eye.

'We have a guest for breakfast,' she said lightly.

'This animal has not a scrap of good manners,' Damian said. 'I will be glad when I find its true owner.'

The dog was probably not going to be happy if that occurred.

They ate breakfast in silence, she sipping her tea and mentally planning menus and a list to send to the butcher as a means of blocking out thoughts about how handsome he looked freshly shaved and the way his hair gleamed beneath the candlelight, while he read his book.

Surprisingly, the silence was perfectly comfortable. Not a scrap of awkwardness.

And not a sly look in sight.

He closed his book and finished his tea. 'Do you have an answer for me?'

Right up until that moment she had not been sure what she would say to his offer of a partnership, but his calm businesslike demeanour had helped her make up her mind.

'Yes. Thank you. I would like to accept your offer of a partnership.'

'Excellent.' He rose and held out his hand. 'Welcome to the business. I will have the papers drawn up at once.'

'There is just one thing before I shake hands on it,' she said.

His gaze sharpened. 'What, pray?'

'The contract needs to include something about the dissolution of the partnership, in case one or other of us wishes to leave. It should acknowledge each person's investment. In my case, it will be my forgone wages.'

She watched him closely, wondering what he would say to her suggestion. She would never forget how angry her father had been when he had discovered that his wife had foolishly invested in a scheme that left the last ones to join paying their money to those who had set up the venture and there were no business profits to be had. Indeed, there had been no business.

Having no head for figures, her father had trusted his wife to manage the family finances and she had always done exceedingly well. That time, Mother had been completely hoodwinked.

Pamela did not understand it very well. He had not wanted to burden her with the details, but she had understood the concept of taking money from Peter to pay Paul and that in the end someone along the line would be out of pocket.

Damian looked thoughtful, as if considering the practical aspect of her proposal. At least he hadn't dismissed her suggestion out of hand. If he had, she would have immediately refused to participate.

'I will consult with my solicitor and show you what wording he suggests when I return,' he said.

Inwardly, she breathed a sigh of relief. To her surprise,

once she had made the decision to join the partnership, she realised she really wanted to be part of it. And the idea of the profits she would eventually make was dizzying.

Not only would she be a woman of substance, one who commanded respect, her future independence would be assured. She would not have to face the prospect of marriage to a man who might, like Alan, call her appetites *unnatural.*

Heat rushed to her face at the recollection. Her stomach fell away, leaving her feeling nauseous.

How she hated that feeling of shame. It made her feel small and worthless.

The new venture meant she never need endure it again. She would be financially self-sufficient and to the devil with any man who thought to denigrate her for her choice.

Three days later she had the contract in her hand.

'Well?' Damian said. 'Does it meet with your approval?'

Pamela looked up from the contract Damian had presented to her upon his arrival from London. 'It seems to cover all of the points we spoke of, though the language is rather difficult to follow.'

'If you are concerned that I am trying to pull the wool over your eyes, please feel free to have your own solicitor take a look at it.'

His voice had a chilly edge as if she had somehow impugned his honour. Which she had, she supposed. Her own solicitor. What sort of cook had her own solicitor? She could ask her stepfather's lawyer. But she had no doubt that he would be off, hot-footed, to tell her mother what she was up to and that would be the end of her foray into independence.

The thought of being forced into marriage made her shiver.

'Oh, no,' she said airily. 'I don't doubt it is all as you say.' She signed it with a flourish.

'I also took the liberty of visiting the employment agency,' he continued. 'I concluded your contract with them on your behalf. I will take the cost of the buy-out from your next draw.'

'Perfect.'

He smiled and held out his hand. 'Welcome to our partnership, Pamela. May we prosper.'

A niggle of doubt constricted her chest for a moment. What if she was making a huge mistake? What if she lost what little she had? It was too late for doubts.

She took his hand, warm, large and dry, and shook it. 'Thank you, Damian. And now I must be getting along. I have a great deal to do before our guests arrive tomorrow.'

'Since you are now a partner, I was thinking you should not need to cook for the staff and you should move to quarters more suitable for your new position.'

Oh, heavens. She surely didn't want the world to know she was a partner. What if her mother learned of it? Right now, she was unknown, like the rest of the women who worked for him, and the mask kept her identity a secret. But she knew the *ton*. They would be far more curious about her if they thought she was of importance.

'I think I would rather keep things as they are,' she said. 'There is no need for anyone to know that I have an interest in the endeavour, is there?'

For a second, she saw a shadow pass through his lovely brown gaze. Had she hurt his feelings?

Then he shrugged in that charmingly Gallic way of his. 'If that is your wish.'

'It is. However, I would like a little more help in the kitchen.'

He chuckled. 'I would say we ought to vote on it, but I know Pip would vote with you, so, yes. Hire more help in the kitchen. And while we are on the subject of duties, I would very much like you to take over the bookkeeping. It is something you can be working on when I am in town. That is if you wouldn't mind.'

'It is a fair trade.'

The study door swung open.

The dog, tongue lolling, trotted in.

'Oh.' She looked at Damian. 'You didn't find his owner?'

Damian winced. 'According to the innkeeper, he is a stray who showed up in the neighbourhood about a month ago. One of the locals in the taproom offered to shoot him. They say he's been stealing chickens.'

'And yet he brought the duck to you.'

'I know. Very odd. Anyway, it seems he's mine and he promised he would behave himself from now on since he is no longer starving.'

'It is kind of you to give him a home.'

He made a gesture of dismissal. 'It is stupid of me. I find myself needing to walk him in the morning in town, because he won't let any of the footmen put a leash on him.'

She stifled a laugh. 'Oh, dear.'

'I thought I would leave him here with you, when I go up to London.'

She looked doubtfully at the dog gazing adoringly at his new master. 'I suppose you could try. Have you given him a name?'

'The Dog.'

'Very original,' she said drily. 'I will see you at dinner. I am off to hire my kitchen maid.'

Damian watched Pamela leave his study with a vague feeling of sympathy

The mouse had taken the cheese, now all that was required was for the trap to shut. It was too bad he liked her, when he had expected to despise her. Of his two victims, she was the one with the gumption.

He still hadn't got to the bottom of exactly why she was hiring herself out as a cook. No doubt it was some kind of rebellion against her family, which was exactly the sort of thing a spoiled brat would do. Also likely the reason she didn't want to advertise her role in their partnership.

Damian was in no hurry. Things like this needed to be accomplished with finesse and he still had one more mouse to catch. The young man was proving elusive.

But now that he had Pamela safely enmeshed, he could focus his efforts on the last of his enemies' children.

The dog thumped its tail on the carpet.

'No. I am not going to take you out,' he said. 'I have work to do.' He huffed out a breath. 'I suppose you do need some sort of name. How about Odysseus? I have a feeling you are a bit of a Trojan horse, old fellow.'

The dog whined.

'Yes, it is a bit of a mouthful. Oddy for short.'

The dog wandered over to the mat beside the hearth, curled up in a ball and closed its eyes.

'Oddy it is.'

Damian tucked the contract in his desk and opened his ledger. If he was going to pass the bookkeeping to Pamela, he ought to make sure it was current first. He sorted the bills into date order and began the tedious task of entering the amounts.

He only noticed the passage of time when he realised it was getting difficult to see properly as the light outside faded fast. He removed his spectacles and stretched.

Time to call it a day. 'Come, Oddy, we will go and check

on my horse.' He had driven himself down in his curricle earlier in the day.

Oddy sprang up, keen and eager, his nose scenting the air.

Damian collected his coat and boots from the mud room. The scent of something delicious cooking permeated the air. Oddy headed in the direction of the smell.

'Come,' Damian said. If he followed the dog, he might be tempted to kiss his cook again and then he might never get out to see to his horse. Besides, Oddy needed to learn who was master here.

He headed for the stables and, with a last regretful look in the direction of the kitchen, Oddy followed.

Outside, clouds covered the evening sky, and only the dark shape of the stables remained visible. He needed a lamp. He unhooked the one beside the back door and almost jumped out of his skin when a form appeared in front of him.

'Pamela? What are you doing?'

She held up a bunch of leaves. 'I needed some sage for the chicken.'

'You gave me quite a start.' He glared at Oddy. 'Why didn't you let me know she was here?'

Oddy wagged his tail.

'I am supposed to be here,' Pamela said calmly and bent to pat the dog. 'Dogs only warn about strangers.'

Why didn't he know that? Because he had never had a dog, or at least not since he had left England, and he barely recalled his mother's pug, who she'd had to leave behind with a friend.

'Where are you going?' she asked.

'The stables. To make sure my horse has all it needs for the night.'

She nodded. 'I meant to ask you earlier how many guests we are expecting tomorrow.'

'Forty.'

'That many?'

'Our parties are so popular I am having to turn people away. I think forty is the maximum number we can entertain comfortably. I don't want people complaining it's a squeeze.'

'Limiting the guest list will only make it all the more popular.'

'And I can pick and choose who I want for a guest.'

'The richer the better, I suppose.'

'No. That would be crass. The key is to invite the most interesting people. Fill the room with a bunch of dullards and our days are numbered.'

'You are very clever about all this.'

'I have had lots of experience. Pip and I both have.'

'While I am a mere babe in the woods. I am still not sure why you want me as a partner.'

'Because you bring an element of the tasteful to the proceedings.'

She made a choking sound of smothered laughter. 'You jest.' Clearly she did not understand her own allure.

'No.'

She shivered.

It was then that he realised she was not wearing any sort of outer garment except for her shawl.

'Why are you not wearing a coat?'

'I only slipped out for a handful of herbs.'

'And now I have kept you talking. Go inside at once.'

She drew herself upright. 'You have no right to order me about, My Lord.'

'It is for your own good.'

She folded her arms over her chest. 'I will decide what is for my own good, thank you.'

'I see. I beg your pardon. Do as you please.'

'I will.' She moved around him and headed inside.

Damian stared after her for a moment. Up to now she had seemed rather pliant. This stand-your-ground sort of attitude was an interesting development.

Interesting and possibly dangerous.

Through the slits of her mask, Pamela watched Rake Hall's guests slowly depart for home. As Damian had predicted, they were turning people away, some even arriving at the door without invitations.

Those, she left to Damian.

A couple of young men on the far side of the room raised their voices. She could see they were becoming belligerent. What was it about young men and brandy that made them argumentative?

It was Mr Long again. She'd had to intervene in an argument he had been having the previous week as well.

She sauntered over. 'Mr Long and Mr Smith,' she said, smiling. 'How are you this evening? How nice to see you both again.'

Long, a portly young fellow with an over-long forelock that flopped in his eyes, turned his angry gaze on her. 'We are having a discussion. Smith here thinks that Oxford is the better university when everyone knows that Cambridge is far superior.'

His words seemed a little slurred. 'I see. It is a friendly argument then.' She linked her arms through one each of theirs and steered them towards the nearest table while continuing to talk. 'So you are both content that you received the best of education?'

They frowned.

'I mean, I am assuming you are not intending to return to your studies?' she said.

'Lord, no,' Smith said. 'Glad to get it over and done with.'

'Me, too,' said Long. 'My tutor was an absolute beast. If I saw him again, I would plant him a facer. Make no mistake.'

'Mine sent me down for putting gin in the water jug in my second year.'

'What a good lark,' Long said, chuckling. 'I got sent down for six months. For fighting. Pater was furious...'

She left them exchanging reminiscences and moved on.

'Everything all right?' a deep voice asked from behind.

She turned and smiled at Damian. 'Yes. Just the usual disagreements about nothing. All forgotten in the blink of an eye. Mr Long seems a bit on the quarrelsome side tonight, though.'

Damian narrowed his gaze on the topic of their conversation. 'Is he giving you trouble?'

'Not really. He is easily distracted as seems to be typical of a young man feeling his oats.'

'Don't hesitate to call me if you need help.'

'I will. He is a recent addition to the guest list, I think. I don't recall seeing him before last week.'

'You are right. His family is very well connected. It would have been difficult to refuse him. Though I will, if you deem it necessary.'

'Not at all. If it happens again, I will have a quiet word with him.'

'Great men stand in dread of your quiet word,' Damian said with a twinkle in his eyes.

'No. Surely not.'

'Lord Stanley said he's terrified of one of your garden bear jaws about his drinking.'

'If he was terrified, he would stop,' she said drily. 'But I notice that he stays well within reasonable bounds since I had that talk with him.'

He put his arm through hers and they perambulated around the room. 'He's a sensible man.' They stopped at the table where Long and Smith had started to gamble. The croupier deftly handled the die.

All seemed well. She smiled at Damian and he nodded and moved on.

Without warning, Long grabbed the croupier by the wrist. 'Let me see those,' he said.

'Is there a problem?' Pamela asked brightly.

'She has been winning an awful lot,' Long said truculently.

A mutter of disapproval rippled around the table.

Pamela winced at the belligerent tone. This needed to be nipped in the bud.

'Perhaps you would like me to have the die broken open?'

Long must have caught the note of anger in her voice. 'I…er…no. I was simply commenting on the bank's good luck.'

It was a dreadful thing to accuse a gentleman of cheating at games of chance. It was a slur against his honour. Indeed, any man caught cheating could expect to be ostracised from polite society. And, whether innocent or guilty, was quite likely to issue a challenge to save face.

In this case, since the profits of the tables went to Damian, he was actually the one being accused of cheating, even if the girl was the one in charge of the table.

Pamela put a hand on Long's arm, a light touch of her fingers. 'I am sure your luck will change.'

Long turned his gaze on her and his lip curled slightly. 'Well, it won't, since I won't be betting any more tonight.'

He swayed as if he was having trouble standing. He had clearly had more to drink that she had originally thought.

'The dancing will start soon,' she said. 'Have you secured a dance with the lady of your choice? Ladies always get claimed very quickly.'

His gaze sharpened somewhat. 'I choose to dance with you.'

'I am sorry,' she said, smiling at the drunken fool. 'I do not dance.'

She didn't need him tripping all over her feet. Or, worse yet, falling down. Besides, now she was a partner in the business, she never danced. Only the girls who worked at the tables danced with the gentlemen. And only if they wanted to. She doubted any of the girls would want to dance with this fellow.

'Perhaps it is time you went home. Shall I have your carriage brought round?'

'I came with Smith. He told me about the rooms upstairs. But I couldn't find anyone to bring.'

Those blasted rooms. While she knew it was a draw for some of the men and that they often spent more money trying to impress the woman they brought, sometimes they were a source of conflict.

'Perhaps you will bring a lady another time,' she said.

He peered at her from under the hank of blond hair. 'You and I could be a couple.'

'No, we could not. I need to look after the guests.'

He leaned closer. 'I am a guest. I want you to look after me.' He grabbed her wrist and started pulling her towards the door.

In all these weeks, it was the first time any of the men had challenged her and certainly none had laid a hand on her.

She glanced up to find Damian already heading her way.

She smiled at him rather shakily as he drew close. 'Mr Long, you know Lord Dart, do you not?' she said, trying to make it sound like an ordinary introduction.

Long glowered at Damian. 'Yes. It is in your pockets where my money ends up.' His voice grew louder. 'I was warned that the house always wins at Rake Hell.'

A few people close enough to hear gasped. And others began to draw closer to see what was going on. The *ton* loved a good scene as long as they weren't the ones involved.

Damian eyed the flushed young man standing before him. He was going to deserve every bit of his comeuppance.

Indeed, one more word and he was going to find himself being called out. And that would suit Damian's purpose even better than simply costing him his fortune. Not that he intended to kill the lad on the field of honour. He would simply make him look a complete and utter fool. It wasn't hard to do, with such a spoiled brat.

'Release Mrs Lamb's arm, there's a good fellow,' he said softly, but with a voice full of icy determination.

Long wobbled on his feet. He took one look at Damian's face and dropped Pamela's arm as if it were hot.

So much for Long being any sort of worthy opponent.

Damian curled his lip. 'Now, what is the problem?'

Long looked around at the staring faces. 'I was saying that the bank here always wins.'

Damian shook his head and looked around at the gathering crowd. 'Not true.' He found the person he was looking for.

'Lord Norris, did you not win one hundred guineas just last week?'

Norris grinned. 'I did. Losing it all tonight, though.'

'I did tell you last week to stop while you were ahead,' Damian said, grinning at the fellow. 'Not one to take advice, are you?'

Norris shook his head. 'It will turn about, you will see.' He headed back to the tables.

Others drifted away.

Pamela, who had looked frightened just moments before, now looked far more relaxed. She had been obviously glad to see him.

'But that wasn't what you were arguing about with Mrs Lamb, was it, Long? You were having a different kind of conversation.'

Pamela slipped away and left him to it.

Long hung his head. 'I wanted her to take me to the rooms upstairs.'

Damian's stomach tightened at the obvious insult. He wanted to throttle the fellow.

To his surprise, Pamela returned with Smith in tow. Long's friend.

'I am going home,' Smith said, clearly primed by Pamela as to his role. 'I have another party to attend.'

Long looked at him owlishly. 'You do?'

'Yes. A private party.' He winked.

'All right,' Long said. 'I will come with you.' He gave an exaggerated bow to Pamela and Damian and left.

'Young idiot,' Pamela said.

'I think he's the sort that is likely to come to a sticky end. Did he lose a lot?'

Pamela shook her head. 'I won't know until later.' The clock chimed midnight. 'Anyway, it is time to start the dancing now.'

And just like clockwork, the tables emptied and the orchestra began to tune their instruments.

Pamela hurried off to make sure everything was in order and he and Pip collected the money they had won.

'What was happening?' Pip asked, clearly referring to the contretemps from a few minutes ago.

'A bit of rudeness from one of our very important guests. I think it is almost time to call an end to the game,' Damian said.

He didn't want it getting out of hand.

When all the guests had departed, the three partners sat in Damian's study with a glass of whisky in hand, while Pip counted the money and Damian worked on the IOUs. It had become a ritual with them since Damian had done it the first time so Pamela could see exactly what was going on. It had worked so well, they had continued meeting and counting after each party.

'So many vowels,' Pamela said, looking at the pile of scraps of paper scrawled with numbers and signatures.

Damien wrote down the numbers alongside the names.

'I see Long lost a hundred pounds,' he said. 'That makes close to three hundred he owes us. I wonder if he can afford to pay?'

Damian hoped not. A man who couldn't pay his debts had to leave the country.

Pip looked up. 'He will have to borrow if not.' He wrote an amount in the ledger and pushed the bundle of notes and coins to Pamela to double-check his counting.

Damien could not help watching the businesslike way Pamela tackled the task. Businesslike and incredibly feminine.

Pamela put down a pile of twenty-pound notes. 'I don't think he should be invited again. I am guessing he drank so much because he is scared.'

Damian shrugged. 'As you wish. But my guess is he will take it very ill if he is not given the opportunity to win back some of what he lost.'

She looked concerned. 'Perhaps you should speak to someone in his family about what is going on.' She started counting the pile of guineas.

Damian gave her a hard look. 'Why do you care so much about the fellow? He came close to insulting you.'

'I believe the Longs were once friends with my family. It has been a great deal of time since I have seen any of them, of course, but I do not feel comfortable about letting him fall into a debt he might never be able to repay.'

'He must repay,' Damian said. 'It is the rule.'

Either that or be forced to flee the country. What a satisfying result that would be.

Pip looked from one to the other. 'Well, my dears, I am *finis*.' He took the register from Pamela. 'It is time for my bed. I am off to Town early tomorrow. If you have finished, Madame Lamb, I will put the money in the safe and collect it in the morning to take to the bank.'

Pamela compared his total with hers and nodded. 'Please leave me twenty pounds in small denominations for purchases for the kitchen.'

He bowed. 'Very well. It shall be as you wish.'

Chapter Nine

Pamela leaned back in her chair with a sigh.

'Tired?' Damian asked his voice solicitous.

'A little,' she admitted. Bone tired, if she was to tell the truth. It might look as if she might do nothing but float around chit-chatting with the guests, but keeping some of these men civil and in order required a great deal of stamina. As well as diplomacy.

'Let me escort you to your chamber,' he said. The kindness in his voice made her feel strangely tearful. It was a long time since anyone had really cared about how she felt. Mother had been too busy establishing herself in London society to really notice much of anything.

Damian helped her to her feet and walked her along the corridor. 'You know,' he said, 'you really ought to move to one of the guest bedrooms. The bed in your current room is small and looks far from comfortable.'

'I like being near the kitchen. It makes it easier to get up and get the fire going first thing.'

'Hmmm. That is another thing. I think that you are really doing far too much. I am going to insist that we hire a new cook and relieve you of those duties.'

'Oh. But—'

'The cook would be under your supervision, of course.

But you go to bed very late after each party and then you must be up very early to make breakfast and such. Lack of sleep must, in time, wear you down.'

It was true. There were some mornings after a party when it was hard to make herself rise and get on with her day. 'Well…'

'There is a chamber in the west wing of the house you could use. It is in pretty good shape. Your scullery maid can make it up and the London staff will add it to their bedmaking duties.'

The west wing was on the other side of the house to the rooms their guests used. It was the wing where he and Monsieur Phillippe slept.

Cooking first thing and then spending the evening tending to their guests was tiring, especially since they continued their work far into the early hours after everyone left. She glanced up at him. There was only concern in his expression. Concern for her. It warmed her. She had the urge to hug him for being so thoughtful.

'You are right. It is tiring. Very well, let us hire a cook to replace me, if you think it is not too expensive.'

'Not too expensive at all since we can't have you looking haggard when our guests come, can we?'

'What will the other girls think?'

'It is not their business to think anything.' His voice was harsh. 'Besides, they are fully aware that you hold quite a different position in the household than you did when you first arrived.'

'Hiring another full-time servant to work for what is really only three days a week seems unnecessarily expensive. I can continue to look after the stocking of the pantry and so on. Why don't I hire someone from the village to come and cook on those evenings when the staff need feeding?'

He chuckled. 'Always so careful with our money. But, yes, if you think that would work, I agree.'

They had reached the door to her chamber. She turned to face him. 'Thank you for being so thoughtful.'

A faintly guilty look passed across his face. 'I don't deserve your thanks. It is more about what is good for our endeavour.'

He would never admit to being kind. He was the same when he was kind to the staff. He always brushed off any thanks.

Without thought, she rose up on her toes, put her arms around his shoulders and kissed his cheek. 'Thank you all the same.'

In a second, his arms were about her waist. He pulled her close and covered her mouth with his in a deliciously gentle kiss.

His breathing was harsh in her ears, his arms strong around her back, but tender, holding her as if she was some sort of delicate flower.

She felt womanly and feminine.

She leaned into him, kissing him back, opening her mouth as their tongues tangled in a dance of passion. Heavenly, heavenly kisses. Her heart beat far too fast and she fell into the dizzyingly lovely melding of mouths and felt the hardness of his body pressed against hers.

It was all too brief.

He broke away, gazing down at her. His gaze was hot, but also stormy, as if he were angry. His shoulders were rigid.

Had her unbridled desire caused her to ruin things between them? 'I am sorry,' she whispered breathlessly. 'I should not have...'

He gave a short sharp bow. 'You are right. It was ill done of me.'

'Oh, no. I did not... I mean...' Why on earth was she stuttering and stammering as if her tongue was too large for her mouth? Perhaps because her heart was still hammering in her chest.

'I will be driving up to London in the morning, please hire the cook as we discussed. Also have a woman from the village come and make up your new quarters while I am gone.'

'Oh.' Disappointment slowed everything to a crawl. 'When will you return?'

'In time for the next party, as usual.' His tone was frigid, almost arctic, as if he resented her questioning him. It wasn't as usual. He often stayed a few days after each party, having dinner with her each evening. It seemed that her kiss, her unwanted kiss, had ruined everything.

He reached around her and opened her door. 'I had forgotten how small this room was. Barely space enough to swing a cat.'

'I have been allocated worse,' she blurted. 'I find it cosy.' It was private, which was always a luxury when you were a servant.

His gaze hardened. 'I bid you goodnight, Pamela.'

He bowed and stalked away.

She watched him go. So tall. So manly.

What an idiot she was. The moment an attractive man came into her orbit, she could not control her desires. No wonder he had turned so cold. He must think her a wanton.

Heat washed through her at the thought of losing his good opinion as he must surely realise she was no lady.

Once more, embarrassment mixed with shame made her feel ill.

Clearly, she had done the right thing by leaving society. No doubt by now she would have made a fool of herself with some gentleman or other and caused her family a terrible scandal.

Obviously, she could not trust herself to behave in a ladylike fashion.

And now, located so close his bedroom, she was asking for trouble. The man was far too tempting for her carnal self.

And that was the problem. *She* was the problem. Something about her made a man forget he was a gentleman. And judging from the way he had withdrawn from her so abruptly, Dart also found her passion unnatural.

Unless she got herself under control, she was going to ruin everything.

No. She could not allow her proclivities to ruin her life. Would not.

No more kisses. No more passion. From now on it must be nothing but business.

Rain on the drive down to Rake Hall from London had soaked Damian to the skin.

Good.

He didn't deserve comfort.

He had almost let a sweet little kiss make him change his mind about the future, to divert him from his purpose.

A few days away from Rake Hall had helped him put things in a proper perspective.

Pamela was attracted to him, as he had intended. The fact that he found her alluring, that he liked her, had no bearing on his objectives. He could not afford to be softhearted. He had promised his father that those who benefited from the destruction of their family would be suitably punished.

He forced himself to recall the way his mother had looked those last few terrible months and how his father had sunk into despair. He had been unable to do anything for his parents while they lived, but he could certainly keep his promise to them now in death.

He finished making his horse comfortable, made sure it had food and water and strode for the house.

Stripping off his wet cloak as he entered the front hall, he made for his study and a nip of brandy to warm him up.

He stopped on the threshold.

Pamela, head bent over a ledger, was occupying his chair.

Instead of her cook's cap, her head was bare and her hair braided and twisted into ropes of gleaming chestnut.

Sensing his presence, she looked up. Her smile was hesitant, as if she was trying to judge his mood. 'Hello,' she said. 'You are a day earlier than I expected. I hoped to have this done before you arrived.'

'This?' he asked,

'Yes. I have been working on these ledgers. They are a bit of a mess and I thought to sort them out for you.' She frowned. 'There are some odd entries that I do not quite understand, but I am sure you can explain.' She turned the book towards him.

He glanced down and saw that she was talking about Long. The son of the man who, along with her father, had stolen his family's wealth. He had been keeping track of the young man's loans from the moneylender Damian had recommended. A man who acted for Damian and who was actually using Damian's money to make the loans. And because of this, Long received a better rate of interest than he could obtain elsewhere. Thus ensuring Damian held all of his debts.

How very clever of her to notice those entries as being different.

'What about them?' he said casually.

'I don't understand how he can be in this much debt. It doesn't seem to tally with his IOUs.'

Far too clever.

'I do not know anything about it. We will have to ask Pip. Do not worry about it.'

She looked inclined to argue.

'Did you manage to find a woman to do the cooking for the staff?' he asked.

'I did.'

'Is she to your liking?'

'She seems very competent. And she was very pleased to have the work. She does not mind at all that she will not live in.'

'Excellent. I hope she cooks as well as you do or the staff will be disappointed.'

She brightened at his compliment. It pleased him more than it should have to see that sweet smile.

'I actually had her make a couple of meals for me as a test before I offered her a position. She prepares good plain food. I am sure the staff will love it. And she is a very nice woman whose children are grown and who was very pleased to have a few days' work every week.'

'And have you settled into your new quarters? Are they to your liking?'

'I have. Thank you. The bed is exceedingly comfortable.' She flushed, as if embarrassed.

A buzz of excitement zinged through his veins at the thought of her in the middle of what he knew to be a large four-poster bed. He imagined all that gloriously coiffured hair of hers un-braided and free around her shoulders with that sweet smile on her face.

Too beautiful to bear thinking about.

'I see.'

She looked a little puzzled. Probably because he had sounded too gruff. Too uninterested when normally he had no trouble striking exactly the right note with the ladies.

'I am glad you find it meets your needs.' That didn't sound much better. He needed to call a halt to the awkwardness. 'I hope you will excuse me, I have some letters to go through and some bills to pay. I am sure you have things to do elsewhere. I will see you at dinner. I assume Cook will be sending our dinner to the small drawing room as you did?'

She shivered very slightly, perhaps chilled by his cool tones.

Chill was what he needed, distance, if he was going to keep his sanity. At least until he was prepared for the final act of her downfall. And that required careful orchestration.

'Yes, of course,' she said hurriedly.

'And you will join me, naturally.' There, that sounded a little more like himself.

'If you wish. Let me leave you in peace. I need to read through the menus I have prepared for Chandon. I can do that in my room.' She hesitated. 'That is, unless you would like to look at them. You know, approve them.'

'I am happy to leave the issue of menus in your capable hands. Why keep a dog and bark oneself?'

He winced. Not exactly the jolly quip he had intended.

With a cool nod, she picked up a couple of pages from the desk and bid him farewell.

Curse it. He had not intended to sound dismissive, where was his easy address? His charm? When it came to her, when he needed it most, it seemed to desert him. It was because of her. She didn't giggle or simper, the way many other ladies did. She was all business.

And yet, despite her air of competence and complete calm, he sensed a vulnerability in the depths of her gaze. Something, or someone, had hurt her in the past, though she tried very hard to hide it. Her bravery made him want to shield her from anything that might offer harm.

Though as far as he knew, the only person offering her harm was him. And he certainly had no intention of forgoing his revenge.

Absolutely not.

He had decided, had he not, that it was time to cease procrastinating and to forge ahead with his plan.

He just wished the idea didn't make him feel quite so uncomfortable.

Pamela gazed at the remains of her dinner, trying to ignore that the gentleman opposite her had barely spoken a word to her throughout the meal. She would have done anything to have been able to turn the clock back and undo their kiss. That brief moment of madness outside her chamber door had ruined everything.

Perhaps if she had not kissed him with such fervour, then they would have continued on in the easy manner they had developed in the weeks since she had arrived. A professional and friendly relationship that she had come to enjoy. No, not only enjoy. That she had come to rely on.

Now it almost seemed he was regretting offering her a partnership. She'd kissed him twice now—he probably thought she was a woman of loose morals who likely should not be trusted in his business. Perhaps he would worry that she would respond in the same way with other men and somehow put their enterprise at risk.

Was she even sure in her own mind that she would not?

The idea was like a hard cold fist squeezing the air out of her lungs.

They had eaten most of their meal in an uneasy silence, apart from the obligatory polite niceties.

'You are right, Pamela. It was ill done.'

She had gone over and over his words in her mind. He had ignored her forwardness twice now, but clearly she would not be given a third chance. Likely, if it was not for their written agreement, he would have been sending her on her way.

Well. She would make sure nothing like that ever happened again and, no matter how he behaved, she was going to continue as if nothing had happened.

'Did you find dinner to your liking?' she asked, unable to bear the heavy weight of silence any longer. 'I thought our new cook, Mrs Maize, did very well.'

She winced at the tentative tone in her voice. She sounded as if she wasn't actually sure. And she was.

'Clearly you have informed Mrs Maize of my preferences.'

She had taken great pains to do so.

He put down his knife and fork and gazed at her intently. 'The meal…' his eyes twinkled briefly '…was not a patch on the food you yourself prepare, but I am prepared to accept it, if it means your spirits are revived. Judging by your looks this evening, this is indeed the case.'

For a moment she did not quite take his meaning. As his words sank in, her face heated. Oh, my Lord, she was blushing. And there was a stupid sort of girlish giggle lodged at the base of her throat.

She swallowed. 'Thank you, My Lord.'

'Come now, Pamela, did we not agree to used our given names?'

'Yes, we did, Damian. I thank you for your compliment and for your forbearance. I agree there was a little too much salt in the soup and the chicken should have been a little more tender, but Mrs Maize is very willing to learn, so I am sure everything will soon be exactly to your liking.'

He leaned back. 'If her desserts are anywhere near as good as yours, I shall be a happy man.'

Happy.

That had been her goal, had it not, to make him happy. Or at least satisfied that he had not made the wrong decision.

She was determined to make this new venture a success. Determined to save enough to make her dream a reality.

He rose and went to the side table. 'May I help you to some trifle?'

'You may indeed.'

He set a dish before her and sat down. 'They say the proof of the pudding is in the eating,' he said with a boyish smile.

Just like that the atmosphere changed. They were easy with each other again, as if the kiss had never been.

'They do. You try it first. I will wait with bated breath.'

He chuckled. 'Are you worried I will send you back to the kitchen, if it does not pass muster?'

'I would like to see you try.'

He laughed heartily and raised his spoon to his lips.

'You will give your *honest* opinion,' she said with mock severity.

He tasted the confection. For a second, he paused, looking at her, laughter in his eyes like some sort of naughty lad bent on mischief. 'Excellent. All is as it should be.'

She let go her breath. 'As I expected. You must know I would not hire anyone who was not up to scratch.'

He reached across to where her hand rested on the table and took it in his. 'I trust you implicitly, my dear. You will pardon my teasing. You were looking just a fraction anxious.'

'Because you are so unpredictable.' She gasped. She had not intended to speak her mind right at that moment.

His eyes widened. Surprise, not anger. 'In what way?'

Heat travelled up from her chest to her face. But she had started this and it was too late to stop. 'One minute you are, well, all warm and friendly. The next you are as cold as ice. I do not know whether I am on my head or my heels.'

He leaned back and picked up his glass of red wine, looked at it reflectively and put it down again, as if he had come to some sort of decision.

'I find myself in somewhat of a quandary. I—' His voice was little more than a murmur.

She leaned forward the better to hear.

'You are a beautiful woman, Pamela. I was your employer and now we are business partners, yet against all social mores, I find myself drawn to you. I was trying…' There was a long pause.

'To protect me.' she put in.

'To protect us both, I suppose. I have a position in society to uphold.'

She frowned. Bewildered. 'As the owner of a hell?'

He chuckled. 'Of course not. I told you. This is not a hell. These are parties, to which only the noblest of families are invited. To receive an invitation to one of my parties is to be recognised as a member of *la crème de la crème*.'

She shook her head. 'I do not understand.'

'As one of the wealthiest men in England, I have no

need to win their money. Therefore, they can trust that I will not cheat them.'

How could that be when this house was decaying from neglect? And if he didn't need the money, then why do it at all? Why count every penny they won as if it was precious? 'Wealthiest?' She could not help the disbelief in her tone.

'Are you giving me the lie?' he asked mildly, but there was an edge to his voice.

'I simply do not understand why you would hold gambling parties if you do not need to make money from them. Why not simply go to White's or Boodle's or any one of a number of respectable gentlemen's clubs?'

'There. You see. You have identified exactly why.'

'I have?'

He got up from his seat, came around to her and helped her out of the chair and led her to the sofa by the fire. 'Let me pour you a brandy.'

She occasionally took a brandy with him after dinner, so his offer did not come as a surprise. 'Yes. Thank you.'

He went to the console and selected one of the decanters. 'You said,' he said as he poured, 'gentlemen's clubs'. No ladies allowed. Some friends and I were discussing this one evening at a ball and one of the ladies indicated that she thought it unfair that ladies were excluded. From there, we talked of opening places like White's to the ladies, much to the horror of the other men present.'

He handed her the glass and sat beside her with a brief lift of his glass in a toast.

She sipped at the brandy and savoured the smooth flavour.

'One lady suggested that they open a ladies' club,' he continued. 'No men allowed. Tit for tat. But where is the fun in that? I wagered that I could open a club where both sexes could mingle and enjoy together what normally they must enjoy apart.'

'But they have card parties all the time. Routs. Drums. Balls. There is always gambling.'

'Under the watchful eye of matchmaking mamas, dowdy dowagers and worried wives. Social strictures. Society's reins. Here, there is only fun in elegant surroundings and no questions asked. Anonymous fun that otherwise can only be had in sordid surroundings. The French are masters of it.'

'The rooms upstairs.'

'Indeed. Discreet rooms for couples who wish to avail themselves of the delights within them.'

'Those silly games are really such a draw?'

'Now you are a partner, I suppose you ought to be aware of *all* we have on offer.'

The dark note in his voice sent a shiver of awareness down her back. She took a quick sip of her brandy and realised she had swallowed it all in one mouthful.

It slid down her throat, warm and bracing. 'Yes. I suppose I should.'

She hoped she sounded more confident than she felt.

He finished his drink. 'Come.' He took her hand and together they walked upstairs.

Chapter Ten

Unto the breach, as his English compatriots were so fond of saying. Damian hoped he wasn't making a huge mistake by revealing this particular secret.

He had not been exactly lying when he said he was one of the wealthiest men in England. He held a great many vowels which, when added together with his own money, represented an enormous fortune. However, the chances of ever collecting on those mountains of debt were slender.

Indeed, he had no intention of attempting to collect on them. Or rather all of them. There was only one young man who would know the disgrace of ruin.

Yet it was hard to believe the recklessness of so many of his fellow peers. Did they even know how much they owed?

Unlike their debts to tailors and innkeepers and other tradesmen, the debts to him were considered debts of honour. Failure to pay a debt of honour had terrible consequences, should repayment be demanded and go unfulfilled. Dishonour was the thing most feared by any English gentleman.

Pamela's dishonour would be of a different sort.

A twinge tightened his heart. It would be hard on her, but it would not change her life so very drastically. At least, not as she lived it now. It would bring dishonour to her family name, however.

She would never be permitted a place in society.

As they passed down the corridor on the first floor on the west wing, he lit the candles in the sconces beside each door. Her hand gripped his arm tightly. Clearly, she feared what he would reveal. Yet she trod boldly onwards.

Each chamber brought a different delight to his guests, as shown on the various pictures hung beside each door. It was through the last door that she would pass this evening. For some, the height of pleasure. And usually the most difficult to obtain except in the grubbiest of surroundings.

He turned the key in the lock and threw open the door beside the picture of a whip and spurs.

He held his candle aloft to pierce the gloom inside. 'Wait there, or you might trip,' he said quietly. 'Let me light some lamps.'

'Oh, my,' she said, as light gradually filled the room and revealed all its glory. 'It's positively medieval.'

He tried to see it through her eyes. The whips and restraints hanging on the walls. The long bare marble table gleaming white. The metal bars of the triangular whipping post. The schoolroom birch twigs in varying widths and lengths neatly hanging from hooks. The velvet cushions strewn on the floor in one corner offering a place for comfort.

She turned slowly around, then walked here and there, touching the implements of pleasure-pain. There was an odd expression on her face. It was not one of shock or horror, but rather of curiosity.

She picked up one of the whips and looked at him. 'They use these whips?'

His body hardened. He turned away from her. He had no wish to scare her off.

'They?'

'The men. They whip the women. I have never seen anyone come down looking beaten. They always look…'

'Well pleasured.'

She wrinkled her nose. 'The women like to be whipped?'

'Some find it exciting, yes. And believe me, it is not always the man using the whip. More often than not it is the woman who has the upper hand, so to speak.'

English school boys and their birch canes. They loved to hate them.

She swallowed audibly. 'I see.'

He spun around at the huskiness in her voice. If his body had responded before, now he was rock hard when he saw the heat in her gaze.

She wasn't just curious or slightly intrigued. She was highly aroused.

In two strides he was at her side, gazing down into her eyes, gently cupping her face between his hands, feeling the flex of her jaw. 'My dear Pamela,' he murmured. 'Have you had some thoughts of a similar nature? Daydreams, perhaps, that leave you hot and bothered?'

She blushed and looked down, as if ashamed.

'It is all perfectly natural,' he said. 'These are adult games that hurt no one.'

'Have you played such games?' she asked, peeping up at him, her eyes wide.

He chuckled. 'I have. Does that shock you?'

She shook her head. 'I had no idea such things were considered so…commonplace.'

Something was troubling her. 'Then you have heard of such things before?' It seemed odd that a girl brought up in such a sheltered household would have come across such knowledge.

She glanced around the room and gave a little shiver. 'Not really.'

She was no longer aroused, rather she was uncomfortable. The shadows in her grey eyes gave him pause.

Had something about this room brought back unhappy memories?

'Come. This is a great deal for you to take in. Let me escort you to your chamber. We can discuss it again another time, if you wish.'

She seemed to relax a little.

Puzzled by her reactions, so very at odds with each other, he took her hand and led her from the room, locking it behind him.

He placed her hand on his arm and felt it tremble. He wished he could understand what was going on in her mind.

The further they walked from the chamber, the more relaxed she seemed.

Was it possible that somebody in her past had whipped her and taken pleasure in it? He tensed. Only with effort was he able to calm his rising ire.

When they reached her new suite of rooms, a few doors down from his own, she stood back as he opened the door for her and gestured her to enter. 'Would you care for a brandy?' she asked. 'I took the liberty of filling a decanter for myself, I hope you don't mind.'

Not one decanter, he noted, but three with differing contents and some glasses neatly set about them on the silver tray on the desk.

'I am glad you did. It is no more than Pip or I would do.'

She poured him a glass of brandy and indicated he should sit beside her on the sofa near the fire. 'Thank you for showing me that room, this evening.'

'Well, now you know the last of my secrets.'

She gave him a sideways glance. 'I think perhaps not.'

He stilled. 'What do you mean?'

She smiled slightly. 'I suspect there is much about you that I do not know. Just as there is much about me that you do not know.'

'What else can there be to know? You are an excellent cook. You have a fondness for animals, dogs anyway, and you are a very intelligent woman.'

She turned slightly to face him, looking doubtful. 'You think I am intelligent?'

'Indubitably. Indeed, far more so than many of my male acquaintances.'

'You are very kind. But I think if you really knew me, you would think I am foolish in the extreme.' She gazed down into her glass for a moment and then tossed back the remains of her drink and set the glass aside.

Regret filled her face.

He took her hand. 'What troubles you? If you do not like the games rooms, then we will do away with them.'

'Oh, no. It is not that.'

'Then what?'

Pink stained her cheeks. 'It was my reaction to what I saw, if I must be truthful. I felt remarkably…' She shook her head as if unable to describe what she felt. 'You must think me…naive.'

He had the feeling that was not the word she had been about to use. Intriguing, indeed. He brought her small hand to his lips and kissed it lightly. 'You do yourself an injustice. Your lack of experience is only to be expected.'

She gave a bitter-sounding laugh.

He frowned 'Has some man taken advantage of you?'

A faint sigh left her lips. 'If that were true, I would feel less stupid.' She shook her head. 'I was engaged to a very nice young man. A soldier. We planned to marry as soon as he received his promotion. Both of our families were happy about the match. Indeed, it had been planned between them since we were children. So I was not as circumspect as I should have been. We were going to be wed, after all.'

Unexpected anger surged through him. 'He did not marry you?'

Her hand convulsed in his. 'He could not. You see, there was an accident during an exercise. A gun carriage broke free. It killed him instantly.'

'Oh, my dear. I am so sorry.'

'He was such a nice boy. Very sweet. Much too good for me.'

He frowned at the sadness in her voice. 'Why would you say such a thing?'

'My father would have been so disappointed in me.'

Her father had no right to be disappointed in anyone.

'So that is why you hired yourself out as a cook.'

'When Mother married again, she decided the only way to be comfortable again was for me to make a good match. She and her new husband had already picked out a groom. How could I tell her? I felt so ashamed.'

So, Pamela Lamb, was no innocent maid after all. Her journey to ruin had started long before Damian came along. She had simply managed to keep it a secret.

Now he would bring it to its natural conclusion. A twinge of guilt twisted in his gut. A feeling of pity hollowed his gut. He could, if he wished, set her free of the trap he had wrought. Let her walk away. He would still have his revenge on the other family.

Yet it was her father who had been the ringleader of the plot to defraud his father of his fortune, he who had turned his back on his father's pleas for help. Now her mother lived at the apex of society, queening it over lesser mortals, while his mother lay in a pauper's grave.

No. Pity had no place in his heart. He had vowed at his father's grave to take revenge on those who had caused his mother's death if he ever had the chance.

He would not turn away from his sworn duty because of a pretty face, a sweet smile and delicious kisses.

Pamela could not believe she was telling Damian her innermost secret. Perhaps it was because she had been unable to tell anyone else all these years.

Despite that he did not seem particularly shocked, he must now think her the worst sort of woman. The sort of woman who had so little respect for herself that she would lay with a man to sate her desires, without any thought of the consequences, for herself or her family.

A selfish, pleasure-seeking wanton.

The trouble was, he would be right.

Her heart squeezed. Misery rose in her throat in a hot prickling sensation. Why could she not follow the rules of her upbringing and behave like a lady?

These past few weeks she had begun to feel at home. As if she had found the place she belonged, where she was respected and valued. Now he would never look at her the same way again.

She wished she hadn't spoken.

Damian gazed down at her, his expression dark, his eyes unreadable.

She swallowed. Would he now demand she leave?

'I am sure you were not the first engaged couple to anticipate their wedding vows,' he said. 'You were both young. You had no reason to expect that you would not marry.'

The kindness in his voice had emotion welling in her

throat, hot and burning. She swallowed down the lump and forced a smile. 'It is kind of you to say so.'

He tipped up her chin and fleetingly kissed her lips. 'You are quite lovely, Pamela. Any man would be tempted.'

Her heart picked up speed. It wasn't the first time he had looked at her with such intensity. Usually, right before they kissed. The attraction between them had been obvious from the start, no matter how they had tried to ignore or deny it.

Since coming to this house, she had realised how lonely she had been in her quest for independence. When Damian was at Rake Hall, she did not feel alone. She felt at home.

When he left, she did not stop thinking about him. Wondering what he was doing, who he was with. Though she tried to pretend she did not care, the thought that he might be with a woman hurt terribly.

'Are you tempted, Damian?' she asked, emboldened by the heat in his gaze and by her own rising passion.

'Constantly,' he said, his voice a little rough.

'And yet you resist.'

'It is not honourable for a gentleman to importune a servant.'

'I am no longer a servant. We are partners. Equals. Perhaps we should stop dancing around each other and enjoy each other instead.'

Oh. Had she really said what had been in her mind for so long? It seemed where he was concerned she had no control at all.

A shadow passed through his gaze. As if he found her words disturbing.

'You think I am too bold.' She shook her head. 'There I go. Making the same mistakes again, as I did with Alan.'

'Your fiancé?'

'Yes.'

'Your boldness is captivating, my dear. But for all that, you are a lady—'

She pressed a finger to his lips. 'No. I can never again make such a claim. And to be honest, I have felt so alone with my secret. And now I have burdened you, too.'

'Alone and lonely.' He spoke as if he understood the feeling. 'You miss the companionship of a friend and a lover. Someone with whom you can share your innermost thoughts.'

'You do understand. Do you have such a person in your life?'

She winced and wished she could call back the words. If he answered yes, she was not sure what she would do. Probably cry.

'I have not known such companionship. As yet, I have been too busy to think of such things.'

'You have Monsieur Philippe.'

'Yes. I have my friend, Pip. He is the very best of fellows.' He gave her a look of deep sympathy. 'But you have no such friend in your life.'

She shook her head. 'We lived very quiet lives at the vicarage, before my father died. You might say my father was my best friend. We spent a great deal of time together. He died not long before Alan. And then my life changed completely.'

'Your stepfather is an earl, I understand.'

'How did you know that?'

'I made discreet enquiries once I realised you were not the common-or-garden cook I had expected. You use your own name. It was easy to discover your true identity.'

'Will you tell my family I am here?'

He shrugged. 'Not unless you desire it.'

'No. I do not.'

'Very well.'

Relief flooded through her. She gazed up at him. 'Thank you. You are a good man.'

His laugh had a sharp edge to it. 'Hardly.'

She turned fully to face him and, in a moment of longing and gratitude, kissed him full on the lips.

For a moment, like before, he hesitated, then he returned her kiss with passion.

Her heart sang. Her body trembled with desire. Instinct said there was no going back this time. And she was glad.

His kiss deepened. His tongue danced with hers. His breathing and hers mingled loud in her ears.

This was what she had missed. The excitement of body and heart and soul. The passion. The desire.

Longing filled her.

He groaned low in his throat, drawing back a fraction, gazing down into her face. 'Are you sure you want this?'

How could he even find the mental capacity to ask?

'Yes,' she managed to whisper. 'I want you.'

Very badly.

'Then you shall have me.'

The words sent a sharp pull at her core. She moaned her pleasure at the long-forgotten sensation.

He kissed her again at length, until her bones felt liquid and her mind dizzied. She was aware of his hands wandering her body in pleasurable strokes and caresses, slowly sliding under her skirts to caress her calves and her knees.

He rose up on one knee, bending over her, gazing into her eyes.

She reached up and pulled at the knot of his cravat, pulling the ends free of his waistcoat and then unwinding it from around his lovely strong throat.

He smiled as she began undoing his waistcoat buttons. 'I think this sofa is too small for the both of us, my darling.'

My darling.

What a chord of desire those words strummed through her body.

He pulled her to her feet, swept her up in his arms with ease and carried her into the bedroom.

The strength of him made her marvel.

She felt feminine and soft and yet strong enough to conquer the world, since he was her world.

Her insides tightened and pulsed with excitement. And the deepest desire she had ever known overwhelmed her.

When he set her on her feet, her knees buckled and he held her while she gathered herself together.

'Turn around, my sweet,' he said. She leaned on the bed while he undid the laces of her gown, then stepped out of it when it fell to the floor. Such a practical garment, not a flounce or a ribbon to be seen. And her chemise was plain cotton, not lace, but he seemed not to notice when he divested her of her stays and spun her back around.

He cupped her face in his hands. 'You are so lovely.'

She relaxed. 'You also.'

'Lovely?' He laughed. 'I do not think so.' He toed off his shoes.

'I will judge.' She helped him pull his shirt over his head. His shoulders were broad, his chest wide, and she ran the tips of her fingers through the triangle of dark curls before kneeling to peel off his stockings.

His fingers busied themselves in her hair, pulling pins until her hair fell down around her shoulders. He brought her to her feet and lifted her on to the bed.

He stroked her hair, spreading it out on the pillow. 'How soft,' he said, his eyes full of appreciation.

He climbed up on the bed alongside her.

He stroked her cheek and kissed her lips, tenderly at

first, but when she slid her arms around his neck and kissed him back, hard and furiously, pressing her breasts against his chest, feeling his hardness against her thigh, he moved over her, parting her thighs and stroking her mons and the little tiny nub within its folds.

Pure bliss. Darkness and waves of pleasure overwhelmed her.

Damian watched *le petit mort* overtake her with a sense of astonished wonder. He had not realised she was so close to the edge.

Carefully he eased his shaft inside her, riding the last waves of her orgasm as her tight passage spasmed around his engorged flesh.

He had never been with a woman so incredibly quickly aroused. Even as her orgasm began to wane, he moved slowly inside her, taking one tight nipple between his lips and suckling gently.

A sound of appreciation came from low in her throat and her hips moved in counter-change to his movements, grinding her sweet soft flesh against the hard bone of his pelvis.

He played with her other nipple with the fingers of his other hand, alternating from one to the other, before moving to her throat, kissing and licking and nipping until he sensed her passion rise again.

He rose up on his hands to look down into her face, her lips full from his kisses, her eyes heavy lidded and soft.

Her hands came up to roam across his chest in small circles, her fingers gently tweaking his nipples every now and then.

She grabbed his shoulders and pulled herself up to kiss his lips.

As she fell back, he followed her down, delving into her

delicious mouth with his tongue, pressing her slender lithe body into the mattress with his weight.

Her legs came up around his waist, opening her hot slick passage to better accommodate his hard shaft, and his mind went blank, aware only of pleasure and the pain of waiting for her to be ready again. It was the purest, most delicious torture.

And then he felt her tighten around him. She made a sound of encouragement and he thrust harder and faster and finally she let go and fell apart.

Pleasured nigh unto death, he followed her into the abyss.

At some point during the night, Pamela had snuggled into Damian's arms. Awaking with the sensation of someone spooned within the curve of his body, one small pert breast filling his palm, the soft fullness of her bum against his groin, was delightfully surprising.

They fit together as if they were made for each other. Only the sound of her gentle breathing disturbed the quiet.

Damian rarely slept beside his bedmates. As a youth, his amorous adventures had been quick stolen moments with ladies of the opera while avoiding the attentions of the local gendarmerie.

More recently, he had enjoyed the company of a couple of wealthy widows who'd been only too pleased to embrace his fleeting attentions while maintaining their independence.

He had avoided any and all lures thrown out by matchmaking mamas who had seen him as fresh meat on the marriage mart upon his arrival in town.

Pamela sighed and stirred in her sleep.

Damian held perfectly still, for some reason wishing to maintain the feeling of oneness for a moment.

Even as the thought occurred to him, he shook off the odd longing and eased his arm from beneath her body and slipped out of the bed.

She stirred again.

He pulled the covers up over her bare shoulder, leaned over her and brushed her cheek with his lips. Her mouth seemed to curve in a smile.

She really was quite lovely.

And the fact that she had not been an innocent maiden made his task all the easier.

Calming maidenly fears had been one of the few things with which he had little or no experience. He had found the thought daunting.

Instead, he had discovered she was a deliciously sensual woman, who had given him one of the most pleasurable nights of his life.

He pulled his shirt on over his head and gazed down at her. With her hair burnished by the morning light spread across the pillow and her face in sweet repose she looked as sweet and innocent as an angel.

Perhaps he should forget about ruining her and her family and simply enjoy their relationship, here in the quiet of the countryside away from prying eyes.

Without doubt, if he continued the course he had chosen, their affair would end instantly and on a very sour note.

He shook his head at his foolishness. His weakness. He should know better than anyone that appearances were deceiving. Pamela was no innocent miss. And her family had played a major part in the ruination of all he had held dear.

The grand crescendo to his revenge was all arranged. The stage set and the play to open three weeks from today at his first society ball in his newly furbished London town house.

The invitations had gone out and the replies were flooding in.

No stopping things now.

Nor did he have the right. For the last ten years of his life his every waking moment had been building towards this end. To stop now not only would be a betrayal of the promise he had made to his parents, but would surely mean he had lost every last shred of his honour by being too cowardly to take action, because he feared being hurt by the consequences. Again.

The recollection of his cowardice all those years ago left a bitter taste in his mouth.

He would never forgive himself.

Damian had watched as his father opened the letter from Vicar Lamb. Watched his hope turn to despair and then rage. The letter had rejected all claims of culpability, denied any knowledge of the scheme that had brought in thousands of pounds and expressed false regret at being without the financial wherewithal to help. Sick at heart, Damian's father had tossed the letter on the fire, but Damian remembered every word.

Not long after that, his dear sweet gentle mother had become ill and when she died Damian had sworn to avenge her death. It had taken him years to reach this point.

The satisfaction of achieving his goal would make the years of struggle worthwhile.

As he had intended, he finished dressing in his room and headed for Town.

Chapter Eleven

Three days later, Pamela, seated in the study, going through the menus for the following day, could not quite believe how easily she had settled into her new life as a partner, both in business and as Damian's lover.

She enjoyed both aspects of her life. Preparing for the parties at the house, making sure they ran properly, was her first priority. Overseeing both the new cook and the rather dramatic Chandon was a challenge she also enjoyed and tested her organisational abilities to the full. Watching her nest egg grow in the ledger accounting for her part of the profits was especially satisfying.

The cottage she had imagined in her mind was no longer a vague fanciful daydream. It was now a possibility which she would soon turn into reality. If only she did not have such nagging doubts about the amount of money their guests were spending.

At least they were not getting as badly dipped as at first. After the evening when she had expressed reservations about the enormous pile of vowels they had accepted, the number had dwindled to very few.

When she enquired about it of Monsieur Phillippe, he had said that she was right to be concerned about the issue, because when they sold those vowels to a money lender, they were hugely discounted. It really was not worth their while to accept IOUs from those who likely were unable to pay their debts immediately, if ever. The fact that Damian and Monsieur Phillippe had listened to and acted on her concern had pleased her enormously.

One consequence of this new policy was that the number of people attending the parties had fallen. Not dramatically, but noticeably.

She glanced down her list of what was in the pantry and decided that the only thing she need order were peas.

The wine order, which was in Damian's purview, had arrived the day before and had been safely put away in the cellars. Fresh-cut flowers for the hall had been delivered this morning and she had arranged them in vases herself. Everything else she required was on hand.

'Good morning, my dear.' Damian's deep voice sent a zing of pleasure deep to her core. It always did.

She turned from her papers to see him standing in the doorway, hat in hand, his hair damp and slicked back, cheeks slightly reddened by the weather and his dark gaze warming when she returned his smile.

She had been expecting him and had dressed accordingly. She had purchased several new fashionable gowns now that she no longer wore her servant's garb and cook's apron.

'Good morning,' she replied, unable to contain her broad smile of welcome. 'All is well?'

'It is. Apart from the weather.' He set his hat and gloves on his desk. 'I really must get out of these wet things, it is raining cats and dogs out there.'

She realised that while his redingote must have kept his shoulders dry, his pantaloons were soaked to the knees. She began unbuttoning his coat, to help him get if off.

'Speaking of dogs,' she said, 'where is yours?'

'I left Oddy in town. He and the boot boy have made friends, thank heavens, and since I will only be away for two nights, he will be perfectly all right.'

'Only two nights.' She could not keep the disappointment out of her voice, no matter how hard she tried.

'Tomorrow will be our last party here.'

She gasped and stepped back. That she had not expected. 'The last?'

'Before Christmas, at least. Many people will be leaving London for their country estates or be busy with other holiday events. Even this week I received a number of declines to our invitation due to other social events.' He shrugged out of his coat and flung it over a chair. 'Besides, I have decided to throw a grand ball at Rake House.'

Rake House was his London town house in Grosvenor Square. That was where he lived when he wasn't here at the estate. He had told her that it was undergoing renovations and unfit for entertaining.

'I see.' Her heart felt heavy. She looked forward to the parties, particularly since it meant he would spend a few days with her. 'When will the parties here resume?' And what on earth was she to do with herself until they did?

'I am not sure they will.'

Her stomach dropped away. What on earth could he mean? The earth seemed to drop beneath her feet. She grabbed his arm. 'Why? What is wrong?'

He pulled her close, briefly kissed her cheek, smiling cheerfully, seemingly unaware of her surge of anxiety. 'We can discuss all this tomorrow night when Pip is here. Naturally I will need your assistance at the ball. Let me go and get out of these wet things.' He hurried off.

Her chest tightened. It was almost as if he was feeling

guilty. And what did he mean about her assisting with the ball?

And how typical of a man to make a dramatic announcement of what sounded like the end of their partnership and then disappear without explaining.

It really would not do.

Her mind in a whirl, she delivered her order for peas to the new cook, who would drop it off with the greengrocer on her way home, and went upstairs in search of Damian.

She entered his chamber without knocking, slamming the door behind her.

He was naked and rubbing at his hair with a towel.

He looked magnificent, broad shoulders, long limbs, dark hair everywhere.

He lowered the towel and gazed at her. His male member hardened and lengthened and rose to stand erect against his belly.

Her body stirred the way it always did when she saw him in all his glory and ready for her.

'Oh, you are pleased to see me,' she murmured, her anger dissipating, her breath quickening.

He laughed and in two strides was across the room and holding her in his arms. 'What a naughty wench you are.'

She reached down and cupped his testes, revelling in their delightfully heavy weight.

He groaned and rubbed his shaft against her hip in an explicitly suggestive thrust.

Feeling the surge of wetness between her thighs, she widened her stance in invitation.

He pulled up her skirts and entered her with one swift thrust. She leaned back against the door and held tight to his shoulders as a pleasure flooded through her body.

With him naked and her fully clothed it felt so erotic.

She reached down to squeeze his hard round bum with one hand while holding tight to his shoulder with the other. She kissed his neck, then nipped it.

With his hands flat on the door, and her pinned against it, he thrust into her hard and fast and…

Pleasure flooded through her even as he reached his own climax.

Somehow he managed to stop her from sinking to the floor and carried her to the bed. They lay side by side, panting.

'Devil take it,' he said. 'I had intended to make love to you after dinner. Long and slow.' He kissed her cheek. 'You undo all my good resolutions.'

'There is no need to forgo your plan,' she teased. 'I am sure you will be ready again by then.'

Oh, goodness, what was she doing? She had almost forgotten her purpose for coming up to see him. As always passion was her master.

But she was calmer now. And ready to listen to his explanation of his earlier remarks.

She trailed a finger through the crisp curls on his chest. 'What did you mean about never having any more parties here?'

'Oh, so that is why you came is it? Not to ravish me.'

She chuckled softly. She loved the way he accepted who she was. 'I was actually going to suggest you might want me to bring up hot water to bathe, since you got a soaking. But, yes, I did have an ulterior motive.'

He grabbed her wandering hand and brought her fingers to his lips. 'At least you are honest.'

'Would you?'

He shook his head as if to clear it. 'Would I what?'

'Like me to fetch water for a bath.'

'If anyone is going to fetch water, it will be me,' he

growled, nibbling her ear. The arousal he had satisfied a few moments before stirred again.

'Don't,' she whispered. 'You know what that does to me.'

He chuckled. 'All right. But only because it is too soon for me. Although there are all those other ways we can resolve the problem.' As he had shown her more than once.

Whereas Alan had been horrified by how easily she was aroused by the slightest touch, even suggesting there might be something wrong with her, Damian thought it wonderful.

'And you won't be entertaining here any more?' she asked tentatively, with a feeling of dread rising up to clutch at her heart.

He sighed. 'The parties are losing their cachet. It is no more than I expected. What was wicked and interesting has become pedestrian and ordinary. Soon enough the *ton* will move on to some new novelty. I would sooner leave them while they still want more than become a has-been.'

She shivered at the thought. Both at the tawdry image he invoked and at the thought of what this news meant. Their business partnership would end. But what about them? Their future. She had not looked beyond each day, until now, preferring to enjoy what she and Damian had, rather than look to what might lay ahead. Would he want her to remain here? Cook for…for whom, if there were not to be any more parties? Her heart seemed to miss a beat. 'What will we do?'

'You may do whatever you wish.'

'What do you mean?'

'You are rich now. You have choices.'

Was he saying they would no longer be together? The thought shocked her. Sent a piercing pain straight to her heart as if she had been struck by something sharp.

He had never made her any promises. Indeed, if she

thought about it, he had almost deliberately avoided talking about the future until now. As she had. Because they both knew there was no future. She was not the sort of woman a nobleman could marry. She had been mistress to two men now. And thoroughly enjoyed it, if she was to be honest.

But now, when it was clear they would likely soon go their separate ways, she could only wish things could be different. That she could be different.

Choices. He made it sound as if it was a good thing. But there was one choice she did not have. To go back and start again. She tried to sound happy, not miserable. 'So I do.'

She hoped her misery did not colour her words.

Damian hadn't thought breaking the news to Pamela would be easy, but he had not expected it to be so damnably difficult. Or that he would feel quite so guilty. Or feel a sense of loss. But then he had glimpsed all of the future.

She took a deep breath as if steadying herself. 'Let us make sure your Christmas ball is the best party any of them have ever attended. Really leave them wanting more.' The bravery in her voice caused his heart to seize as if it had been stabbed by a knife.

He wanted to hug her and tell her everything would be fine. But that would be an outright lie. He never lied when he could tell the truth. Or at least some of it.

'That's the ticket,' he said. 'You do not know what the future will bring.' He knew. Some of it.

'When is your ball to be held?'

'In three weeks' time. It will be one of the biggest social events of the season. A masquerade, of course.'

It would also be the last time anyone in London would admit to knowing him, if it all went well.

'You will act as my hostess, of course.'

She rose up on her elbow, looking down at him, her expression angry. 'Certainly not. That will not do at all. Everyone will recognise me as the woman who runs your gambling hell. Your ball will be considered beyond the pale, should you attempt to foist me off on the *ton*. No one will attend.'

He sat up with a frown and cupped her cheek in his hand. 'None of my guests has ever seen your face.' He kissed the tip of her nose.

She jerked away. 'It will take them but a moment to recognise me. It is impossible.'

He lay back down and stretched. 'Leave it with me. Nothing is impossible.'

'I mean it. I will help you from behind the scenes, but that is all I will do.' She lay down with her head on his shoulder and was quiet for a while. 'Will there be gambling, the same as here?' She wrinkled her nose, no doubt thinking there were those among the *ton* who would likely not be impressed.

'There will be a card room. It is expected. But nothing like our parties here. Just tables available for people to play cards. No croupiers.'

She chuckled. 'No special rooms upstairs, either. We don't want to shock all the old denizens.'

But that was exactly what would happen, but for a completely different reason.

She snuggled closer, her lithe body fitting along his side, her leg resting on his thigh in a most erotic manner.

His body hardened. 'We will go over the details later—right now I have other things on my mind.' He rolled towards her and kissed her cheek.

She glanced down at where his erection pressed against her thigh. 'So I see.'

Such an earthy woman. Direct. Honest. Incredibly passionate. He was going to miss her terribly when they parted. And that was not all he would miss. He would miss her companionship. A strange pang caught at his heart.

Not once in his adult life had he felt any regret about ending an affair.

For some reason Pamela was different. It was almost as if they were made for each other. He shook his head at himself for his maudlin thoughts.

She was not the woman for him. Their pasts made it impossible.

She reached for him.

'Slowly does it,' he murmured. He wanted to savour what might be some of their last moments together. 'Let us take our time. I want you out of those clothes first.'

The next evening, the three of them sat in his study counting the proceeds of the last party Damian would ever hold at this house.

'What will you do with Rake Hall, now that you won't be holding any more parties?' Pamela asked once the ledgers were closed.

He couldn't sell the house, because of the entail. 'The farm already has a tenant, so I suppose I will put in in the hands of an agent and try to rent it out also.'

'You do not want to live in it yourself? You must have so many memories of your childhood here.'

Pamela had an uncomfortable way of getting to the heart of things that troubled him.

'I was very young when I left here. Most of my youthful memories are from France.'

A stricken expression crossed her face. 'Will you return to France, then?'

'Perhaps. I am not sure when, though. I thought I might travel to the Americas.'

'America is a wonderful country,' Pip said. 'I have a cousin in Canada. He writes of its vastness. There is a lot of opportunity, I think.'

'It is so far away. It will take weeks to get there.' She sounded sad.

'Many weeks,' Pip agreed.

'Especially during the winter,' Damian added. 'I hear the Atlantic storms are quite fierce.'

A shudder shook her slight frame. 'I prefer to remain on dry land.' She looked unhappy.

As unhappy as he'd begun to feel these past few days. He half wished she hadn't been so easy to find. It would have been easier if the Vicar had left behind a son, instead of a daughter. A very beautiful daughter who… Regrets had no place in his thoughts.

There was nothing he could do, even if he wanted to, except take comfort in the fact that she would not be left destitute. What he must do was focus on his plans

'Pamela, you will travel to London with me tomorrow,' he said. 'There are a great many arrangements to be made if the ball is to be a success. In addition, you will need several new gowns.'

'Why? I told you, I do not plan to go out in public.'

'Damian tells me that you fear you will be recognised,' Pip said.

'I do not fear it, I know it. Many of your guests have met me over these past few months.'

'Not if you listen to me. Wear a dark wig. A touch of make-up, a change of accent, not even your mother will know you. Trust me in this.' He looked very pleased with himself.

She looked to Damian for his opinion.

'It will only be for a couple of weeks,' he said, with an encouraging smile. 'I will introduce you to all as a distant cousin acting as my hostess. I certainly hate to think of you shut up in the house, when we could be going about together.'

Despite being clearly tempted, Pamela still looked doubtful. 'Your distant cousin?'

'My distant widowed cousin. We will give you a new name, change your appearance, and no one will know the difference.'

'I can darken your eyelashes a touch and your brows, add a beauty spot,' Pip continued, clearly enthused. 'Indeed, you will not know yourself.'

'Do not forget,' Damian added, 'you have been masked all this time. It is quite likely you would not be recognised even without these changes.'

'You sound as if you have experience in such matters,' Pamela said to Pip, clearly intrigued by the idea.

'*Ma mère*, she was an actress,' he said. 'I spent many hours as a child watching her put on her *maquillage*. Sometimes even helping her.'

'Oh. I see.'

'I see you think I am not respectable,' Pip said with an easy chuckle.

'Not at all. For some reason I thought you were of noble birth.'

He shrugged. 'It is possible. On my father's side. But how is it one could know?'

'It doesn't matter one whit to me,' Damian said. 'You are my friend.'

'New clothes will make a difference, too. They must be the height of fashion. You will see. You will dazzle them into blindness.'

She smothered a laugh as if the idea was madness, but Damian could see she was beginning to weaken. After all, it was a chance for her to shine.

He felt slightly ill at the thought of all that brightness he saw in her eyes being snuffed out in an instant.

Dammit. He would not think like that.

She hesitated, then finally nodded.

Instead of feeling delighted, he felt…sad.

'So,' Damian said, forcing himself to sound carefree, 'it is decided. We will close the house for the season and you will travel up to town with me tomorrow.'

'The furniture should be put under holland covers,' she said. 'The pantry emptied and the remaining food donated to those in need.'

'Do not worry about it. I will put all in the hands of my agent.'

'Wonderful,' she said. 'Then all I need to do is pack.'

'Exactly,' Damian said. He pulled her close and kissed her lips. 'But not tonight. It has been a long day and I need you in your bed.'

Her gaze turned hot.

Pip threw up a hand. 'Excuse me. I will retire. I bid you goodnight.'

He closed the safe, locked it and left.

'Poor Pip,' Pamela said. 'He needs a wife.'

'I think he would be horrified by the very idea. He is too much of a butterfly to ever settle down.'

Pamela laughed.

Damien reached for her hand. 'Come here, my lovely. I have been looking forward to holding you in my arms all day.'

And that really was the absolute truth.

* * *

Pamela clung to the side of Damian's curricle as they bowled along the frosty country lanes with high hedges and tight corners at a pace she could only describe as foolhardy. His vehicle was of the high-perch sort. Exceedingly fashionable among young blades, but, in her view, exceedingly unstable.

Damian must have sensed her concern because he snaked an arm around her shoulders and pulled her closer. 'Do not fear, my dear, I am an excellent driver.'

'You cannot possibly know what is around the next corner.' she said, 'You are going too fast.'

'If there is something around the next corner, there is lots of room to pass. I have travelled this road many, many times and not once have I run into problems.'

Even so he slowed their pace.

For which she was grateful.

She was grateful for a lot of things. The improvement in her financial stability, the passion she had found in his arms, the joy she had found in his company, even though it was coloured by the sadness of loss. She could not deny she would miss him. Or that the thought of him leaving made her heart ache.

She could not imagine wanting another man, the way she wanted Damian.

What she had felt for Alan paled in comparison for the emotions twisting her heart every time she thought of Damian's departure.

Then she really must not think. It was simply too painful.

At the next junction, a finger post pointed one way to London and the other to Brighton. They had reached the main road. Twenty miles to London. By mail coach the journey always seemed interminable, but in this vehicle it would take no time at all.

The highway was wider and straighter than the country lane and she felt able to relax in her seat and enjoy the journey.

A mail coach lumbering in the other direction reminded her of the discomforts she had endured travelling from one position of employment to another. Now she was enjoying the comforts of a well-sprung vehicle that ate up the miles and provided lovely views of the countryside.

The horse settled into a trot and Damian manoeuvred around several slower vehicles with ease and skill.

'It is a long time since I was in London,' she said to fill the silence.

'Did you miss it?'

'Not at all. I prefer the country.'

He grimaced. 'I prefer the city.'

'Why is that?'

'There is too much solitude in the country. I like people. You never speak of your family. Do you not miss them?'

She froze. How to answer such a question? 'There is only my mother left and she married again. I do not particularly like her new husband.'

'Because he replaced your father?'

She sighed. 'Perhaps. It annoys me, how she fawns over him. She never did so with my father. They were always arguing.'

'About what did they argue?'

'I was not party to their discussions. I mostly heard heated voices, but I believe it was about money. Father was a hopeless spendthrift. For the most part, Mother managed the finances. Except now and then and he would spend money without discussing it with her. Then they would argue. Anyway, Mother does not approve of me and my choices, so I am better off as I am.'

'I would give anything to speak with my mother again.' He sounded terribly sad. 'She died not long after we arrived in France.'

She touched his arm in sympathy. 'How old were you?'

'Ten.'

'I am sorry.'

'It was a difficult time. My father never got over the loss.'

'Whereas my mother happily skipped on to the next man who would keep her in the style to which she had become accustomed.' She could not keep the bitterness out of her voice.

'You resent her for marrying again.'

She huffed out a breath. 'I thought at the very least, she should have waited out the mourning period. I can't even think where she might have met him, to be honest.'

'She did well to capture an earl. He doesn't seem like a bad man to me.'

Startled, she stared at him. 'Do you know my stepfather?'

'I have met him once or twice at social events.'

Why had he never said anything? 'And my mother?'

'We were not introduced, but she was pointed out to me quite recently as being the widow of the late Reverend Lamb. There is a family resemblance and I put two and two together.'

'Oh.'

'She looked to be in fine fettle, if you are wondering,' he said.

'I was not.' She tried to rein in her anger.

'So you do not think she chose well?'

He seemed to understand her concerns without her saying anything. She sighed. 'I do not know what to think. I feel as though it is a betrayal of my father. And yet she has a right to be happy. Perhaps in time I will get used to it.' While she had seen no evidence of it, she sometimes had the sense that her mother and the Earl had known each other for a long time. As if they had secrets.

She could never forget how her father had collapsed during their last argument. It was hard not to blame her mother for his untimely death.

And then there was the way Mother had tried to marry her off to a rather elderly friend of her new husband. A man in need of an heir. Her mother could at least have stood up for her against her stepfather.

There was a pause, as if he was waiting for her to tell him more. For a moment, the full story was on the tip of her tongue. She swallowed the urge to unburden herself. While her mother might have sided with her husband against Pamela, making her life with them untenable, it was none of Damian's business.

'This part of the country is very beautiful,' she said, instead 'But rather hilly.'

'It is. We will stop at Streatham to rest the horse and for us to take some refreshment.'

An extravagance. No doubt he could afford it, given how much he won from his fellow peers. It was too bad that she had joined his enterprise such a short time before he brought it to a conclusion. Still, all good things came to an end eventually and she had put away a nice little nest egg. One that would keep her comfortable for a long time into the future, if she was careful.

'Will you miss Rake Hall when you leave?'

She really could not understand anyone wanting to abandon their ancestral home. Her father had been a younger son and had never owned a home of his own. The vicarage had been theirs as long as Papa lived and it had been very dear. Being forced to leave had been a terrible sadness.

'I haven't spent enough time there to miss it,' he said.

'But you did live there as a child.'

'I think I mentioned before that I scarcely remember those days.'

'Or you do not wish to?'

His grip tightened on the reins and the horse broke stride. 'Easy,' he said softly.

The horse settled.

'I do not remember them,' he said, his voice tight, 'because they are more like a dream than reality. My life changed a great deal when we arrived in France.'

'In what way?'

'It is a long story of little interest and here we are at the Red Lion.'

They had indeed arrived at the inn. As they pulled into the courtyard of the old Tudor building with its timbered walls and red-tiled roof, an ostler ran to the horse's head.

The man touched his forelock. 'I got him, Yer Lordship,' he said, looking at Pamela with curiosity.

How stupid of her. She should have asked Monsieur Phillippe to help her with her disguise before she left for Town. Or travelled in a closed carriage. Stupid indeed.

Damian jumped down and helped Pamela to alight.

The innkeeper bustled out and his eyebrows rose to his hairline as he saw Pamela.

'Mrs Clark and I would like a private parlour,' Damian said, using the name they had decided upon for his widowed cousin. There were several branches of Clark in his family.

The innkeeper bowed. 'Certainly, My Lord.'

They followed the innkeeper inside.

Chapter Twelve

In the inn's coffee room, Damian sat at a table by the window, waiting for Pamela to join him. Until meeting Pamela, he had deliberately not thought about his childhood before going to France. What had been his had been wrenched away by unscrupulous scoundrels. From then on, he had been forced to think only about survival as his mother's health declined and his father barely eked out a living from his tutoring.

Walking with Pamela in the grounds of Rake Hall *had* reminded him of happy times with his family, but the pain of what came afterwards had tainted those memories.

For a moment, he had thought about telling her the truth about his life in Marseilles. No doubt she would think he was looking for sympathy. He didn't need anyone's pity. He needed to implement his revenge.

And if it meant losing her, at least he would have the satisfaction that he had done his duty and kept his promise. Perhaps, then, the guilt he felt over what had happened to his family would be less burdensome. How bad would a few years in prison have been, if it would have saved their lives? Every time he thought about it, he felt like such a coward.

He rose when he spotted her entrance. 'I took the liberty

of ordering a light luncheon,' he said. 'We breakfasted very early and I thought you might be hungry.'

'That is kind of you,' she said. 'Thank you.'

He seated her opposite him. 'The food here is quite good, actually. I usually stop for a bite on my way through.'

'I am glad you thought to break the journey,' she said.

'From here, we should reach London in about two hours.'

'I am looking forward to seeing your town house. Monsieur Phillippe says the renovations you have undertaken are a marvel to behold.'

'Pip is the main architect of those improvements, so I am not surprised he is pleased.' He grinned. 'But, yes. The house is much improved.'

'Will you sell it, when you go to America?' Her grey eyes held a hint of sadness.

He could not let it trouble him. 'I will. Fortunately, it is not part of the entail.'

'And what happens with the Scottish estate?'

'It isn't worth much. I would be lucky to find a buyer. There is no house, only a swathe of poor land occupied by a few crofters and a section leased to a sheep farmer. The only other property was a house in Edinburgh that was sold years ago. Rake Hall is the only property included in the entail. I purchased the house in Grosvenor Street when I first arrived in London.'

It had cost him a pretty penny, but he had needed to do it to prove he wasn't some poverty-stricken bumpkin out to make a splash.

The waiter arrived with a pot of coffee and a tray containing bread rolls, butter, slices of ham and an assortment of sweet pastries.

To her professional eye, it all looked beautifully prepared.

She poured the tea and they helped themselves from the plates set before them.

'It sounds as if your plans are set then,' she said wistfully. 'I envy you going to America, but I do not envy you the journey to get there.'

'It will be a new adventure for Pip and me.'

'Will you ever return to England?'

Much as he hated to do it, he had to make it clear that once the ball was over, he would be gone from her life. He shook his head. 'If we decide to come back to the old world, we will go to France. We both grew up there.'

The pain in her expression almost brought him to his knees.

'And the title?' she asked. 'Your responsibilities as a peer of the realm. If you have a son, he will inherit.'

Clearly she was hoping something would make him want to stay. The irony of it all was a bitter taste. Sadly, eventually she would be glad to see him go.

'By the time I leave, I will have fulfilled all the responsibilities I deem important. As for the title, it can go into abeyance for all I care.' That was how he was supposed to feel.

'You are a republican at heart, then.' She chuckled. 'A revolutionary.'

He wasn't anything so grand.

'Politics do not interest me. *You* interest me.'

She blushed. 'Not enough to keep you here in England.'

'Would you want to go to America?' He froze. Why had he asked that question, for heaven's sake? What would he say if she said yes? His heart thudded in his chest as he awaited her answer. Hope or fear. Either way it could not come about once she realised he had deliberately brought about her ruin.

'No. I have other plans.'

He breathed a sigh of relief. Or was it regret? No. Not regret. He had no room in his life for more regrets. 'What will you do?'

'A small cottage in the country. A few chickens. Perhaps I will bake pies and cakes and sell them at a local market.'

'I am sure whatever you choose to do, you will do very well.'

She gave him a smile edged with sadness. 'Thank you.'

They finished their lunch and were soon back on the road.

As they both looked to the future, neither said very much on the rest of the journey.

Sitting at her dressing table, preparing for her day, Pamela could not quite believe she was enjoying herself. The moment she had arrived in London, the whirlwind had begun and she hadn't once been near a pot or a pan or a sink full of dirty dishes.

She recalled her come out as months filled with stress. This was altogether different.

Sukey stepped back from pinning her wig and nodded in satisfaction. 'Right as a trivet, Mrs C.'

The two of them had forged a friendship during their time at Rake Hall and Sukey had been more than happy to take on the role of ladies' maid during Pamela's visit to London. Apparently, becoming a ladies' maid had been Sukey's girlhood dream.

Now Pamela was trying to train Sukey, so she could find a job working for another lady, once Pamela returned to being a cook or whatever it was she decided to do once Damian left. Trouble was, she hated thinking about his departure.

'You could say *it looks perfect*,' she suggested.

'It certainly does,' Sukey said carefully in ladylike tones.

Pamela grinned at her. 'That's the ticket, Sukey.'

They laughed. 'I was thinking,' Pamela said, 'that you should call yourself Susan, it sounds more like the sort of name a ladies' maid would use and dressers use their last names only.'

Sukey looked doubtful. 'I don't think I can learn all this in three weeks.'

'Of course you can. You are doing brilliantly. I promise.'

The young woman smiled proudly. 'We best hurry up, if you want breakfast. You have the dressmaker coming for fittings this afternoon.'

'I was hoping to visit the glover before Madame Celeste arrives. Do you think you can accompany me? I would sooner you than a footman.'

It had turned out that Sukey—no, Susan—had instinctive, impeccable taste and Pamela had taken full advantage of it.

'Of course.'

Pamela took a last peek in the mirror, happy with her reflection, though the wig was still taking some getting used to, along with the darkening of her eyebrows and eyelashes, but if she was quite honest, she would not have missed this trip to London for the world. She was having so much fun!

And her nights with Damian were heavenly. She was determined to make the most of these last few weeks with him, and it seemed as if he felt the same way.

Damian was already seated at the dining room table when she entered the breakfast room. He looked up from his paper and rose as she entered.

He took her hand and kissed it. 'You look lovely this morning.'

Her face warmed at the compliment. 'Thank you.' She filled her plate from the buffet with eggs, ham and toast.

'What do you have planned for today?' he asked when she was seated.

'First Bond Street to buy some evening gloves and then a fitting with the dressmaker. Why?'

'I thought I might take you driving this afternoon.'

They had agreed that they should be seen out and about in Town, so people would become used to seeing his widowed cousin on his arm. When she looked in the mirror and saw how different she looked, she had become sure neither the people she had met at Rake Hall nor her old acquaintances would recognise her. Pip had done an amazing job and Susan had no trouble repeating the effect each morning.

'Why not?' she said. 'My new redingote arrived yesterday and I am dying to wear it.'

'Perfect.'

'Pass me your cup, if you would care for more tea.'

He did so. 'Thank you. How is the rest of the wardrobe coming along?'

They had also agreed that she would wear nothing but clothes of the highest fashion. After all, their masked ball was to be the event of the season. They had already chosen their costumes. They would go as Antony and Cleopatra, the theme of the party being Shakespeare's plays. The *ton* was already vying for invitations.

'I have my last fitting today. Madame Celeste is not only an excellent dressmaker, she is also very quick.'

'So I should hope at her prices.'

'I have only ordered what I think I must have, nothing more.'

He reached across the table and took her hand in his, giving it a gentle squeeze. 'A man must grumble, must he not? It is expected.'

She laughed. 'You are teasing. I should know that by now.'

'I like to see you rise to the bait.'

'Were you thinking we would attend Almack's?' she asked. 'I need to make sure I have a suitable gown, if so.'

Almack's was always the fussiest of the various events the *ton* attended. There it would be easy to make a mistake and get oneself excluded from the higher echelons of society. Men were required to wear old-fashioned knee breeches, but for every young miss new on the town it was a must visit.

'I don't think so. Neither of us is on the lookout for a spouse.'

'It will not look odd, if we do not put in an appearance? You, at least, are considered a good catch.'

'It will not look odd. I have made it clear I am not on the marriage mart. Not this Season. If ever.'

She chuckled. 'Never say never.' The girl he chose to marry would be a fortunate young woman. A little sadness stole into her heart. Sadness that it could not be her.

She shook it off. She had given up on the idea of marriage a long time ago. She was quite happy as she was. And would be even happier, once she had her own little house in the country. Would she not?

And yet the thought of Damian leaving, of never seeing him again, left a very empty feeling in her chest. More like a huge hole. What if they had met under different circumstances? If she had been a proper lady, not so wanton, would there have been a chance that he might have wanted more than an affair? Had she kept him at bay, acted the prim and proper miss, would he have thought more of her?

It seemed she had squandered the one thing any lady owned: her honour.

It seemed so unfair.

A man could sow his wild oats without any consequences…indeed, he would be thought peculiar if he did not. But a woman became a pariah. Unworthy.

He said he did not want to marry, but she had no doubt he would change his mind. When he met the right woman. Some young innocent, with stars in her eyes.

Something painful twisted beneath her breastbone.

She squeezed her eyes shut. What was the point in regrets? She could not change her past.

He finished his coffee and rose. 'Enjoy your shopping, I have an appointment with my man of business, but I will be back in lots of time to take you driving.'

He bowed and left.

She rang the bell and asked the butler to notify Susan she was ready to leave, then finished her second cup of tea.

It didn't help with the empty feeling inside her heart.

She forced herself to get up and get on with her day.

Susan was waiting in the hall, dressed in a cloak and hat, and she helped Pamela into her dark blue spencer.

Albert, who in London served as the butler, opened the door. 'I don't believe it will rain, Madam,' he said, 'but I think Susan ought to carry an umbrella just in case.' He handed one over.

'I don't believe that will be necessary and besides we are going shopping. There will be a great many parcels to carry, I have no doubt. Susan won't be able manage an umbrella also. Besides, you are unfailingly correct about the weather, Albert, so I do not think we need worry.'

Albert bowed. 'As you wish, Madam.'

Outside, Susan huffed out a breath. 'Thank you. I half expected him to insist we bring John along when you said I couldn't carry the umbrella.'

John was Susan's bane, because he wanted Susan to walk out with him and Susan had developed other ambitions.

* * *

Damian drove his phaeton around from the mews and drew up at the front door.

By the time the groom had gone to his horse's head and Damian had jumped down, Pamela was already on her way down the steps.

He really liked that about her. She never shilly-shallied and was always ready on time, if not a little before.

This afternoon she looked stunning. The new redingote she had spoken of at breakfast was made of dark burgundy wool with black velvet at the collar and cuffs. She carried a black fur muff on one arm and her hat, a small affair with peacock feathers, was set at a jaunty angle. The lip rouge and blush on her cheeks were so subtly applied one could not be sure it was there at all. The light net suspended from its brim to cover her eyes made her look mysterious.

Not to mention that the coat hugged her figure in all the right places. Places he knew all too well. Desire struck him the way it did every time he looked at her and especially when she gave him back glance for heated glance as she did now.

He fought to control the urge to take her indoors and say to perdition with driving in the park.

But driving in the park was all part of his plan. To be seen by the *haute monde*.

It was beyond a doubt that any man would be proud to be seen with her, although on occasion he found himself missing her more natural self, the chestnut-haired, fresh-faced young woman he had walked with in the countryside.

But that young woman wouldn't fit with their roles of young sophisticates out on the town.

He handed her up into the carriage.

'Congratulations on your choice of costume, my dear,' he said as they started off for Hyde Park.

'Thank you. It was very costly, but Madam Celeste gave me a discount, because I promised to let everyone know where I purchase my gowns.'

'Do not bother your head about the cost.'

'Why should I not? I think you forget that the cost eats into my profit as well as yours. I prefer to consider it as an investment and I need to get the best value for my money.'

Such an independent woman. She deserved… He forced himself not to think about what she deserved. That had already been decided. 'I beg your pardon. You are right, of course. And what do you plan to do with your ill-gotten gains.'

'Ill gotten? I thought you said—'

He put up a hand. 'I speak figuratively. In jest. I mean, what will you do with your share of our profits when we part company? Invest it?'

He shouldn't be asking, shouldn't care, since he was the one forcing them apart, but he couldn't help caring.

He was going to miss her when they parted. Badly. Far more than he ever would have expected. Somehow he had allowed her to get under his skin, to steal a part of him he hadn't known existed. His heart. Too often he found himself wondering what she would think about a particular matter he was dealing with. Or how she would react to something someone said. It gave him an odd pain in his chest to think of leaving her behind.

It should not matter one whit.

Her father certainly hadn't worried about his family. And yet… The thought of her destitute and alone had recently reared its ugly head and he found it disturbing.

'I will buy a house, somewhere close to the sea. I have

always wanted to live near the coast. And if there is anything left over, perhaps invest it.'

'So you will not continue as a cook?'

'I will continue cooking for myself. I suppose it will depend on whether I will have enough to live on, as to whether I will hire out to cook for others.'

Wouldn't humiliating her family be enough of a revenge? After all, she had not been directly involved in his family's downfall. Did he really need to ruin her utterly?

Devil take it, he did not need to be having second thoughts at this stage of his plan. Everything was set. Nothing would stop it now. Nor did he want to.

Well, he might want to, but that would be letting his family down, yet again. By being selfish. By thinking about himself instead of thinking of them. The guilt from his decision not to take the risk of imprisonment, a risk that if successful would have saved his family, was a heavy weight in his chest. The only way he could make up for it in some small measure was to keep his promise.

'I see,' he said steering them through the busy streets of Mayfair and to the entrance of Hyde Park.

Carriages were lined up along the street waiting their turn to enter.

'It is busy today.'

'The dry weather has brought everyone out.'

It was dry and crisp, if somewhat smoky from all the surrounding chimneys.

They followed a barouche through the gate and made their way along Rotten Row. Several gentlemen on foot tipped their hats when they saw him. These were men who had visited Rake Hall, but he also knew them from White's, a far more respectable gentlemen's club.

He waved a hand in greeting.

When their gazes fell on Pamela, however, their expressions turned puzzled. Would they eventually realise where they had seen his *cousin* previously?

He hoped not. Not yet.

A young couple waved a greeting. Long and a young lady, with her maid trailing them at a discreet distance.

'Dart,' the young man said.

Damian leaned down to shake his offered hand.

'Have you met my fiancée, Miss Frome?'

A fiancée. This was news. 'I have not had the pleasure. Miss Frome, I am honoured.' He bowed to the lady. 'Allow me to introduce my cousin, Mrs Clark.'

Pamela inclined her head.

Long, all smiles, bowed and Miss Frome dipped a curtsy. 'Pleased to meet you, Madam,' Long said with not a glimmer of recognition. He grinned shyly. 'I received your invitation to your ball, Dart. I did not expect it.'

'Did you not?' Damian said. 'I cannot think why.'

The young man looked relieved and slightly embarrassed. 'I was wondering if you would also invite Miss Frome.'

Whereas Damian could not have been more delighted. 'Of course. If you would be good enough to furnish me with your address, Miss Frome, it will be my very great pleasure to send you and of course your parents an invitation.'

The young woman blushed and handed over her calling card. 'You will find Father in *Debrett's*,' she said primly.

Pamala was delighted that Damian had invited Long. Since their altercation in Rake Hell, he had been back only a few times and was more subdued and polite towards her, having imbibed less of his drink, clearly atoning for his awful behaviour that night, although he had not been seen there recently. Likely because of his engagement.

Perhaps he deemed that he had sown all of the wild oats and now it was time to settle down. He was one of those who initially had been getting deeper and deeper into debt. One of those on Damian's list.

They bid the young couple farewell and the carriage moved on.

Aware of many curious stares and some of outright disapproval, she kept her back straight and her smile firmly pinned on her lips. No one would possibly recognise her as Vicar Lamb's shy, awkward daughter.

Not even her mother.

She hoped. Fervently. For that theory was about to be tested. Mother and her new husband were headed straight towards them.

She resisted the urge to tell Dart to turn the carriage around and gallop out of the park.

He glanced at her, clearly sensing her concern. 'Look them straight in the eye,' he said with a pleasant smile as if he wasn't discussing her immediate ruin. In a moment the two carriages passed each other and Pamela was proud that she met her mother's haughty gaze without flinching. There certainly wasn't a hint of recognition in that frosty glare. And if her mother didn't recognise her, no one else would.

A few moments later, a gentleman on horseback drew alongside them. 'Monsieur Phillippe,' she said, beaming at his handsome face and warm expression. 'Good afternoon.'

'My dear, Mrs Clark. May I say how delightful you look?'

'You may,' she said. And blushed at her boldness. Something about this disguise made her say things she would never have dared say as herself.

'I do wish you would call me Pip, as Damian does. We are friends, are we not?'

'Very well, Pip it is.'

Pip beamed and accompanied them along the Row when Damian set his horse in motion.

Pamela did her best to ignore some of the rather pointed looks askance. Once the party was over she would never see any of these people again.

She certainly would never tell her mother or anyone else for that matter about this adventure, but she did not regret it. Meeting Damian had added something to her life that had been lacking for a long time. Affection.

She was fond of Damian.

More than fond. He seemed to be the only person who valued all the parts that made her who she was: her skill in the kitchen, her organisational abilities and, of course, their compatibility in the bedroom. His passions seemed to match hers perfectly. He had given her a sense of accomplishment. A feeling of pride in herself as a person.

When she thought about him leaving, of never seeing him again, something hot and painful rose up in her throat. She was desperately trying not to let him see how the thought of losing him was hurtful, but it was getting more and more difficult each passing day.

If she said anything, she was sure he would be astonished.

Apart from their mutual passion, she had no real sense that he felt anything deeper than a mere liking for her. For him, theirs was a primarily a business partnership, with additional benefits.

For her, it had definitely become something more. What had begun as mutual passion had gradually changed into a deep-seated need that had grown tendrils around her heart. The idea of saying goodbye was almost too painful to contemplate.

She still could not believe that in two weeks' time their association would end.

She forced herself to be practical, calm, exactly the same as him.

'Do you know anyone who could assist me with the purchase of a property?' she asked.

'You are thinking about your cottage in the country.'

'I am.'

'My man of business ought to be able to help you, if you would like me to ask him?'

'Do you have an idea of where you would like to buy this cottage?' Pip asked.

'Somewhere quiet, near the sea. Perhaps Dorset.'

'A long way from London.' He shook his head. Such a waste. 'How sad.'

She laughed at his nonsense.

An older man driving in the opposite direction doffed his hat and smiled at them. Pamela recognised him from the club. Lord Luton. Would he have acknowledged her if he had recognised her? Likely not.

They turned at the end of the Row and Pip left them to greet some others who had gathered there, while they promenaded back.

A dashing woman driving her own phaeton drew up with a flourish of her whip. Her hair was jet black and her eyes bright blue. She wore a coat the same colour as her eyes. She was stunning.

'Dart,' she said. 'Back in Town, is it?'

A faint Irish accent, Pamela thought.

'I am.'

The woman eyed Pamela up and down and seemed to dismiss her. 'Call on me tomorrow. I will be at home.'

She cracked her whip and the horses moved off.

'Who was that?' she said.

'Lady Leis.'

'She is beautiful.'

'Do you think so?'

His voice was casual. Too casual. Pamela had a strange feeling in her stomach. 'Is she—?' She did not know how to phrase it.

He glanced at her face and then back to watching the traffic ahead. 'Is she what?'

How did one ask such a question?

'Someone you know…well.'

'Well enough.'

Now what on earth did that mean? And why would it matter?

Somehow it did. She felt bruised.

Oh, now she was being stupid. They were lovers. No doubt he had other lovers in his past. As she had Alan in hers. And if he had others in his present, why would she be surprised? Had she not seen how men behaved away from their wives while working at the club? Why would she expect him to be any different? Especially since she was not even his wife.

To give it a second's thought was foolishness. Besides, from his perspective, their relationship was based purely on lust. It would be better if she thought of it that way also. Perhaps that way she could stifle the ache around her heart.

And if she had a twinge of jealousy now, it was because of the other woman's beauty, not because she had a place in Damian's life.

'A penny for your thoughts,' he said.

Not even if he offered her a hundred pounds would she tell him what she was thinking. 'I was admiring that woman's hat,' she said, nodding towards a lady wearing a high poke bonnet festooned in silk flowers.

He grimaced. 'I prefer yours.'

And from that she had to draw what little satisfaction she could.

They were almost out of the gate when a town coach cut them off.

Pamela couldn't see its occupant, because the blinds were drawn down.

She looked at Damian to see what he thought of it.

'The Duke of Camargue,' he said softly. 'I wondered if he would be here today. Excuse me for a moment.'

He handed his reins to the driver of the other coach and climbed inside.

The Duke's coachman sat with impassive expression as the two carriages remained blocking the carriageway. Other drivers began complaining loudly.

A constable strode over to see what the commotion was about.

'Move along,' he said.

The driver looked at him down his nose. 'When the Duke is ready to move on, he will do so.'

The policeman backed away.

Oh, goodness.

'Perhaps if you moved a fraction to the side...' She began to suggest.

The driver shot her a scathing look and she subsided into silence.

A good five minutes passed and Pamela felt her face getting hotter by the minute.

One passer-by even reached for the bridle of the Duke's lead horse, but the same look from the coachman that had defeated the police officer sent the fellow scurrying away.

Finally, the carriage door opened and Dart jumped down.

In a trice both carriages were moving and the traffic began to flow.

'Wasn't that a bit rude?' she said as Damian guided his horse into the street.

'When you are the Duke of Camargue, one of the wealthiest men in the world, no one ever calls you rude.'

'Well, I do,' she said.

Damian laughed. 'You would. The Duke wants to buy my land that adjoins his property. He wasn't exactly pleased when I didn't jump at his offer.'

'Why didn't you?'

'He says he will put the crofters off the land to run more sheep. I am not keen on the idea. Those people have lived on that land for centuries. In truth, the land is more theirs than mine.'

He cared. About people he had likely never met. Her heart seemed to stop beating. A painful awareness swept over her. It wasn't just that she cared for him, she had fallen in love. If they hadn't been in so public a place, she might have blurted it out without thinking.

They had both made it very clear there were no strings attached. He might think she was trying to hold on to him. Or trying to get him to admit to something he really did not feel. It would spoil the rest of their time together, when she only wanted him to have good memories.

He was leaving for the New World. She had her own plans. And he had never shown any sign of feeling anything but mere fondness. How could he? After all, she was a fallen woman.

'Besides, he isn't offering nearly enough,' Dart said.

She didn't believe him. His words were merely a front. She would not let him make her think he cared only about money.

Chapter Thirteen

The next day, when Damien entered the breakfast room after his early morning ride, he was surprised to find Pamela there ahead of him looking delicious in a morning gown of dark rose.

'Good morning, my dear.' He kissed her cheek.

She turned a beautiful shade of pink. 'Good morning, Damian.'

'You look ravishing, I must say. Good enough to eat. Where are you off to?'

She chuckled. 'I am going to Covent Garden this morning to see about the floral decoration for the ball.'

The hairs on the back of his neck rose. 'Send for the nursery man to come to you. Covent Garden is no place for a lady.'

'Really, Damian. A lady? I have already met with the nursery man. He is outrageously expensive for the particular item I am seeking. I am sure I can get it much cheaper at one of the smaller stalls.'

'There is no need to scrimp and scrape.' He browsed the buffet and helped himself to eggs and ham.

'I am not scrimping and scraping, but I refuse to be cheated.'

When he heard that tone of voice, he knew she would not be put off.

'Very well. I will accompany you.'

She looked surprised and pleased, then shook her head. 'Oh, dear, I would not put you to so much trouble. I know you are busy. I won't go alone, I promise you. I have already arranged for my maid to accompany me.'

'I will drive you,' he said firmly. 'After all, the ball is my project. And I am intrigued as to what it is you need to acquire.'

Her naughty little smile stirred his blood, as it always did. 'You will have to wait and see.'

'Because?'

'Because.'

He frowned. 'Whatever we do, it must be in the very best of taste.'

'Of course.'

He could tell from her expression he was not going to get any more out of her, likely because she thought he might try to veto her purchase.

As if he actually would. Unless he was concerned for her safety, he had discovered he could not deny her a single thing she wanted. It pleased him to make her happy, when he knew it should not. He was indulging himself in the short few weeks left to them. Perhaps hoping that they would both have some happy memories, before the sword of Damocles landed. He would feel its cut as much as she would. But he could not stop now. Could he?

Once before he had let his parent down so badly. If he had been less cowardly he would have had all the money he needed to pay for doctors and medicine. They might even have been alive today, living in comfort.

He could not now go back on his word to avenge their deaths. If he did not keep his word, what sort of son would he be?

If only he didn't like her so much.

Unlike his previous ladies, who wanted jewels or money, Pamela asked for nothing other than what was due to her. But then as his partner, she lacked for nothing in the money department. However, she could have asked for more. Most women would.

He was going to miss her very much when they parted. She was the most honest, sweetest woman he had ever met. And if he allowed himself to think about it, the thought of ruining her made him feel sick to his stomach. She would hate him when the truth came out.

A strangely hollow ache filled him.

It twisted painfully inside him. Devil take it. Sentimentality had no place in his plans.

'I will get the carriage put to.'

She gave him a puzzled look as if she sensed his disquiet. 'Very well, it seems there is no dissuading you. I will fetch my coat and hat and meet you at the front door.'

As he strode for the mews, he realised he had barely touched his breakfast. He shrugged. What did it matter that he wasn't particularly hungry?

Oddy greeted him wildly for the second time that morning.

Damian patted him. What on earth was he to do with the animal when he left for America? Perhaps Pamela would take him.

When the coachman put the horses to the barouche, Oddy immediately jumped aboard.

'I don't think I need your company today,' Damian said. 'Ladies don't like dog hair all over their clothes.'

The dog stared at him mournfully, reminding him that he always went with Damien when he took the barouche.

It was their agreement. He could not go in the phaeton, but he could go in the carriage.

Damian sighed. 'Very well. After all, it is her fault that I own you in the first place.'

'Will you be wanting the canopy raised, My Lord?' the coachman asked.

He had not bothered purchasing a town coach, since he did not plan to remain in London for more than a year and the barouche had come with the house.

The day was fair, if a little chilly. They weren't going far and he preferred not to be shut up inside unless it was pouring rain. 'Leave the front down, but put a couple of extra blankets in, please.' He could always change his mind if it was too cold.

With the carriage ready to go, Damien returned to the house to get his hat and coat.

Pamela was on her way down the stairs when he reached the front door.

Her coat today was of a bright peacock blue and the way her bonnet framed her pretty face made him want to kiss her. And perhaps forget the trip to Covent Garden.

Instead, he took her arm and walked her out of the house and across the pavement to the waiting coach. 'I hope you don't mind Oddy's company. He refused to be left behind.'

'Not at all. He can serve as our protection.'

Damian chuckled as he handed her up. 'I am all the protection you need.'

'I was not thinking about me.'

He laughed. 'I assure you, I am quite capable of defending both of us. However, Oddy has been known to show his teeth at people he doesn't like the look of upon occasion, so perhaps he will serve a purpose.'

Pamela beamed. 'Good boy.' She patted Oddy's head and the animal grinned at her.

Damian gave the coachman the go ahead and soon they were wending their way through the city traffic.

Covent Garden during daylight hours was a very different prospect than Covent Garden at night when the streets milled with the carriages of those attending the theatre and rubbing shoulders with those who hoped to take advantage of them.

During the day, the square behind the Church of St Paul was abuzz with a whole different sort of trade and person.

The predominant goods on offer were, of course, fruits, vegetables and flowers. Many of the flower girls one found selling their wares on street corners came here to buy the blooms for the posies they sold. But at this time of year there was not much on offer.

They left the carriage with the coachman and he and Oddy followed Pamela to the far end of the market.

'You have been here before,' he said, seeing that she knew exactly where she was headed.

'Only once.'

A rough-looking fellow edged closer.

Damien gave him a hard look and a grim smile. The fellow shrugged and walked off. But he wasn't the sort Damian was most worried about. It was the small lads who dodged in and around the stalls who caused him the most concern. Boys who were not unlike what he had been at that age. Boys with quick fingers and bad intentions. Though they also seemed to be giving them a wide berth.

He glanced down at Oddy whose hackles were up and whose ears were pricked. Ha! Here was the reason no one had attempted to pick his pocket or cut Pamela's purse. And he hadn't had to raise a fist or grab a collar.

While he did not relax his vigilance, he did welcome the reinforcements. At last, the dog was earning its keep.

Later, he was going to have a long talk with Pamela about coming to a place like this with only her maid for company.

A youngish woman with dark hair neatly pinned under her cap and a bit of sacking for an apron tied around her waist rose from the upturned bucket she was using for a seat to greet them.

On her stall, she had twigs of holly with berries and mistletoe sprigs tied in little bundles ready for hanging and a pile of evergreen boughs.

Relief shone in her smile. 'I hoped you would come today.'

'Good morning,' Pamela said. 'I promised I would, did I not?'

'Well, you did. But not all keeps their promise.'

'Were you able to obtain any?'

'I was. Me pa skinned both knees he did, shinning up all the trees in the woods.'

She ducked beneath a ramshackle wooden table on one side of her stall. She reappeared with a large, roughly woven carrier loosely rolled around its contents. 'Here they are.'

She set the carrier on the ground and unrolled it. Inside were a mass of tangled strands of ivy.

'Perfect,' Pamela said. 'Thank you. It is just what I was looking for.'

'Ivy?' he asked. 'What is so special about that? I am sure any nursery could supply you with that.'

The young woman looked anxious. ''Ere, it took me da hours to collect that there.'

'Well, of course we will buy it now you have obtained it, but Pamela, really? Why endanger yourself for anything so common-or-garden?'

'If the nurseryman could have supplied it,' Pamela said, 'I would have ordered it. It is not the sort of thing they grow. Not in the lengths I wanted.'

'I see.' He didn't, but if a huge bunch of ivy made her happy, then so be it. But next time she wanted to foray into the stews of London, she had better request he go with her.

'How much?' he asked the woman.

'The lady already paid, sir,' the woman said. 'Though you can pay again if you like.' She laughed.

'No. Once is enough,' Damian said. 'Thanks all the same.'

The woman rerolled the mat and tied the string. Damian carried it back to the carriage.

Quite honestly, Pamela thought Damian might have made more of a fuss when he saw what she had bought. The idea had come to her while looking at a picture of ancient Greeks at a party.

He laid the bundle on the seat opposite, leaving just enough room for the dog.

'Was there anything else you needed while we are out?' Damian asked.

'Nothing I can think of at the moment.'

'You could have sent one of the grooms to pick this up,' he said.

'When I ordered it, she wasn't sure she could supply what I needed. No one had ever asked her for ivy before.'

'And yet you paid her in advance.'

'She would have returned the money.'

'You are very trusting.'

'Too trusting, you mean?'

He seemed to freeze for a moment. As if her words had struck an unpleasant chord. A twinge of anxiety tightened her stomach. The only other person she had trusted was him.

'It seems on this occasion your trust was well founded, but I would suggest that you take a little more care about who you trust with large sums of money. Even if you do not care about the money, it is highly reckless to endanger your person in that way.'

'I thank you for the advice.' She grinned. 'I told her if she cheated me, I would send you after her and she would highly regret it.'

'You didn't?'

'No. I didn't. Actually, our housekeeper knows the family. They are from the same village and it was she who recommended I go there with my special request. She recalled a copse full of ivy nearby the village. She also told me they were well respected and honest.'

'I am sorry I called you reckless.'

'I probably should have explained.'

'Yes. You should have.'

While his words were harsh, his voice and gaze were soft as butter. The look in them melted her insides. Her heart picked up speed as he took her gloved hand and raised it briefly to his lips. 'I cannot help but be concerned about you.'

How was it that he made her feel so feminine? And cared for. 'I am well able to take care of myself.'

She didn't mean to sound defensive, but she was afraid she was beginning to rely on him, on his caring, on his protection, far more than she ought.

After all, very soon he would be departing for distant shores and she would once more be alone. She had only herself to rely on. She would never ever go back to live with her mother.

Besides, she had grown used to her independence. She liked it. Most of the time. On the other hand, she had enjoyed these few weeks of companionship.

He released her hand and she felt the loss of his touch.

'I am sorry,' she said quietly, thinking she might have hurt his feelings.

'I am sorry, too.'

'You have no reason to be sorry. I shall never forget your kindness. You and Pip. If not for you I would never have had the opportunity to—'

'Hush.' He touched a finger to her lips. 'Do not say any more. I think you may regret it if you do.'

Puzzled by the note in his voice, as if the words hurt him to say, she gazed into his eyes.

He looked away. 'Have you ever been to Vauxhall Gardens?' He gestured across the river.

'Is that where it is? I have never been there. My mother did not think it suitable. Have you been there?'

'I went there this past spring. It is quite the experience. It is too bad it is closed or I would have taken you.'

She laughed. 'Just my luck to come to London in the winter time.'

'Perhaps there are other places you would like to go that are open.'

'I would like to see the Elgin Marbles at the British Museum.'

'Ugh. Just a bunch of broken old statues. I'll take you if you wish.'

He made it sound as though she was asking him to undergo torture.

'I thought I might like to see it after I read about it in the newspaper, but I won't trouble you if it is not something you would like to do.'

'What about taking in a play? Would you like to go to the theatre?'

'That I did do when I was here and I enjoyed it immensely. I have never been to the opera.'

'Very well. The opera it is. I will see if I can borrow a box. I know a couple of people that have them.'

'Do you know what is playing?'

'I do not. I will find out.'

'Oh, dear. I am not sure I have anything suitable to wear.'

'Then you must order something right away.'

'Perhaps I should not go. An opera gown is a great extravagance and I will likely never need it again.' She sounded sad.

'All the more reason to purchase it. A memory to savour when you retire to the country. Do you think you will miss living in London?'

'I think it is the people I will miss, rather than the place.'

I will miss you.

The words hovered on her tongue, but they had always avoided speaking of feelings.

She smiled brightly. 'I am a country girl at heart. London is exciting, to be sure, but, no, I will not miss living here.'

'I'm glad.'

The fervency in his voice was genuine, and she was grateful that he cared that much.

'Will you miss England?' she asked.

He grimaced. 'I have spent so little time in England, missing it would not be logical. I may have some regrets, I suppose.' He sounded slightly wistful, then laughed. 'I think I will miss France more.'

He didn't say anything about her being one of those regrets. Hurt stabbed at her heart. But she knew he did not care for her the way she had come to care for him, so she would do well to keep such feelings at bay. What was the point of longing for something that was out of reach? Nothing could change the choices she had made in the past and she needed to accept that, enjoy what moments she had with him and when he was gone move on with life. As hard as that would be.

Oddy jumped up and scented the air.

'It seems we are almost home,' Damien said drily. 'He always knows.'

'Clever boy,' she said. 'What will you do with him when you leave?'

'I haven't decided.'

'I will take him, if you wish.' It would be something. A reminder of their time together.

'Would you? I would certainly feel better knowing he was with someone I trusted to look after him.' There was a note of longing in his voice.

And he trusted her. Even if it was only in the matter of his dog. Well, that was something, wasn't it? They would still have a connection. Perhaps he might even return to see how the dog was doing, some time in the future.

'Wonderful. Thank you. I can always rely on you, can't I?' He pulled her close and kissed her, hard, as if it was the last kiss they would ever know.

When they broke apart, she gazed up at him. And for one brief moment she was sure she saw regret in his gaze.

He looked away, as if he saw more in her face that he wanted to see. 'Now, what do you want done with this greenery?'

Jolted back to earth, she looked around. 'Perhaps the servants can find a cool place to keep it, until we decorate the ballroom. So the leaves don't drop?'

'Did you hear that, Sam?' he said to the coachman.

'Yes, My Lord. I will speak to the gardener about it.'

'Good.'

While she and Damian entered the town house through the front door, the dog seemed perfectly happy to go with the coachmen. When she said this to Damian he laughed. 'He knows he will get a bone or some other treat the moment he arrives.'

'Ah, like a man, the way to a dog's heart is through his stomach.'

'Is that why you became a cook?' He was teasing as he so often did, he knew she was not in the market for a husband.

She smiled brightly. 'How did you guess?'

He helped her out of her coat and handed it to the waiting footman.

'Well, if I am to have an opera dress made, I need to get in touch with Madame Celeste right away.'

He looked a bit disappointed.

'What? Did you have other plans?' she asked.

'They can wait until later.' The wicked gleam in his eye caused her cheeks to heat.

'That is good,' she said repressively, 'since the opera was your suggestion.'

'Oh, I thought it was your idea,' he said mildly, but his eyes were smiling.

She laughed. 'Whosever idea it was, I need to get the gown ordered right away, if we are to go.'

He tipped her chin and kissed her lips. 'Then later will be worth the wait.'

Feeling suddenly hot, she fled upstairs.

Excitement stirred Damian's blood as he waited in the drawing room for Pamela to come downstairs. He just hoped she would be pleased and not disappointed tonight.

She had been startled when he had asked her to come as herself and not as his cousin.

He had promised not a single soul would see her in the box he had rented and the hood of her opera cloak would keep her hidden from prying eyes, especially since they would enter the theatre by way of the stage door.

The doubt on her face made him wonder if she would do as he asked or ignore his request.

Footsteps on the stairs alerted him to her imminent arrival. He tossed back his drink and went to greet her.

On seeing him, she paused a few steps up.

He gazed at her in awe.

She was a vision of loveliness.

'Will I do?' The breathiness of her voice betrayed her nervousness.

'You look stunning.' He held out his hand and she continued on down.

'It is too bad it is not raining,' she said. 'It might have been easier to hide.'

'I am glad it is not raining,' he said. Glad and grateful. His plans would have been ruined. He took the white velvet-lined cape he had purchased for her from the footman. 'Have them send the carriage around, please, Jeffrey,' he said.

He held out the cape.

'Oh, my. Where did that come from?'

'It is a gift from me. You may need it this evening. It is a little chilly.'

She stroked the soft material. 'It is far too fine for a cook.'

'But tonight you are not a cook. You are my guest.'

She looked a little sceptical, but let him put it around her shoulders. She snuggled into the deep pile like a kitten seeking somewhere warm to sleep.

The cape fitted her perfectly.

'It is beautiful, thank you.' She stood on her tiptoes and brushed her lips against his in a gesture of affection.

It warmed him from his head to his toes.

Damn, he was going to miss those little kisses of hers. Not just those. All the kisses. All the loving.

So it was a good thing he was leaving soon, or he might be diverted from his purpose.

It was not long before the footman returned to say the carriage awaited them at the kerb and they stepped out into December's cold evening air and climbed aboard.

He had hired a town carriage for this evening's outing. His grooms had spent the afternoon making sure it was spotless inside and out.

'How was your day?' he asked.

'Busy. What with cooking dinner and getting ready to go out.'

'*Sacre bleu*, why did you say nothing? I could have hired someone in to help.' He should have thought of it for himself, if he was honest.

'I prefer to cook myself. What I don't prefer is last-minute invitations that require heaps of visits to the dressmaker and last-minute requests to change my appearance.'

That told him. He laughed.

He took her hand, turned it over and pressed a kiss to her pulse. Her little shiver of pleasure caused his blood to heat. He ignored his desire and said in teasing tones, 'I apologise for inviting you to spend the evening with me.'

She laughed ruefully. 'You are not the smallest bit sorry. And neither am I.'

'I want this evening to be special. I want you to enjoy every moment.' He put his arm around her and she leaned into him.

'How can I not when I am with you?'

A pang in the region of his heart made his breath catch. The knowledge that eventually she would hate him nigh brought him to his knees.

He cursed his ill luck. Why was she the one woman he had come to care for so deeply?

It wasn't until they turned on to the bridge that she noticed they were not headed for the Haymarket.

Pulling free of his arm, she leaned forward to look out of the window in the door. 'Where are we going?'

'Oh,' he said casually, 'didn't I tell you? There are no operas on offer tonight in Town, we have to go a little further afield.'

'No. You didn't mention it. Are they playing in Southwark?'

'We are not going to Southwark. This is Regent Bridge.'

She turned and stared at him. 'Regent Bridge? So we are going to…?' She tilted her head. 'We are not going to the opera, are we?'

'No. I hope you will not be too disappointed.'

'But… I can't believe you would…'

'Take you to Vauxhall Gardens? Believe it because I am.'

She shook her head. 'You said it was closed.'

'It is closed to the public, yes. But I have rented it for the evening.'

Her eyes widened. 'That must have cost a fortune.'

He shrugged. 'Since tonight will be our only opportunity to visit the gardens, I thought the price well worth it.'

'You spendthrift.' She threw her arms around his neck and kissed his cheek. 'But I love you for it.'

They both froze.

His heart pounded in his chest. Usually, with such a demonstration of affection, he would have nuzzled her neck, kissed her silly and who knew where it might have led, but right now he felt as if there was a hole in his chest where his heart ought to be.

He straightened. 'Good,' he said stiffly. 'I am glad you are pleased.' God, that sounded so stilted. He forced himself to smile, but even that felt stiff and awkward. He cleared his throat. 'Wait until you see what else is in store.'

She took a deep breath as if to steady herself. 'Who else will join us? People who know me from the club? Do you think they will put two and two together when they see me in all this finery? Oh. I should have brought a mask. They only ever see me with a mask.'

'Do not worry. We are the only guests.'

The coach drew to a halt and the door opened to reveal a man in red livery. 'Welcome to Vauxhall Gardens.'

They stepped down and went through the entrance. Thousands of multi-coloured lanterns swinging in the branches of trees and on lamp posts lit the buildings and the Grand South Walks ahead of them.

Damian glanced at her face, trying to judge her reaction. Why the hell had he turned into a block of wood when she had said those words? It wasn't as if they actually meant anything more than she was happy with his surprise.

They were lovers, yes, but love, true love, didn't enter into it. How could it, given what he had planned? His throat dried.

She would hate him once the truth came out.

He felt as a huge hole had been carved in his chest. And he deserved it. He certainly didn't deserve love. He had proved that when he had decided to save himself rather than save his family.

An emptiness hung between them. There was nothing he could think of to say.

'They lit all these lights for us?' she said, finally breaking the silence.

'Yes.'

'How pretty it is. Magical.'

His shoulders loosened. 'It is quite the sight.'

She cocked her head on one side. 'Do I hear music?'

'You do.'

'Come, let us see.' She quickened her pace.

They entered the grove, and gazed at the Gothic Orchestra pavilion where a quintet was playing a waltz. He had given the order that they play nothing but waltzes.

She spun around, looking at the supper boxes and the lights in the trees strategically placed on the dance floor. 'I can just imagine it full of people.'

It should be full of people. He would take pride in showing her off.

Devil take it, where had that thought come from?

His stomach fell away. He would be showing her off at the ball. But he knew without question that there would be no pleasure in keeping his promise to his father. There would only be pain.

He pushed thoughts of the future away, caught her in his arms and they effortlessly came together into the dance, twirling and gliding among the trees, her face glowing in myriad coloured lanterns.

It was as if they had been partners all their lives. Of course, he was holding her closer than he ought, but there was no one here to see or care.

When the dance ended he led her away from the orchestra to one of the overlooking supper boxes.

Chapter Fourteen

Pamela had heard about the famously shaved ham at Vauxhall, but now here she was, eating it in a private box in the Gardens.

She could scarcely believe that Damian had gone to so much trouble on her behalf. The moment she realised where they were, what he had done, she had entirely lost her heart.

She knew she had fallen for him, but now she knew he was the only man she would ever love. Not that she could ever tell him so.

His reaction to her words earlier had made it perfectly clear he did not feel the same.

It hurt. Terribly. But she wasn't going to let her sadness spoil the evening. It was not his fault she was the only one in love.

He was her friend and her lover. And neither of them had wanted more. She was going to treasure the memory of this evening for the rest of her life.

She glanced around the box. It was delightfully decorated with paintings of scenes from the tempest.

A waiter brought them champagne.

'To my beautiful partner,' Damian said, raising his glass.

For a moment her heart seemed to stop beating. Business partner, he meant. She blinked back the hot moisture that had welled in her eyes and sipped at the wine while the waiters delivered a salad and roast chicken among other dishes.

'Thank you so much for doing this. How on earth did you manage to get them to open for just two people?'

He looked a little guilty. 'The owner is indebted to me.'

'Oh. Don't tell me. You forgave his debt.'

'I did. Not very businesslike of me, but worth every penny. Besides, who knew when he would be able to pay me back, if at all. I am pleased you like my surprise.'

'It is wonderful.'

While they ate, a soprano joined the orchestra and sang a selection of songs from various operas.

'Will you dance with me again?' he asked when she finished her dessert, a delicious cheesecake.

'I would love to.' She would dance with him as many times as he wished, because after tonight she would likely never dance with him again. After the ball, she would find and leave for her seaside cottage and he would be travelling to the other side of the world.

This evening was like a fond farewell.

Her heart ached.

But how could she be sad when he had gone to so much trouble to give her such a wonderfully special gift? She gave him her brightest smile as he led her on to the dance floor.

They did not talk as they danced. The music and the movement of their bodies seemed to be the perfect conversation. A harmony of spirits.

She closed her eyes and sank into the pleasure of being held in his arms as if the world no longer existed.

Reality would return tomorrow, but tonight she would enjoy the dream.

A bell rang in the distance and it seemed to be some sort of signal because the orchestra ceased playing.

'There are some sights you should see while you are here,' he said, tucking her arm under his and matching her steps perfectly. He led her away from the pavilion and down one of the lantern-lit walks.

They strolled along the Grand Walk and when they turned into a narrower walk they discovered a beautiful waterfall in a bucolic country setting and lit by strategically placed lights. This was the famous cascade.

'It really does look like water,' she said in amazement, knowing full well it was a mechanical display. 'And sounds like it, too. Oh, and the water wheel actually turns. How wonderful. How very clever.'

For a full ten minutes they watched as the water cascaded down into a pool and mechanical people, carriages and wagons crossed over a bridge.

She was so wrapped up in the spectacle that it was a while before she glanced up at Damian to see his reaction. He was looking at her with an odd expression on his face.

'It is quite marvellous, isn't it?' she said.

He smiled. 'Yes. Marvellous.'

Why did she have the feeling he wasn't talking about the mechanical wonder before them?

The performance came to an end and curtains painted with a country scene closed over the tableau.

'That was lovely,' she said. 'Thank you.'

'There is more.'

They crossed to the South Walk to admire the triumphal arches. As they walked, the sound of music once more floated across the gardens.

They wandered in the opposite direction admiring the statues, groves and piazzas as they went.

At the end of the South Walk the lanterns ended, though the walk continued to the right and left.

'The infamous dark walk,' Damian said.

'Infamous?'

He chuckled, led her a short way along the walk where the trees seemed to close over them and she could barely see a hand in front of her face. He pulled her close and kissed her.

Deeply, sweetly and somehow full of longing.

Carried away on his passion, she put her arms around his neck and kissed him back.

Finally, he drew back, his breathing heavy, his voice husky. 'You see? Infamous.'

She laughed at his nonsense. 'I think it is you who is infamous. The walk is quite innocent.'

He tipped her chin with a fingertip. 'I wish you were wrong.'

She frowned and peered at his expression, but already he was leading her back to the lit path.

When they returned to the grove, a waiter handed them glasses of champagne and the singer performed for them once more.

'One last dance, my darling girl, and then we must go.'

'One more,' she agreed.

One turned into two and then three. And then it really was time to leave.

They strolled hand in hand back to their waiting carriage.

'I think that is the best evening of my life,' Pamela said, when they climbed aboard and she was wrapped in his arms.

'I am glad,' Damian murmured against her hair. 'You deserve it. I—'

She waited for him to finish.

'I wish I could do more,' he said finally.

'You have done a great deal for me,' she said. 'I cannot believe I made enough money to actually buy a house so close to the shore. It is a dream come true. And it is all thanks to you. I shall never forget your kindness.'

'You may not think that way, once we part,' he said. 'But I hope, in time, you will remember this evening with some sort of pleasure.'

His voice was full of regret.

'I don't understand.'

'You will.'

Back at the town house, he escorted her upstairs and they made love, slowly and with great tenderness.

She realised as he got up and left her room that this had been his way of saying goodbye.

She tried not to cry.

But eventually, she had to turn her pillow over, it was so damp.

As the next few days passed, and the ball drew ever closer, Damian found himself in his study, supposedly working on his wine inventory, but pondering how Pamela was going to react to the upcoming unmasking.

He had seen her expression of anxiety when her mother had approached them in Hyde Park. And he could not help but admire the way she had straightened her shoulders and met the other woman's gaze head on.

Pamela had backbone. And the thought of what he was about to do to her was niggling at his conscience day and night.

Especially at night, when she lay sweetly in his arms. She trusted him. And he was about to destroy that and more.

He kept telling himself that his plan would not affect her as badly as how her father's actions had affected his family. She had no interest in remaining in society. It was her mother and stepfather who stood to lose the most.

Her mother would feel the sting of the *ton*'s wagging tongues and would certainly not be welcome in society for a very long time, if at all.

And nor would Damian, of course.

It wasn't that society would care that he had a mistress—what they cared about was that they had been duped by him and by her and her family.

Pamela would, of course never speak to him again. And nor did he deserve that she should.

Next Thursday would be the end of the Earl of Dart's rule of London. The end of Rake Hell.

And he would walk away whistling.

The only fly in the ointment was Camargue's sudden appearance in the park.

Camargue had apparently been surprised to discover someone using a title that had been thought to have gone into abeyance and had hotfooted it to London to meet the new Earl—something Damian had not been expecting, since the old fellow hadn't left his castle for ten years or more.

Camargue been strangely pleased to think the title had found a successor and had begun talking in earnest of plans for the future for their adjacent lands.

Damian hadn't had the heart to inform the old man he had no intention of actually going to Parliament to substantiate his claim to his father's title and that instead he and Pip would be off to the Americas.

The butler knocked on the door and announced, 'The Right Honourable Mr Long.'

Surprised, Damian leaned back in his chair. 'Long,' he said, ignoring the young man's outstretched hand, except to notice it was trembling. 'I was not expecting you, was I?'

'Perhaps you should have been,' Long said with more force than Damian would have expected.

'How can I be of assistance?' Damian drawled, gesturing to the seat in front of the desk.

Long sat. 'It is about the vowels of mine you hold.'

Damian frowned. 'Yes.'

'I heard from one of my friends that you let him pay his debts off at a heavy discount.' He smiled shyly. 'I would like to do the same. I admit I got in way over my head, but I have stopped gaming now that…' he blushed '…now that I am about to be married. I would like to pay off my debts at the same discount you offered my friend. I believe I can do it over the next three months, if you will allow me the time.'

This was exactly what Damian had been planning. He leaned back and shook his head slowly. 'You clearly do not recall the terms of our agreement. The club manager refused to accept any more vowels from you and I personally loaned you the money with which to play. Are you now saying you will go back on your word to pay me back in full?'

'Oh, but, surely the club and you are the same thing?' His voice had risen a notch. A note of panic.

'Not at all. You borrowed from me personally, not the Rake Hell. It is a debt of honour. I have your vowels.'

'I have to pay the full amount?' He sounded completely shocked.

'Of course.'

'I—oh. I see.' His voice shook, but he straightened his shoulders. 'I assume you will give me time?'

'One is expected to redeem one's vowels in short order,' Damian said. 'But I can wait a day or two. After all, we are friends, are we not?' He smiled benignly. 'Naturally, since it is a debt between gentleman, I won't be charging you any interest on the delay.'

The young man's face blanched. 'Thank you. A day or two?' He sounded breathless. 'Yes. Yes of course.'

'The day of my ball will do. You are coming, of course.'

He looked frozen, but managed to speak. 'Yes. Miss Frome is looking forward to it immensely.

'Wonderful. I shall look forward to meeting her again.'

Long hurried off.

No doubt he would be scurrying around town, trying to find someone to loan him the money to pay Damian off.

A gentleman's debts of honour must be paid before any others. If they were not, a man could not hold up his head. He would become *persona non grata.*

The way his father had.

But there wasn't a money lender in London who would give Long the amount of money he needed. Damian had seen to it personally.

Damian, frowned. Why didn't seeing the culmination of all his plans gradually unfold make him feel good?

Nonsense. He was delighted. This was exactly what he wanted.

On her way downstairs, Pamela was surprised to see Mr Long in the hall by the front door putting on his coat.

'Good day,' she said. 'What brings you here so early?'

'Mrs Clark.' He bowed. 'I am here about some business with His Lordship,' he choked out. His expression was distraught, almost tearful.

'Is something wrong?'

'I owe His Lordship a great deal of money and I do not know how I am going to pay.'

Puzzled, she frowned. She had thought Damian had resolved all of those issues at the club. 'Oh, I see.'

He squeezed his eyes shut for a second. 'I was a fool

to allow myself to fall into debt. I have very little time to come up with the money. Excuse me.' He grabbed his hat, bowed and left.

Determined to get to the bottom of his obvious upset, Pamela made her way to Dart's study and entered without knocking.

The dog lying beside the hearth wagged its tail in greeting.

Damian withdrew his gaze from the view from the window into the street and it settled on her face. 'Good morning.'

'Good morning. I just met Mr Long on his way out. Apparently he owes a great deal of money.'

'Indeed he does.' He seemed completely unperturbed. 'He was absolutely sure his luck would change, despite my assurance it would not.'

'He is little more than a boy.'

Damian's face hardened. 'I doubt he would thank you for that descriptor.'

'Can you not come to some sort of arrangement? As the club did with some of the others?'

'My dealings with Mr Long are really none of your business.'

She recoiled, shocked at his harsh tone of voice.

'As a part-owner in the club—'

'You have no say in the matter. The club refused to accept any more of his vowels. As you yourself requested, I might add. He borrowed my money. Begged me to lend it to him. It is a debt of honour.'

The words struck like blows. She had never heard him speak so harshly.

'Do not look at me like that, Pamela. I cannot afford to let it go. Am I to be ruined to save him?'

How had she been looking at him? 'How can him not paying his debt land you in ruin?'

'How do you think I came up with such a large sum of money?'

'From the club?'

'Please. Do you think I would go behind my partners' backs and lend money that had already been refused?'

She frowned. 'You borrowed it?'

'Exactly.'

She sat down. 'Oh, my good Lord. Is it a really large sum of money?'

'Some might call it a king's ransom. Forgiving would leave me horrendously in debt.'

Her stomach fell away. 'Why would you do such a thing?'

'He asked me.'

She frowned. 'There is no possible way he asked you for such an enormous amount of money.'

'He was in debt already. He owed money all over town. He thought it would be better to consolidate his debt. He begged me to help him. The young fool needs to learn a lesson.'

The vengeful note in his voice sent a spike of fear down her spine. 'I think he has learned his lesson. And surely you knew when he borrowed the money that it was far more than he could ever repay.'

Eyes cold as ice, he shrugged. 'He said he could. I took him at his word.'

For the first time in a long time, he was shutting her out. Hiding something. And she did not like this version of Damian one bit.

'You want to hurt him.' The words shot out of her mouth before she could think about them. They were instinctive. A sense that he was doing this on purpose.

She waited for his scathing outburst at her accusation.

And waited.

He merely looked bored. 'What do you think gives you the right to take me to task about a matter of honour?'

The remark cut deep as she realised that he was implying she had no honour so therefore how could she judge.

She glared at him. 'I know the difference between right and wrong.'

'Do you? I wonder. I hope you will excuse me, I have a meeting at my club.'

He got up and walked out of the room with the dog trailing behind him.

She paced across the room and stared out of the window, down into the street. She heard the front door close. Watched him saunter down the street without a care in the world. Her head hurt. But worse than that, her heart hurt.

Damian, who she knew as kind and generous, was showing not a scrap of mercy to poor young Mr Long.

Why on earth would Damian have let himself get into debt for the sake of someone else? There must be some reason he had loaned such vast sums of money.

On the other hand, Damian had given him time to pay when he could have asked for it back immediately. But apparently now he would wait no longer. Men were strange creatures with regard to their honour and vowels and all that nonsense.

Perhaps Mr Long could borrow it elsewhere and pay Damian back.

She thought she'd been helping Mr Long when she told Pip to stop accepting his vowels. Instead he had gone to Damian for a personal loan.

What a disaster.

And it was partly her fault.

There had to be something she could do to help. She

could give him her share of the money she had earned. Her stomach fell away. It would be the end of her dream of a cottage by the sea.

But would it be enough?

And would his honour allow him to accept her offer? She had to at least try.

The first thing she needed to do was find out where Mr Long lived. She couldn't actually call on him, but she could send him a note asking him to meet her somewhere.

As long as she had her maid with her and it looked like a chance meeting, there shouldn't be any problem.

It took longer than she expected to arrange a meeting with Mr Long. But finally he had replied that, yes, he would meet her at the British Museum in the room devoted to the Elgin Marbles. She had always wanted to see them, so she had decided she might as well accomplish two things at once.

And as she sat on a seat amid the statues and friezes, she was very glad she had. It was awe inspiring to know that these stones had been carved so long ago. How sad that they had suffered so much damage. Surrounded by them, she could almost imagine herself cast back to ancient times.

'Mrs Clark.'

Mr Long looked as if he hadn't slept or eaten since she saw him last. He seated himself beside her. There were a few other people walking around the room inspecting the statues, but no one within earshot.

'Mr Long. Good day. Thank you for agreeing to meet me.'

'I am sorry I did not get your note right away. I went out of Town. To Newmarket.'

Her stomach gave a little flip of dismay. 'Newmarket?'

'There was a horse. A sure thing, I was told.'

'And?'

She waited for the worst.

'It won.'

'You mean you are solvent again? You can repay your debt?'

'Some of it.'

'Although I cannot entirely feel comfortable about you taking such a risk, I suppose it is good news.'

He shook his head. 'His Lordship seemed determined I should pay the full amount. Perhaps with a partial payment I can convince him to wait. If not… Do you think you can put a good word in with him for me?'

Damian had told her to mind her own business. 'I can try. I am not sure he will listen. Can you not ask your father for help?'

'My father is experiencing some financial difficulties of his own.' His shoulders slumped. 'I will have to leave the country if it becomes known I reneged on a debt of honour.'

'I don't understand.'

He groaned. 'I will be beyond the pale. Blackballed. Even my family will turn their backs on me. And no doubt they will also be affected by the scandal.'

'Oh, dear. How much can you pay back?'

'A little over half.'

'Very well. I will speak to Lord Dart on your behalf.'

He took her hand and kissed it. 'Will you indeed? I am in your debt for ever.'

'I think it best that from now on you do not owe anything to anyone.'

He groaned. 'I won't. I still don't understand how I could have been so foolish.'

Chapter Fifteen

Finally, the evening of the ball had arrived. Damian knew Pamela had been trying to speak to him and he had no doubt it was about young Long, so he had taken an unplanned trip to Rake Hall and stayed overnight, and now, arriving in a downpour in the dark and soaked through to the skin, he had arrived barely in time to change into his clothes for the evening.

While at Rake Hall he'd spent his time wandering the rooms, trying to think of a way of accomplishing his goal without involving Pamela.

No matter which path he began on, it always led to the same place. He could not destroy the Lamb family name, the way his family's name had been ruined, without Pamela also being dragged down.

The Lambs were not as important to his revenge as the ringleader of the fraud, Long, but when confronted all those years ago, Vicar Lamb had refused to even acknowledge his guilt.

A groom dashed out of the stables to take charge of the horse. Wearily, cold to the bone, he climbed down to discover Pip awaiting him.

'Mon ami,' Pip said, his face grave. 'I am glad to see you.'

Damian's heart skipped a beat. His thoughts went to Pamela. 'What has happened?'

'There is this Duke. Camargue. He has been asking for you.'

Damian let go a sigh of relief. 'Camargue. You don't need to worry about him. He is pressing me to sell him land.'

'He is in haste, apparently. He demands that you attend him. I told him you are out of town. He demanded I get you back. *"It is urgent,"* he said. But he will not say what he wants. So I cannot help him. So now he sends a fellow to camp out in the hall. Awaiting your return. Naturally, he goes to tell his master you have arrived, the moment you pull up. Therefore, if you are hiding from this Duke, you had better hide now.'

'What the devil? I'm not hiding from him. I will go and see him in good time. Right now, I need to get out of these wet clothes.'

Pip looked at him. 'Why did you go in an open carriage in December?'

'I needed some fresh air.'

'And is Pamela in need of fresh air also? Is that why she looks so pale?'

He frowned. 'Are you telling me she is ill?'

'She does not say so. She wanted to know where you were, also with some urgency.'

A cold fist seemed to clutch at Damian's heart. A sense of something about to go wrong. Nothing would go wrong. He had planned every last detail.

'Leave me to worry about Pamela.'

Pip nodded. 'Then all is in train.'

'It is.' They walked together into the house. 'First and foremost, I need a hot bath.'

Damian gave instructions to the butler for water to be brought up and went to his chamber.

He had removed all but his breeches when Pamela strode in. 'There you are.'

'Indeed. I am here.'

And there she was, obviously annoyed and very beautiful. He had not seen her so angry before. Her grey eyes were no longer clear calm pools a man could drown in, but dark with storms swirling in their depths.

'Please. Do not sound so innocent. I have needed to speak with you these past three days and you have deliberately been avoiding me.'

'Why would I do that?' he drawled. 'But if you do not mind, I am about to bathe. I am soaked through from the rain.'

As if to prove his point, a footman entered with the tub followed by a couple more with buckets of hot water.

They ignored Pamela.

'I don't mind at all,' she said, placing herself in a chair and crossing her arms. 'We can talk while you bathe.'

He waited for the tub to be full and the servants to be gone before he stripped himself off and climbed into the steaming water.

Under other circumstances, he might have invited her to join him, but somehow he didn't think such an offer would be appreciated.

As the door closed behind his valet, she jumped up and prowled towards him.

He held out the soap. 'Would you?'

She gave him a blank look. 'Would I what?'

'Wash my back.'

'I need to speak to you about Long.'

He sighed. No back wash then. 'Again?'

'Yes. It seems he can repay half the money he owes you and…'

'He needs to repay all of it.'

'I am sure he will. But he needs more time.'

'When he asked me for the money, I did not ask for more time. I gave it to him when he needed it. Now I need it to repay my debt. If I don't, I will be paying a great deal in interest.'

Or he would be, if he had in fact borrowed it.

She threw up her hands, picked up a washcloth and the soap. Damien leaned forward to give her better access.

She worked up a lather and began vigorously scrubbing his back.

It felt wonderful.

'There must be something you could do,' she said. Her tone was matter of fact, not wheedling or whiney.

She was asking him to help because she was a kind and generous woman.

And he had planned her ruination. He felt ill.

He snatched the washcloth from her hand. 'What is this young fellow to you? Why are you taking such an interest in him?' The words tasted sour in his mouth, but he could no longer bear to have her this close and not give in to her demands and forgo the revenge he had worked so hard for these many years.

She recoiled. 'What are you talking about?'

'It seems to me that you are taking more interest in his problem than in mine. There must be some reason for it. I know you met him in secret at the British Museum.'

Her face turned fiery red. 'What? How do you know?'

'I asked a footman to keep an eye on you.'

'How dare you?'

'How dare I? You were the one who went wandering off to Covent Garden without a moment's thought. You don't think I would let that happen again, do you?'

'You have no business telling me what I can and cannot do. And to answer your question, no, I am not having an affair. Mr Long is engaged. You know that. He is about to be married. But if he cannot repay the debt, he will be forced to leave the country and the marriage will be called off. I simply want to find a way to help him.'

'At my expense.'

'You must think I am a complete fool,' she snapped. 'I know you could easily afford to forgive part of the debt, if you wished. I am not sure why you are doing this, but I get the feeling you are doing it on purpose. I had no idea you were so cruel and unfeeling.'

Astounded, he stared at her. She wasn't angry, she was furious. As if it really mattered to her what happened to young Long.

Long's father hadn't given a damn about what would happen to Damian's family all those years ago.

If she knew the truth, she wouldn't ask. Would she? But then if she knew the truth, she would learn of her own father's complicity in the scheme.

He hesitated.

'Well?' she snapped.

'This is business. The man owes me hundreds of pounds. You are not being logical.'

'Logical?' She handed him the washcloth. 'I know you could find a way to get your blood without a pound of flesh.' She stalked out. Left him feeling…bereft. Alone.

Well, he had been alone for years. It was nothing new. She should be grateful that he had decided that only Long would bear the weight of his retribution, not treat him like some sort of ogre.

But then he would never tell her that, would he, or she

would guess at his original intentions. Intentions he would not be able to carry through.

Damn. He should have guessed that whereas most women would have given up upon realising he was serious, Pamela would stand by her guns.

And his accusation of unfaithfulness had been a low blow indeed.

Damn it all.

A tap on the door made him look up. Hope leaped in his chest. Had Pamela changed her mind?

His valet entered.

Hope dissipated. 'Pass me a towel, please. I'm done here.'

His valet obliged. 'Apparently His Grace, the Duke of Camargue, awaits you in the drawing room.'

Good Lord. What now? Dukes did not normally show up on one's doorstep like common men. They summoned lesser mortals. Clearly the matter of what the Duke had described a worthless tract of land had become a matter of urgency.

'Then I must hurry.'

Pamela entered the drawing room and stopped in surprise at the sight of an elderly gentleman rising to his feet. 'I beg your pardon. I was unaware that Dart was entertaining.'

And she wasn't prepared for visitors. She'd been coming for her reticule containing her calling cards. She needed to send a message to Mr Long.

She could see it on the table containing her needlework bag.

'I am Camargue,' the elderly man said, peering vaguely at her over the top of his spectacles.

Camargue. The Duke. She dipped a curtsy. 'Mrs Clark.'

'Delighted to make your acquaintance.'

The Duke spoke with a heavy Scottish burr and leaned heavily on a cane.

'Please, be seated. I am sure His Lordship will not be long.'

She eyed her reticule. Should she grab it and leave? Come back later or—?

'Good afternoon, Your Grace,' Damian said from behind her.

'Dart,' the Duke said. 'Good of you to see me so soon after your journey.'

'I didn't realise the Duke had come to call and came to fetch my needlework,' Pamela said, scooping up both bag and reticule. 'I will leave you to your conversation.'

'You are Dart's hostess,' Camargue said. 'I have heard about you.'

She gave Damian a panicked glance.

'Mrs Clark is a distant cousin,' Damian said. 'She serves as my hostess while I am a bachelor.'

Camargue looked from one to the other with a knowing expression. 'Cousin, eh? Dear me. Is that what they are calling it now?' He put up a hand when Damian opened his mouth to speak. ''Tis no matter. Perhaps Mrs Clark can convince your butler to provide a cup of tea for an old man who is fair drookit after walking here in the rain.'

'You walked?' Damien sounded astonished.

'No sense in spending an hour putting the carriage to for the sake of a ten-minute walk.'

'Perhaps you would prefer something stronger,' Damian said. 'I have whisky if you prefer.'

'No, no. Tea will be perfect.'

'Of course.'

Pamela rang the bell and ordered tea. No doubt the Duke

would expect her to pour it also. She looked at Damian whose expression was one of resignation.

She sat down and waited for the tea to arrive.

Damian seated himself on the sofa near Camargue's chair.

'To what do I owe the pleasure of your call, Your Grace?' Damian said.

'My man of business said you returned our offer unsigned. I came to find out why. You won't get more elsewhere. It is more than generous for such a scabby bit of land.'

Damian smiled briefly. 'Possibly.'

'If you think you will wring more out of me, my boy, you are off by a mile,' the old man growled.

'I have no intention of selling the lands at the moment.'

'Is that right?' The old man chuckled. 'Then you are a fool. There is no access to that land except by way of mine.'

Damian's shoulders stiffened very slightly.

If she had not known him so well, Pamela might not have noticed.

Damian expression remained mild and polite. 'Not fool enough to believe you are going to so much trouble for a half a dozen sheep.'

'A half-dozen, is it? More like a hundred dozen. There's money in wool.'

The butler entered with a tray followed by a footman with a plate of petit fours.

The Duke rubbed his paper hands together. 'Tea. Just what I need.'

Pamela poured him a cup. Damian waved his off and she poured one for herself.

'No, lad, I will not be put off. You will sell me the land and the longer you wait the lower the price will be.'

Damian's eyes twinkled. 'Your Grace, I believe you are neglecting one salient fact.'

The Duke looked up sharply, the vague, decrepit old man seeming to disappear in an instant. 'And what would that be, pray? Oh, is it the future of a few miserable crofters now occupying the land? My man tells me most of them haven't paid their rent in years. I have a plan to solve that problem.'

'And that would be?'

He grinned triumphantly, revealing a mouth full of broken teeth. 'Send them to America.'

Damian's face revealed nothing of his thoughts. 'I see.'

'Well? Will it serve?'

'What about the coal?' The calm in Damian's voice was so cold it made Pamela shiver.

The Duke waved a dismissive hand. 'Coal? Who said anything about coal?'

'I sent a man north to take a look at the land after you approached me in Hyde Park. He says the locals believe there is a seam of coal that runs from your pit right under my land.'

'Not such a fool after all,' the Duke muttered and took another swig of his tea.

'The price you offered for the land is a pittance and I will not sell.'

'It won't do you any good. Your access to the sea is blocked. If you mine it, I'll not give you permission to cross my land.'

'Then I suppose I will have to go around it.' While Damian sounded calm enough, Pamela had the sense he was furious with the old fellow for trying to dupe him.

The Duke gave a nasty chuckle. 'Then you will lose more than ye gain. That land is not worth a penny more than I offered. I bid you good day, young fellow. When you are ready to talk business, you may send word to my man of affairs.'

The Duke snatched up his walking stick and rose to his feet.

Pamela got up to ring the bell.

'No need, Mrs Clark,' Damian said with a grim smile. 'I will show the Duke out myself.'

Pamela watched the two men leave. All that animosity over a little bit of coal. She had not been able to help feeling pleased that Damian had not wanted to dispossess the people who lived on his land. But now it seemed that he was holding out for a better offer, since, as far as she could tell, Damian cared for no one but himself, given the way he was behaving towards Mr Long.

'There,' Susan said, putting the finishing touches on the glossy black wig Pamela had chosen for the evening. This one fell long and straight down her back. 'Is it to your satisfaction?'

'It looks lovely. Thank you.' If only she felt more confident that no one would see through her disguise. To her eyes it looked patently false.

Still everyone would be wearing wigs and masks and other forms of disguises this evening so she would not stand out.

'It is I who should be thanking you,' Susan said. 'Without your help, I would never have even dreamed of becoming a ladies' maid. I am very grateful for everything.'

Pamela had written her an outstanding reference letter and Susan had already landed another position, starting after Pamela and Damian's planned departure.

'It is nothing that you do not deserve,' Pamela said.

'I just wish I could continue working for you. I will miss you.'

They had become friends long before Susan had become her maid.

'Once I am settled you must come to visit me when you have some time off. Promise me.'

'Oh, I will. You will send me your address the moment you know it.'

Pamela's stomach sank a little. She had no idea where she might end up next. 'Of course I will, but give me yours now so I can reach you.'

Susan wrote out her address on a piece of paper and tucked it into Pamela's jewellery box.

'Time for us to get you into your dress,' Susan said. She picked up the gown laid over the bed and stroked the silky gold material. 'Queen of Egypt. You will make a fine queen.'

They both laughed.

She couldn't wait to see Damian as Antony. Though she was still angry with him, she had come up with an idea to solve the problem, if Damian wouldn't change his mind.

This was the last evening she would appear as Mrs Clark, the Earl of Dart's cousin. After today she would simply continue her life as herself.

Strangely, she had the feeling she would miss it. She had already begun to miss Damian. These last few days she had hardly seen him and when she did they had argued.

She stepped into the tunic-like dress and held still while Susan fastened it down the back.

She still didn't know how she would fare living alone in the depths of the countryside. Nonsense. She would manage as she had for years, only this time she would be pleasing only herself.

'Where does this go?' Susan said, holding up a belt fashioned to look like a snake.

'It ties around the hips, quite low. Look, here is the picture of what it is supposed to look like.' The dressmaker had drawn up the design for her and Damian's approval.

'Oh, yes. I see now.' Susan fastened the belt around her hips.

'Now for the jewellery.' Susan fastened bangles around her arms and a golden headband across her forehead, then stood back to admire the effect. 'This is so much fun. I don't think I would recognise you if I didn't know you.'

Pamela laughed. No one actually knew her. Not any more. Except perhaps Damian and he really didn't seem interested any longer.

'Now for the make-up.'

Susan looked at the picture. 'I can do it like this, if you wish.'

Kohl-rimmed eyes, ruby lips and darkened eyebrows. 'Perfect.' If only her eyes weren't such a distinctive shade. They were the only thing about her that she could not change.

When Pamela went downstairs an hour later, she felt certain she would not have recognised herself, but still she was glad of the mask she held in her hand. She would put it on before their guests arrived.

Tonight there would be several people here that she knew well, including her mother. Quite possibly, they would be a lot closer than they had been when they passed each other in the carriage.

Damian was in the drawing room, looking like a god in his Roman robes and the crown of olive leaves on his brow. It was the first time he had ever appeared in costume. Clearly, he was set on making this event a success.

He also had not yet donned his mask.

He gazed at her for a long moment and nodded his approval. 'You look like every man's dream of Cleopatra.'

She wasn't quite sure if it was a compliment or not, he sounded so grim. 'Thank you.'

He handed her a glass of sherry. 'Fortifications before the hordes arrive.'

She smiled and swallowed a mouthful. 'I need it. I just hope I haven't forgotten anything important.'

'Everything is just as it should be. And I have to say that the ivy-clad columns are a very nice touch.'

'I am glad you like them.'

He tossed back his brandy and held out his hand for her glass. She finished it and handed it over.

How distant they were with each other, how restrained. No doubt he did not want her losing her temper the way she had the other evening.

Together they climbed the stairs to the ballroom.

They stood at the double doors waiting to greet the guests as they arrived and she gazed at him. Soon they would part and would never see each other again. 'I am sorry if I have been a bit of a trial to you recently,' she said.

He closed his eyes briefly. 'I am sorry, too. Very sorry. I hope you will remember that.'

He turned away to speak to one of the footmen at the drinks table.

What on earth did he mean?

But there was no time to enquire. The butler was announcing the first of their guests.

And if an evening's success was to be judged by how many people could fit in a ballroom and the various antechambers, the ball was definitely the event of the Season.

There was just enough space left for people to dance

and that was only by dint of footmen judiciously moving people back from encroaching on the dance floor from time to time.

All evening she had tried to find Mr Long to let him know about her lack of success with Damian, but so far she hadn't seen him or his fiancée. Either that or she hadn't recognised them.

She should have asked him about his costume. There were a great many Romeos and Juliets, a quantity of Macbeths, not to mention Titanias and Oberons, with the odd donkey-headed Bottom thrown in.

There were even two other couples dressed as Antony and Cleopatra, but neither of the men looked anywhere near as gorgeous as Damian, who stood head and shoulders above the crowd.

She had danced a good few dances, too, none with Damian though, sadly. He had been busy charming their guests.

As he should, of course.

'He is magnificent, is he not?' Pip said, handing her the glass of champagne he had offered to fetch.

He must have seen her staring at Damian like some sort of lovesick fool. 'As always.' She hoped she sounded light-hearted, not miserable.

'And yet you are not as happy as I have seen you.'

Clearly she was not much of an actress. She took a deep breath. 'I suppose I am a little sorry we will soon go our separate ways.'

Pip glanced across at where Damian was in the middle of a group of ladies and gentlemen, regaling them with some story or other. They seemed to hang on his every word.

'I do not think he is so glad about it either.'

'Really? He seems perfectly happy to me.'

'Yes. He wears his mask well.' He gave her a look. 'A quiet cottage by the sea will be welcome after all this excitement?' He sounded doubtful.

'Indeed.' Strangely the cottage was a good deal less appealing than it had been as an impossible dream. Perhaps she had become too accustomed to all the excitement around Damian. Or perhaps it was the thought of living there without the man himself.

She tried to shake off her sadness. 'I am looking forward to it immensely.'

'It is a bargain *incroyable*, according to my agent. You must finalise the purchase before another snaps it up.'

'First thing tomorrow.' she said, realising that he had noticed she had been procrastinating.

She sipped calmly at her champagne. He was right, it was an incredible bargain. To keep the agent waiting was unfair.

She smiled at him. 'I think you better dance with Lady Simpson, she has been staring at you for the past five minutes.'

He grinned. 'Ah, yes. We have an assignation later. She does not like me to speak with other ladies.'

'You are going to miss your lady friends when you depart.'

'There are always new friends to be made,' he said with a wink and headed for the lady in question.

She took a deep breath. It was time to go back into the fray. Once last round of being charming and then she would leave, she did not want to be around for the unmasking. There was really no point—with or without her mask she was not herself.

Finally, there was Mr Long. Alone. His fiancée must be elsewhere.

She eased her way through the crowd to Romeo's side. 'Have you made your arrangements with Lord Dart?' she asked.

'Mrs Clark, I scarce knew it was you,' he said.

'Good. But did you?'

'I haven't been able to see him, but I sent a message saying I could come up with half of it…'

A gentleman dressed in Tudor robes, muttered something to his companion wearing a tricorn and powdered wig. 'It is Long,' his companion replied. 'The effrontery of the fellow.'

They made a show of turning their backs.

A gap opened up around her and Mr Long. A circle of disdain.

Long turned fiery red. 'Someone must have learned about me not meeting my obligation. Did he not agree to receiving a partial payment?'

Pamela's stomach fell away. 'No, but I have thought of a plan. I did not expect people to know… '

'Everyone knew tonight was the deadline.' Long looked mortified. 'I would not have come if I had known he refused to wait. You should have let me know.'

'I had no idea the deadline was tonight. You did not tell me.' Her mind raced. She had to do something. 'I will speak to him.'

'It is too late.' Long strode away, his head held high, but the view of the *ton* was made perfectly clear as they moved aside as if his touch could cause contamination.

She felt slightly ill. Only one person could have let fall that Long had failed to discharge his debt of honour by the appointed time. Damian. She scanned the room, looking for his imposing presence. There. Near the orchestra.

She started towards him.

The clock struck midnight.

Oh. No. She did not want to be here for the unmasking. She would have to speak with him after the ball. She was not going to allow this to happen to poor Mr Long.

It would be even more of a disaster if she was recognised.

She turned to make her way out of the room.

A hand caught her arm. Pip.

'Where are you going?' he asked.

She tugged to free her arm. 'Pip. You know I always leave before the unmasking.'

'Not this time, I think.'

'What?'

She glanced down the room to where Damian was already making his way up on to the dais with the orchestra. About to announce the unmasking.

'Pip. Let me go. What are you doing?'

But he wasn't looking at her. His grasp remained firm and he was watching Damian.

Chapter Sixteen

As arranged, the orchestra was finishing up a waltz a few minutes before midnight. Damian glanced around for Pamela.

This was the moment he had chosen to reveal her identity. To ruin her in the eyes of society.

He gave a sigh of relief as he saw her making her way to the ballroom doors. His plan had been to ask her to dance with him. One last dance, right before the unmasking, and then—

But of course he had not. Could not do so.

The thought of hurting her, of causing her any sort of pain, made him feel physically ill.

Call him a coward, dishonourable, whatever it was his father would have thought of him, he wasn't going to ruin an innocent woman because her mother and father had behaved badly to his parents.

At least Long had not escaped his net. He had arranged for his man of business to drop a word or two in several gossips' ears and they had done the rest. He just wished he didn't feel sorry for Long. Or regret that Pamela would never forgive him.

Dammit all.

He smiled at a lady dressed as a shepherdess, leaving

the floor with a gentleman dressed as Pan. 'Ready for the unmasking?' he asked.

She giggled.

Pleased that no harm would come to Pamela, Damian felt suddenly lighter and happier as he strode for the dais.

Everyone was chattering and laughing excitedly as they waited to remove their masks.

Something made him glance over towards the double door. A sort of stir among the crowd. To his horror he saw that Pamela had not left.

She was standing alongside Pip. It took a moment to realise that the reason she had not departed was because Pip had hold of her arm.

The clock struck twelve.

Pip looked over at him, expectantly.

Devil take it, he had not told his friend he had changed his mind. Had not thought to. He shook his head.

He saw comprehension dawn on his friend's face and his grip on Pamela's arm relax.

She looked from Pip to him and back. Her eyes widened.

He made a shooing motion with his hand and saw her move toward the door.

He breathed a sigh of relief. 'Let reason prevail. Let all our revellers be revealed,' he called out as expected. He removed his mask.

Around the room people untied the strings of their disguises, laughing and exclaiming as the people around them were revealed.

Footmen moved among the guests with trays and drinks.

'A toast, ladies and gentlemen. To King and Country.'

'The King,' everyone said.

'To our host,' someone called out.

'Dart,' chorused around the room.

A commotion beside the doors caught his attention. He stared in shock. Pamela was standing in the entrance, her mask gone, held in the hand of a drunken reveller dressed as Henry the VIII, if he wasn't mistaken. The man was trying to snatch a kiss. As he pulled her close, her wig came off and her chestnut hair cascaded around her shoulders.

'Unhand me,' Pamela said.

'Oh, my goodness,' a woman said in the sudden silence. 'Pamela Lamb, is that really you? But I thought you were...' Everyone looked from Pamela to Damian.

Damian's heart went cold like ice and his stomach fell away.

A buzz of shock rippled through the room. He could see her mother collapsed against her stepfather with shock.

By the time he made it across the room, Pamela was gone.

Dear God. What had he done?

Exactly what he had set out to do.

Although the *ton* had been thoroughly titillated by the scandal at his ball, two days later, Damian was still dealing with the aftermath of what in his mind he could only think of as a debacle.

After long and hard reflection during his sojourn at Rake Hall, he had returned to London having decided that punishing the Longs would be revenge enough, since it was Long's father who had been the chief instigator of the fraud. That he was still alive to see his only son ruined made it doubly sweet. Pamela's father, on the other hand, was long gone, so would not know the sting of shame.

He had felt as guilty as hell, coming to such a conclusion, but had been able to rationalise it as justice, a fair punishment for a guilty man, rather than revenge on an innocent woman.

But, despite his best efforts, he had failed to save Pamela from his own machinations, because some drunken lout had taken a fancy to seeing her unmasked. If only he had let Pip in on his decision, all might have been well, but truth to tell he'd been somewhat ashamed of his weakness when it came to Pamela. He'd thought she would simply slip away as she had planned and that would be an end to it.

To Damian's astonishment, the following morning, Long had come up with the money he owed and demanded that Damian let everyone know he had not reneged on his debt of honour.

Although Long was one day late, no one among the upper one thousand would fault him for that and so Damian had been forced to spend the last two days making sure the damage was undone.

The fact that Pamela had been unmasked and that the Longs had got off scot-free after all had been a bitter pill.

Knowing Pamela would have been pleased Long was not ostracised, did not make it any easier to swallow. To make it worse, she and everyone associated with her had been turned into pariahs.

And he'd thought he'd had it all under control.

He hadn't felt like such a failure since the day his mother died.

He'd been too much of a coward to save his mother and now he'd all but destroyed the woman—he had to face it—the woman he loved. This time, no matter what it took, he was going to set things right.

The moment he could break free of the Long nonsense, Damian had set off for the cottage she had purchased. Only to discover she had not purchased it at all. Another family had moved in.

Where the devil had she gone?

He had tried her mother's house, but she had been shocked when he asked about her 'wayward daughter' as she called her and denied any knowledge of Pamela's whereabouts and never wanted to see her again.

Clearly all she could think about was salvaging her own reputation by distancing herself from her child.

And so, here he was back at his town house, trying to guess where Pamela might have gone while Pip regarded him with sympathy. 'Have you tried the agency where you found her before?'

'I did. No luck there.'

Pip pursed his lips. 'Let me see what I can discover.'

'If I have failed to find her, I don't know why you think you would succeed,' Damian flung at him. 'Why the devil did she not buy that cottage? She was so taken with it. I suppose she must have bought something else.'

'I have the answer for that, *mon ami*. After a few discreet enquiries, I have discovered that it was Pamela who gave Long the money to pay his debt.'

Damian groaned. 'I should have known she would do something like that.'

'Indeed.'

The pain in his chest felt as though a knife had pierced his heart.

And now she was out there somewhere without a penny to her name and no doubt hating him.

The pain grew worse at the thought of where she might be with no friends and no money.

Pip frowned. 'You know, she is very friendly with her maid, Susan, who left when she did. She said she had no reason to stay, now her mistress was gone. Perhaps they are together. Or her family might know something.'

A tiny seed of hope germinated in his heart.

'Why did you not say so before?'

'I did not think of it before.'

'Do you have an address?'

'As luck would have it, I do.'

Seated on Susan's bed in the tiny attic chamber in a tenement in the Seven Dials, Pamela stared blindly at the newspaper she had in her hand. A week had passed since the ball and she still felt numb from the realisation that Damian had intended to reveal her true identity. He and Pip had planned it all along.

She had seen the guilty looks on their faces. They had known exactly what they were doing.

Her heart squeezed painfully. Why on earth would he do that? What had she ever done to him? Surely not because he had discovered she intended to help Long.

How cruel. Even the enveloping numbness could not dull the pain.

But she could not remain here sobbing her heart out because of Damian. She was imposing on Susan and her family and that she must not do for any longer than necessary.

She made herself read the notices for cooks wanted. Naturally, all of them required references. And where was she supposed to get those?

Certainly not Damian.

She had her references from earlier positions but a gap would always be seen as a red flag to a potential employer.

'You should open a pie shop,' Susan said from her chair by the window, where she was mending her stockings. 'Your pies are delicious. I would eat it every night, if you did. You would make a fortune.'

She had been cooking for the family over the fire as a way of paying her rent.

'It costs a great deal to set up a shop,' Pamela said. 'Money for rent and pots and pans and food to cook.' She had not a penny to her name. She had given everything to Mr Long. And she was glad she had stopped Damian from his cruelty.

A commotion in the street brought Susan to her feet and peering down from the tiny dormer window.

'Oh-ho! Who is this a-parking a carriage outside?'

Pamela ran to look. 'Oh, no. Dart. Why on earth did he think of coming here? Don't let him in.'

Susan ran downstairs to the front door. Pamela could hear the sound of arguing voices, but not what they said.

Heavy footsteps on the stairs told her that Susan had not been successful in keeping Dart out. She froze.

Should she hide?

Why? She had no reason to hide. She had no reason to be ashamed. How dare he come chasing after her!

He knocked on the door.

'Who is it?' she called out.

'You know very well who it is.'

Her heart was racing so hard she could scarcely utter another word. 'Go away.'

'No.'

Typical Dart.

'What do you want?'

'I want to explain.'

She frowned. That she had not expected. Rather she might have expected him to demand an explanation for her sudden disappearance. 'Explain what?'

'Pamela, may I come in?'

'And if I say no?'

'Then I will wait out here until you say yes.'

She sighed. 'Very well, come in if you must.' She folded her arms over her chest.

The door opened to reveal Dart with an anxious-looking Susan peering around him.

'It is all right, Susan. I will speak to His Lordship. Please give us a few minutes.'

The girl nodded. 'I'll be downstairs. Give a shout if you need me.' She gave Dart a pointed glare and left muttering something about people barging into other people's homes.

Damian winced. 'I couldn't do anything else. She was determined to keep me out.'

'You should have taken no for an answer.'

'I needed to speak with you.'

'I don't think we have anything to say to each other. Not only did you try to ruin poor Mr Long, you intended my ruin also.'

'About that—'

'I do not care to hear your excuses.'

The thought of it somehow seemed to penetrate the cold. It hurt. Badly. All over again. She turned away. Pretended to look out of the window, but could see nothing because her vision was blurred.

'You don't understand,' he said.

'No. I don't. And I do not care to either. Please leave.' Somehow she managed not to start sobbing.

'Please. Give me a few minutes. To explain.'

'Very well. Five minutes. I have a great deal to do today.' Five minutes was about all she thought she could bear of the pain of seeing him here.

'I made a promise to my father, when he was dying,' he said softly, with a note of pleading in his voice. 'I promised I wouldn't let the people who ruined my family get away with it. My mother might have been alive now if they hadn't cheated my father.'

She turned back slowly. 'Long cheated your father? He couldn't have.'

'Not him. His father. He offered my father a chance to invest in a scheme he said would make him rich. Another man, a man my father thought was a good friend, encouraged him to borrow the money to invest. He couldn't pay it back when the scheme collapsed. The scheme was a fraud.'

'That is why you were brought up in France?'

'Father was ruined. Left with nothing. We had to flee to France to avoid our creditors. To avoid prison. My mother was delicate. She could never have survived in prison.' He gave a bitter laugh. 'She didn't survive the awful conditions in Marseilles either. Nor did my father for very long. I was fourteen when he died.'

'How did you survive?'

'I lived on the streets. Doing what I had to do. That is where I met Pip. But I swore to my father as he lay dying that I would avenge Mother's death. That I would have justice for the way my father was cheated. It took me years to reach the point where I could return to England and keep my promise.'

The pain in his voice was tangible.

She sat down on the bed and gestured for him to do the same. 'So you are punishing Long's son? That hardly seems fair.'

'It hardly seems fair that his son got to live a life of ease while I was forced to steal to eat.'

'I see.'

'My father said the sins of the father's should be visited upon the children, as they were visited upon me.'

She frowned. 'Are you saying my father was involved? Is that why…?'

Damian grimaced. 'He was the one who talked my father in to borrowing the money to invest in the scheme. While he profited, my father lost everything.'

She shook her head. 'I don't believe you. He wasn't the sort to— What sort of investment was it?'

'Each person who brought a new person into the group got that person's money less a percentage that was paid to Long and to the person who brought them in. My father was supposed to get someone else to join to get his money back. But shortly after he paid his money, he was told the group collapsed.'

'That sounds like robbing Peter to pay Paul.' And it also sounded very familiar.

'Exactly. It was a scam. Only the people who invested early profited. The ones who came later lost their money. It was your father, a supposed friend, no less, who convinced my father to join.'

'So I was another of the children of a sinner, to be punished. I will have you know that my father would never cheat anyone. Not knowingly. He wasn't that sort of person.'

'I couldn't do it. I—I care for you too much. I—'

Hearing him say he cared for her would have made her heart sing only a couple of weeks ago, but now she didn't know how she felt.

'Well, you accomplished your goal. I am well and truly beyond the pale now. So I hope you are happy.'

'I am not in the least happy.'

'And you continued with your plan to ruin Mr Long despite telling me you would think about it.'

'To keep my promise to my father. You must see that I had to avenge my mother's death. I swore I would.'

'And now you have. I hope you are happy.'

He looked miserable. 'Long paid his debt. So I achieved nothing.'

'You achieved my ruin.'

'In the end, it was not what I wanted. I had decided justice would be served if only Long fell. Please. You have to believe me.'

'Believe you or not, it is done.'

He took a deep breath. 'Not necessarily. If we marry—'

She stared at him, incredulously. 'Marry? Why would I marry you?'

The pain those words caused in Damian's chest robbed him of speech.

Why indeed?

He couldn't actually think of a good reason, except that it would salvage her reputation in the eyes of society. He was losing her and he had to somehow find a way not to.

'When it came to it, I realised I could not do anything that would hurt you. I did not intend for your identity to be revealed. If Pip—'

'Pip knew what you were about? He was in on the plot? I trusted you both.' She could not keep the bitterness out of her voice. They had lured her in with the promise of money. 'What a fool you must think me.'

'No! I do not think you a fool. I think you are the most wonderful woman I ever met.'

Her expression was incredulous.

'I don't blame you for being angry, but please do not blame Pip. It was all my doing. Please. Let me make amends.'

She shook her head. 'It doesn't matter to me. I care nothing for what society thinks of me. It doesn't make the slightest difference in my life as a cook. The only thing I need from you is a letter of reference.'

'I—I love you,' he blurted out. The only thing he could do now was to be absolutely honest. Anything less would be an insult to her intelligence. And if she did not feel the same way about him, then so be it.

And the pain at that thought seemed ten times worse.

'I love you,' he said again, this time with more confidence. More conviction. 'And so I will tell you every day until you believe me. And I will never stop trying to win you, unless you marry someone else. I mean it. I will be on your doorstep every day.'

She stifled a rueful chuckle. 'I can just imagine my next employer putting up with so determined a follower.' She turned her face away. 'How can I know you mean it? How can I trust you? As far as I can see, you are driven by guilt, not love.'

He cupped her cheek in his hand and turned her face towards him. He gazed into her eyes, the soft dove grey that held so much pain. Pain he had put there.

'Never in my adult life have I ever told anyone I loved them. I have been too busy planning how I would accomplish my goals. With you it is different. I need you. Unless you are near, I am not happy. You make me want to be better than I am.'

Her expression remained doubtful. He truly had lost her trust. Until now he had not realised how important that trust had been.

His case was hopeless.

How could he even consider forcing her to do anything she did not want to do? 'I'm sorry. I am being selfish. If you do not return my feelings, if marriage to me is not what you want, then I will accept your decision. Leave you in peace even though it will break my heart.'

She sighed. 'You would truly leave me in peace?'

A pain squeezed in his chest. He closed his eyes briefly. 'It will not be easy, but I will do it, if that is what you want. It is as simple as this: my happiness is yours to command, but your happiness means more.'

She stared at him for long moments as if trying to read what was in his heart.

'I love you, Pamela,' he said softly. 'I want only what is best for you. If you want that cottage of by the sea, it is yours. If you want to be a cook, I will arrange for a position with a friend. If there is some other dream you wish to fulfil, I will do my best to bring it about.'

'What about your promise to your father?'

His heart ached at the doubt he heard in her voice. 'Long's father should have been punished. He should not have been allowed to hide what he did behind the skirts of respectability. But… I let my quest for revenge take over my life and it has cost me the best thing that ever happened to me.'

She sat silent for a while, staring into space, her hands clasped tightly in her lap. He did not know what he was going to do when she told him to leave.

'I need to know the truth, Damian. I don't believe my father would have had anything to do with a scheme to defraud others of their money.'

'That is what you want?' How the hell was he to find the answer to that?

'My father was judged guilty by your father, by you. If he did what you said he did, then will it not always stand between us?'

A smidgeon of hope filled his chest. 'I would not allow it.'

She pursed her lips. 'The past would always be there whenever you think of your mother, when you visit your childhood home. It would be there, lying in wait, like some dark vengeful beast, waiting for a moment of weakness.'

'You paint a grim picture of me.'

'You loved your mother. You lost her when you were still a child. You still carry the pain of her loss. Can you forgive those who caused her death?'

He closed his eyes and for the first time in a long time remembered the days before she died. The slow wasting away of a beautiful soul. The anger rose inside him. He hung his head. 'I cannot forgive.'

'Then I need to know the truth.'

'There is only one person who might know the truth of it.'

'My mother.'

'Are you willing to ask her?'

She let out a breath. 'I am.'

Damian tamped down his hope. After his earlier conversation with Lady Malcom, he feared she would not be helpful.

Chapter Seventeen

'Her Ladyship is not at home,' Mother's butler pronounced when Pamela and Damian showed up on the doorstep.

'Not at home to me or actually out of the house?' Pamela asked.

The butler looked down his nose and started to close the door.

Damian stuck his booted foot out. 'We will wait in the hall while you ascertain the truth of the matter.' He shouldered past the man and Pamela followed him in.

Damian was not a man to be stopped by a mere butler. Pamela tried not to smile at the thought. Their errand was serious.

Much depended on what Mother had to say, because she did not believe that Damian could truly put the past behind him. And if she married him with this cloud hanging over their heads, she had no doubt that it would come back to haunt them.

And she could not live with the doubt.

To her astonishment, Damian followed the butler up the stairs. He glanced over his shoulder and she hurried after him.

The butler looked back at them full of indignation, but one glance at Damian's face had him hurrying onwards.

And still Damian reached the drawing room before him.

He walked in.

'My Lady!' the butler said from behind him. 'He would not take no for an answer.'

Her mother, seated on the *chaise longue* with an embroidery hoop in her hands, glared. 'What do you—?'

Her mouth snapped shut at the sight of Pamela squeezing around the butler to stand beside Damian.

'How dare you bring that—?'

Damian stepped towards her.

Mother pressed her lips together with a little shake of her head.

She swung her feet down and sat up. 'That will be all, Willers,' she said to the butler.

The man left.

Damian closed the door.

'Well,' said Mother. 'To what do I owe this…this intrusion?'

There was no sense in beating about the bush. 'Did you know that Father defrauded Lord Dart's father?'

Her mother's eyes widened. She made a face. 'I—' She shook her head. 'I know nothing about it.'

Her expression said she was not telling the truth.

'Mother, please. You must tell us.'

'I think you owe me that much,' Dart said.

Mother stiffened. 'I owe neither of you anything. Do you know how furious Lord Malcom is with me after your behaviour at the ball? He is most displeased with the pair of you. Several people have already rescinded our invitations.'

Damian gave her a hard look. 'Do you not owe it to your daughter to let her know the truth about her father?'

He still believed her father guilty, no matter that Pamela

was sure he was not. She was right to see the matter as an insurmountable difficulty.

'The truth, Madam.'

Her mother looked from one to the other as if trying to work out what it was they wanted to hear. She let go a breath. 'Dash it all. If you must know, Pamela, your dearest papa was an idiot with money. We were badly dipped for most of our marriage, living from one disaster to another. He was always giving money to anyone who begged for his aid. I do not know how we managed to stay out of debtors' prison.'

Pamela's stomach sank. 'I knew my father was kind to all he met. I did not realise his kindness was a problem.'

'Of course not. Do you think we would have let you worry about such things? That was why I was so upset when you refused to entertain any of the suitors I suggested after Alan died. I did not want you to go through what I went through with your father. You were a very stubborn and foolish girl.'

Shocked, Pamela stared. She had never suspected her mother of wanting to protect her.

'When Long explained his investment proposition, your papa refused to have anything to do with it. He told me all about it later. It seemed to me like a wonderful opportunity.'

Pamela shot Damian an 'I told you so' look. Her mother seemed not to notice. 'As I said, your father never did have a head for finances.' A guilty expression crossed her face.

Pamela's heart stilled. 'Mother. What did you do?'

'What was I supposed to do? Half the time we didn't have enough money to pay the butcher. I wrote to Long, explained that after some thought Lamb had changed his mind and sent him a sum of money to invest.'

'Where did you get the money without Father's knowledge?'

'I sold some jewellery. It was mine. Inherited from my mother. I received a good return on our money, too.' She grimaced. 'Of course, your father was too busy looking after his flock and reading all those dusty books of his to notice our situation had improved.'

'What about my father?' Damian asked. 'It was Lamb who got him drawn into the scheme.'

She shook her head. 'No. I wrote to him. Without my husband's knowledge.'

'What?' Pamela said. 'How could you?'

'Long was threatening to remove us from the plan if we did not come up with more investors. I didn't want that. I wrote to several of my husband's old friends. I was doing them a favour, I thought.'

'Why on earth would they listen to you, Mother?' Pamela said.

Her mother waved a dismissive hand. 'I was quite adept at writing as your father. I had to. To stave off tradesmen when necessary.'

'You mean you committed forgery?' Damian said in chilly tones.

She glanced at Damian. 'Lord Dart's father was the only one who responded. He had been falling into debt and saw it as a way to repair his fortunes.' She wrung her hands. 'I thought I was helping, Pamela. Then the money dried up and no one could get their investment back.'

'So that is why Lamb denied any responsibility for the scheme,' Damian said. 'Because he truly hadn't been involved.'

Mother winced. 'If he had known, he would have wanted to pay the money back. We would have been paupers. We were barely making ends meet once the investment failed. It was a disaster.'

Sick to her stomach, Pamela stared at her mother. 'But he did find out, eventually, didn't he? I heard you and him arguing the day before he died.'

'He found the ledger I had been hiding in my sewing room.' Mother looked sad. 'His heart gave out…' her lips pursed '…leaving us to fend for ourselves. I was lucky Malcom came to our rescue, but you, you ungrateful hussy, had to ruin everything.'

'Mother!' Pamela looked at Damian, who was staring at her mother. 'I am so sorry for what happened to your family. It seems it is our fault, after all.'

His gaze left her mother's face and came to rest on hers. 'Your father did not betray mine.'

'My mother did.'

He shook his head. 'What hurt my father most was the way your father cast him to the wolves, when they had been such close friends in their youth. It was the one thing that made him so angry. So vengeful. I think he would be happy to know your father was an innocent in all of this.'

'Well, he has had his vengeance now,' Mother said. 'Our family name is ruined. We will have to leave town for several years. Malcom is very angry, might I say.'

The truth was not quite what Pamela had expected, but she was happy to know her father was not responsible for the downfall of Damian's family. 'It serves you right.' She got up. She could no longer bear the sight of her mother.

She glanced at Damian. 'It seems that justice has been served after all.'

And since there was no more to be said, she walked out of the room and down the stairs.

She was aware of Damian following.

At the front door, she turned around. 'I really am sorry.'

He took her hand and brought it to his lips. 'It was not

your fault. And it seems my father and your mother were equally fooled by an unscrupulous fellow.'

'Who has, because of me, not been punished. But I am glad the young Mr Long was not made to pay for his father's crimes.'

'You are the sweetest, nicest person a man could ever wish to meet. I had spent so long being angry, I could not see what I was missing from my life. I meant what I said, earlier. I love you and would be honoured if you would become my wife.'

The sincerity in his gaze held her entranced. She shook her head. 'I am beyond the pale.'

'I put you there. So it is only right I join you. Besides, I care nothing for London and its society. And after what happened at my ball, I doubt they care much for me. I am off to the New World. Please. Won't you come with me? I love you beyond anything.'

She had never cared about society. Not for a moment. A sense of a new beginning welled up inside her. And looking into his eyes she knew he was telling the truth. 'Yes.' She smiled. 'Yes, I will.'

He swept her into his arms. 'I love you so very much.'

She pressed her hand to his cheek gazing up at him. 'I love you too.'

His mouth came down on hers in a long hard kiss.

A cough behind them broke them apart. The butler was holding the door open. 'Good day, My Lord. Madam.'

They laughed and stepped out into the street.

Epilogue

Susan pinned the pale pink silk rose in Pamela's hair and stepped back to admire her handiwork. 'You look beautiful.'

Pamela smiled at her friend and erstwhile maid. 'I am so glad you agreed to come with me.' She had also agreed to stand as a witness to her marriage.

Susan touched her arm. 'Me, too. It will be quite an adventure.'

Pamela took a deep shaky breath. Butterflies seemed to dance in her stomach. Was she right to trust Damian? Was it love, or a sense of duty that had made him offer marriage? He said it was love, but… It was too late for second thoughts now.

She straightened her shoulders. 'Let us go.'

Damian was waiting downstairs with the Vicar who had agreed to wed them at short notice once Damian obtained a special licence.

When she descended, Damian and Pip were waiting at the bottom of the stairs. Damian looked up and smiled. As usual he looked so darkly handsome in his impeccably fitted coat. The pink rose in his lapel matched the rose in her hair. But it was the sweetness in his smile that tugged at Pamela's heart and it slowed to a steady beat. Together they would face anything.

He ran up to meet her and put his arm through hers.

'You look lovely,' he murmured, kissing her cheek. Feeling as if she was floating, she walked the rest of the way down the stairs.

At the bottom, Pip offered his arm to Susan and, to Pamela's surprise, she saw a secret little smile pass between them. Oh, dear. Perhaps she would be wise to warn Susan about Pip's butterfly ways. But not today.

As they entered the drawing room a sliver of pale winter sunshine chose that moment to find its way into the room and illuminate the spot before the Vicar.

Her heart lifted.

She glanced at Damian to find him looking down at her, the love in his eyes clear for anyone to see. Her heart welled with joy and confidence. 'I love you,' she whispered.

He gave her hand a squeeze. 'Always and for ever, my darling,' he murmured.

* * * * *

If you enjoyed this story,
be sure to read Ann Lethbridge's
previous Historical romances

The Wife the Marquess Left Behind
The Viscount's Reckless Temptation
A Shopkeeper for the Earl of Westram
The Matchmaker and the Duke
A Family for the Widowed Governess